PRAISE ~~FOR DON GUTTERIDGE'S~~
MARC EDWARDS SERIES

"He mixes real with historical characters . . . in clever ways."
—Margaret Cannon, *The Globe and Mail*

"As Edwards discovers the complexities, subtleties, and brutalities of
Upper Canada, so do we."
—Joan Barfoot, *The London Free Press*

"Don Gutteridge has taken up his quill and written a riveting yarn
of 1830s Upper Canada, steeped in conspiracy and political intrigue.
Gutteridge is not only a master of this historical period, he writes
like a veritable visitor from it. Canadian history has never been more
gripping and enlightening. The story burns, the pages turn, and the
reader learns. Fans of Bernard Cornwell and Patrick O'Brian will
love Don Gutteridge and his Marc Edwards mysteries."
—Terry Fallis, author of *The Best Laid Plans*

"Don Gutteridge has created a fascinating cast of historically accu-
rate characters as he follows a trail of murder and political intrigue
with a bit of romance thrown in. Great mystery, great history, and
a terrific read."
—David Cruise and Alison Griffiths, authors of *Vancouver*

"Gutteridge weaves his tale perfectly, with believable characters and
perfect scene-setting."
—*The Globe and Mail*

OTHER MARC EDWARDS MYSTERIES BY DON GUTTERIDGE

Turncoat

Solemn Vows

Vital Secrets

Dubious Allegiance

BLOODY RELATIONS

A MARC EDWARDS MYSTERY

DON GUTTERIDGE

A TOUCHSTONE BOOK
Published by Simon & Schuster
New York   London   Toronto   Sydney   New Delhi

Touchstone
A Division of Simon & Schuster, Inc.
1230 Avenue of the Americas
New York, NY 10020

This Touchstone export edition June 2013

TOUCHSTONE and colophon are registered trademarks of Simon & Schuster, Inc.

For information about special discounts for bulk purchases,
please contact Simon & Schuster Special Sales at 1-800-268-3216
or CustomerService@simonandschuster.ca.

Manufactured in the United States of America

1   3   5   7   9   10   8   6   4   2

ISBN 978-1-4516-9050-7
ISBN 978-1-4516-9051-4 (ebook)

For Gene Burdenuk, friend and longtime supporter

PROLOGUE

It is July 1838. The provinces of Upper and Lower Canada have suffered through two rebellions, both summarily put down. Although there is peace, it is an uneasy calm that hangs over both colonies. The grievances that fomented revolt remain unresolved, principally the oppression of the mass of farmers at the hands of legislatures that are tipped in favour of the established order. For more than a decade, reform movements in both provinces have tried unsuccessfully to introduce more democratic, less authoritarian forms of governance. The mother country has at last woken up to the issues and is taking steps to alleviate the situation. A new governor, Sir George Arthur, is appointed for Upper Canada, replacing Sir Francis Bond Head. More important, Lord Durham, a Whig sympathizer, is named head of a commission of inquiry and temporary governor of both colonies, tasked with finding a possible solution for the troubled provinces. In July of 1838, he visits Quebec City, Montreal, Niagara, and finally Toronto, consulting with dozens of locals from every level of society. Months later he will make a report that will forever alter the nature of the Canadas.

ONE

Briar Cottage
11 Sherbourne Street
Toronto, Upper Canada

July 17, 1838

Dear Uncle Frederick:

I was happy to hear that you've almost wound up Uncle
Jabez's affairs and the settling of his estate. No doubt you
are looking forward to your return to France and the bosom
of your family. That they are all healthy and thriving must
provide you with some consolation during this period of
mourning for your brother.

As you know from my previous letters, a number of which
likely arrived simultaneously in April—the mails here are as
unreliable as the roads—my life since last October when the
troubles began has been both hectic and harrowing. Thus it
is only in the past two months, since my marriage to Beth,
that I have had time to reflect on what now seems "my other
life" in England and the role that Uncle Jabez played in it.

I miss him more each day, and have long ago forgiven him for his faults, as he was kind enough to overlook or indulge mine. His generous annuity on my behalf is more than I deserve. I wish to thank you for arranging its transfer to my bank here in Toronto. As you know, Beth inherited money and property from Joshua Smallman, her father-in-law, so we are well situated financially.

That being so, you may wonder at our purchasing a "cottage" here in town rather than a "residence," or even having one built to our specifications and fancy. In fact, Briar Cottage suits us both just fine. For the moment there is only Beth, me, and Charlene Huggan, a young woman whose sisters have gone off to homestead in the Iowa Territory. Charlene is our "housekeeper" (the local term for an all-purpose female servant). Should our ménage expand, as I devoutly hope it will, we shall add additional rooms on the back of the house. We have better than half an acre of land, minuscule by the standards of the English gentry, but that is sufficient for a considerable vegetable garden and a coop full of chickens. There is a small barn as well, which will shelter a carriage horse before summer.

You will be surprised to hear that Beth looks after the garden herself (she ran a farm on her own after her first husband died), with occasional assistance from a "hired man" (another localism) and her own husband. The latter, however, has been branded "hopeless" by his employer, who seems at a loss to explain how he could wield a sabre and dodge bullets (well, most of them) and yet be utterly inept with sickle and hoe.

You asked again about my war wound, and I am pleased to report that I have fully recovered. My stamina

*and physical strength are returned to their former "glory"
and my limp is slight and barely noticeable. (It seems
to worsen only when I am in need of an infusion of
sympathy.) And thanks to the law books you were so
thoughtful as to send, I have been exercising my mind once
more. As you know only too well, I abandoned the solicitor's
inns for the life of a soldier with your timely assistance,
and have never regretted doing so even though, for reasons
I outlined in my last letter, I felt compelled to resign my
commission. A life of petty, if profitable, conveyancing was
not for me. However, the notion of becoming a barrister
someday has its attractions. At any rate, the thought of such
a career and the necessity of burrowing deep into the tomes
of jurisprudence are enough to keep me out of trouble for
the time being.*

*It is mid-afternoon on a July Monday as I write this.
Just a few hours ago, one of the more memorable and happy
events of the year took place, and I am eager to describe it
to you while it is fresh in my mind. Down at the Queen's
Wharf this morning, more than a thousand citizens of every
political stripe gathered to witness the arrival, from his
stopover in Niagara, of Lord Durham, governor of all the
British North American provinces, special envoy of Prime
Minister Melbourne, and the man chosen by the Whig
government to broker a lasting peace among the warring
factions of Upper and Lower Canada.*

*The pomp and panoply were worthy of a monarch's
progress through his dominions. I have seen nothing more
splendid or exquisitely intimidating at Hyde Park or more
festive and convivial at Brighton racecourse! In front of
the early-morning crowd at the wharf and behind them*

*on the open ground above Front Street were arranged
the colourful ranks of the King's Dragoon Guards and
the 43rd Foot (force-marched up from Fort George at
Niagara) as well as our own 23rd from Fort York. The
immaculate tents of the dragoons, who had bivouacked
along the bay and the spit to the west, fluttered in an
approving breeze.*

*Then, about ten o'clock, a blast of trumpets behind us
proclaimed the sighting of sails beyond the southeast shore
of the peninsula-cum-island that acts as a buffer for our
beautiful bay. A huge hurrah went up. Even our most
skeptical Tories are overawed by the "divinity that doth
hedge" someone who's hobnobbed with kings and czars. The
schooner ferrying His Lordship then weighed anchor some
leagues offshore. After an agonizing and well-judged pause,
a longboat was lowered, soon to be joined by others from
ships we couldn't quite see, and the flash of oars in perfect
unison left the throng momentarily stunned. They spoke to us
humbled onlookers of the might and relentless precision of the
British Empire.*

*As the band struck up a martial air behind us, the
longboats came silently and with deliberate ease towards
the end of the wharf, where an honour guard flanked
Lieutenant-Governor Sir George Arthur and his liveried
minions. When the leading longboat drew near, the oars
flipped up as one and stilled. In the middle of the boat, a
tall and majestic figure rose gracefully into view and posed
for posterity. Neither it nor the impeccably dressed oarsmen
moved again as the demi-royal craft floated on its own
glamour towards the tip of the quay and, while the crowd
held its breath, nudged the pier as softly and meticulously*

as a caress. Then the air reverberated with the thunder of a twenty-one-gun salute, during which Lord Durham put first one foot then the other upon Toronto soil, before extending a hand to Lady Durham and drawing her up beside him. I thought of Caesar putting a Roman toe upon the simple shingle of ancient Britain.

The effect of this gesture upon the Upper Canadian populace was, I am certain, a calculated one. Lord Durham—the man you know as Radical Jack at home—is in the eyes of the Tory Compact here a thoroughgoing Whig. They know about, and are appalled by, his "coddling" of the miners who toil for him in Durham, his permitting them to form workers' associations, and his dastardly role in designing and carrying through the Great Reform Bill six years ago. They also keenly disapprove of his dismissal of the Tory Council in Quebec, his lenient treatment of the French rebels, and his even-handed attempts to sort out the various claims of grievance. Hence His Lordship seems to realize that a little pomp and ceremony and a reminder that he is after all a peer and a member of the "real" Privy Council will go some way towards cowing the local gentry and petty aristocracy. Indeed, the first affair of state will not take place at Government House but rather at one of our native "palaces," Spadina House. Nor will it be a business meeting. At nine this evening, Lord and Lady Durham will play host to the town's elite at the Governor's Ball—gourmandizing and dancing till the wee hours! More on this in the next letter. Till then, I remain,

Your devoted nephew,
Marc

P.S. The only discordant note at this morning's extravaganza, for me, was the appearance at Lady Durham's side of a young gentleman who flinched at every cannon shot and bugle blast. My heart went out to him. When I asked who he might be, a man beside me said, "That's Lady Durham's nephew, Handford Ellice, and a burden he's been to her ever since they come here." Unfortunately for the curious, no more was said, but I subsequently learned that he is the son of the commercial adventurer Edward Ellice, a man with his own bold interests in our fair colony. Strange that his offspring should appear so timid.

Eighteen three-letter words with no vowels:

CLY	SWY
CWM	SYN
HYP	TSK
LYM	TWP
MYC	TYG
PHT	VLY
PYX	WYN
RHY	ZZZ
SNY	

TWO

A few hours later, in the household of Mr. and Mrs. Marcus Edwards, Charlene Huggan, the maid and all-purpose servant, was giggling so heartily she could barely remove the last of the pins from the hem of her mistress's gown without damage to herself or the lady in question.

"If you don't stop teasing the girl, we won't get to Spadina before midnight, at which time—according to the brothers Grimm—we all turn into pumpkins." Marc did not seem displeased that both women turned at this witticism to notice how resplendent he looked in his top hat and tails. He did half a pirouette, just in case.

Beth fixed him with that blue-eyed stare of hers. "Am I Cinderella or one of the ugly stepsisters?"

Charlene giggled again, and spat pins in several directions.

"With that look, you could pass for the heartless stepmother."

"Don't she do the dress proud, sir?" Charlene stood back and gave Beth and her ball gown a worshipful scrutiny. "And missus thinkin' she couldn't put herself beside any of them ladies up at Spadina!"

"The only genuine lady up there will be Lord Durham's wife, who was born a lady and whose father was prime minister of the

United Kingdom." Marc leaned back and surveyed Beth like a tailor approving a perfect seam. "The rest of them, Charlene—and you mustn't ever forget this—are just ordinary women dressed up as titled ladies and hoping to pass as such. And their husbands likewise."

"As ladies?" Charlene's eyes danced impishly and she gave Beth a conspiratorial glance.

"As pretend *gentlemen*," Marc said patiently. "And Mrs. Edwards, as usual, will be herself in that company and, for all that, will be thought a true lady."

"Why don't you try flatterin' me?" Beth asked with a cautious peek in the mirror that Charlene had set against the nearest wall.

"If I didn't know better, darling, I'd accuse you of carelessly droppin' yer *g*'s."

Charlene, who could have stood and listened to this conjugal banter all evening, was rudely brought back to her duty by the sound of a carriage drawing up outside the house. "It's here!" she cried, and raced to the window.

Marc went over to Beth and placed a woollen shawl across her bare shoulders. "I'm glad you decided to come after all," he said with sudden seriousness.

"So am I," she said. "I know how much it means to you to meet Lord Durham."

"I truly believe he is the only person in Christendom who can save this dominion and begin to salve the wounds that have been inflicted."

"Even though he's a Whig," Beth said, smiling.

Marc smiled back. "I've come a long way, haven't I?"

Beth squeezed his arm, and they walked briskly towards the hired gig outside their front gate. Only Beth noticed that as her husband moved like the born gentleman he was to the waiting vehicle, there was still a perceptible limp in the left leg—a memento of the personal injury he had suffered in the civil turmoil of the past nine months.

When the invitation to the ball at Spadina had arrived five days before (Durham's advance men had been busy orchestrating his tour through the Upper Province), Beth had simply refused to take it seriously. "It has to be a mistake," she informed Marc when he got back home from his afternoon walk. "We don't hobnob with the Family Compact—or any other compact." Marc noted that their surname had been spelled correctly and the messenger from Government House knew perfectly well where Sherbourne Street was. Indeed, most of the town knew exactly where the "hero of St. Denis" had taken up residence with his bride in the middle of May, even though he no longer graced the thoroughfares of the capital in his officer's uniform with its glittering sabre and the green-feathered shako of the 23rd Regiment of Foot. "Invalided out" was the story in circulation, despite Marc's futile attempts to scotch it: he had bought out his commission as a gentleman was obliged to do and had abandoned his military career without regret and with good reason, in his view. Soon after, he and Beth had purchased the substantial stone cottage on Sherbourne Street, near the outskirts of the town proper, complete with barn and extensive garden.

Marc's assumption that the invitation was the work of Colonel Margison, the kindly commanding officer who had attended Marc and Beth's wedding in full regalia, was borne out the following day. But Beth's initial no was as unshakeable as it was succinct. Marc gently reminded her that she would not be alone or unbefriended at the gala. Major Owen Jenkin, their best man and faithful ally, would be in attendance alongside the colonel and several other officers whom she had met at the wedding breakfast and taken up willingly as dancing partners afterwards. Among the local ladies there would be perhaps a dozen whom she knew from her days as co-proprietress of the millinery shop on King Street, an enterprise Beth and her aunt Catherine had expanded to include dressmaking, utilizing the designs and sewing talent of Mrs. Rose Halpenny. Alas, the Rebellion and its fallout had caused its closure, and Aunt Catherine had returned to her native United States.

"I'll wager that a third of the gowns up there will be products of your own enterprise," Marc had declared, a tad too effusively.

"And I'm sure the good ladies of Torytown will be happy to see their dressmaker do-si-doing with their hubbies," Beth had shot back, silencing him.

A day later he tried another tack. After luncheon with Major Jenkin at the mess in Fort York (his first trip back since his discharge), Marc informed Beth that the principal reason for the colonel's encouraging Marc's attendance at the ball was to have him meet and, with luck, talk to Lord Durham.

"What in ever for?" was Beth's disingenuous response.

Marc plunged ahead. "Lord Durham is in Toronto for four days only. Colonel Margison feels that he should meet a broadly representative group of citizens and be exposed to a wide spectrum of opinion. In fact, the governor himself has asked that this be so. The colonel has put forward my name as someone to be consulted, and feels that if Lord Durham has an opportunity to meet me, even informally at the gala, he might decide to include me in his official consultations."

"I don't suppose yer 'wide spectrum' includes citizens who drop their *g*'s or who aren't the right sex to vote."

"This is serious business," Marc said, miffed.

"Don't pout; I know it is. And I know you've got a lot more

sense to talk than most of those Tories with half a brain and twice the prejudice. So go on up there by yourself. Talk sense. You don't need a dancing partner to distract you."

Marc knew when he was defeated and when to keep his counsel. To his surprise, though, that night as they were getting into bed, Beth announced quietly that she would go. They both knew the real reason behind her initial reluctance, and thus he appreciated the courage her acceptance entailed. Beth was as bright and politically astute as any gentleman likely to be found fawning over Lord Durham. She had operated a farm in the rural districts where the folly of government policies were keenly felt, then helped to found a successful business in the heart of Toronto's commercial district. Marc could not help appreciating too that she was more naturally beautiful than any of the overdressed and cosmetically improved chatelaines of the town, their native accents no less flat-vowelled or uninflected than her own. But she was most comfortable in her own home and especially in her garden, where she had spent her days since late May preparing the neglected soil and planting spring vegetables. In the house she worked alongside Charlene, whom she thought of more as a favoured niece than a servant. She had no desire to mix with her so-called betters, abashed by the notion that she might be mistaken for one of them.

Marc had tried in vain to persuade her that this attitude was an inverted form of snobbishness and that if only she were to meet and get to know some of these women, she might change her mind. "I met most of them in my hat shop," she'd reply, and no elaboration was deemed necessary. Marc also realized, but was too tactful to say, that Beth missed her brother and her neighbours, including the other Huggan sisters, from her days on the farm at Crawford's Corners. All of them were now homesteading in the

Iowa Territory, victims of the recent upheavals. She missed too the easygoing, unpretentious women of the Congregational church in Cobourg. As a compromise, but with scant conviction, they both now attended St. James on most Sundays.

So, improbably but happily, Beth and Marc found themselves speeding along King Street in the July gloaming, en route to the splendours of Spadina House. Once Beth made up her mind that something had to be done, she accepted it with grace and executed it with a will. If her husband required a pretty wife to decorate his arm and send the hearts of hopeful dancing partners aflutter, then so be it. She would smile and chatter as lightly as could be expected in such frivolous circumstances and dance the midnight down. After all, the cause was critical. And it was partly her own.

CONSTABLE HORATIO COBB WAS IN A vile mood. And the fact that he had been put in such an uncharacteristic funk—being by his own admission a man of cherubic good cheer—had made him even more irritated at the world in general and at Constable Ewan Wilkie in particular. Wilkie had been inconsiderate enough to take to his bed on the one day in the year when every officer of the Crown, from pig warden to assistant sheriff, and every soldier and resuscitated militiaman had been pressed into service to protect and otherwise coddle the newly arrived earl of Durham. Cobb had spent the morning being elbowed and cursed by the citizens' mob down at the Queen's Wharf, frantic in their efforts to catch a glimpse of His Lordship's haughty chin. Cobb's capture of two pickpockets and a cutpurse had earned him a bruise on the left cheek and not a lick of thanks. After a mandated two-hour afternoon nap, the four regular constables and their chief were expected to return to their street patrols and remain there with utmost vigilance until the last carriage or ambulatory gentleman-drunks had found their way safely home from the governor's gala at Spadina House. That is, unmolested by any thieves, rabble-rousers, or garlic-breathing gawkers who might be tempted to take advantage of the hubbub and inadvertence excited by the earl's hospitality. As for Cobb and his fellow constables, it guaranteed them a long, foot-wearying night.

Cobb's regular patrol was the southeast sector, below King and east of Bay as far as the city limits beyond Parliament Street to the Don River. It was an area he knew well, having superintended it for the three years he had been a member of the newly formed Toronto constabulary. It included his own home and half a dozen congenial watering holes that supplied him with a steady flow of useful information from a cadre of thirsty snitches, along with the odd meat pie *avec* flagon. He knew every alley and service lane where a miscreant might hide or contemplate ambush. If a window curtain were out of place or a shop door abnormally ajar, he would spot it in a wink and spring into fearsome action. This in spite of his unspring-like shape, which placed a bit too much rotundity just above the centre of gravity. Like his fellow patrolmen, he had learned to navigate in the dark or the shadowy near-dark—there were feeble candle-lamps only along King Street for a few blocks—preferring to deploy his keen sense of hearing rather than use the cumbersome lantern recommended by the chief. What did one do with it when the right hand reached for the trusty, wooden truncheon: hold it up to give the thug a clearer target?

But Cobb was not on Cobbian ground this evening, thanks to the perfidy of Wilkie. It was not that he had not covered for Wilkie before or that this area of town was totally unfamiliar. But given that the bigwigs' ball was being held at Dr. Baldwin's extravagance way out on the northwest edge of the city, Cobb's own southeast patrol would have been as peaceful as a teetotaller's picnic. So peaceful in fact that when Wilkie's wife reported him sick at suppertime (he'd somehow managed to force down a roast-beef dinner before collapsing from the effort), Chief Sturges had reassigned Cobb to the stricken man's area without a thought to the safety of the abandoned southeast sector.

It was now early evening. Two or three carriages had already passed him, heading west along Newgate Street, their occupants sitting sedately as if in their Sunday pews. How different, Cobb mused, would be their demeanor on the return trip, when the broughams, barouches, and democrats departing Spadina would be abulge with the whooping and dishevelled or quietly inebriated representatives of Upper Canada's upper crust. At the corner of Newgate and Yonge, with the lingering acidities of Barnett's tannery prickling his nose, Cobb turned and plodded dutifully past Hospital Street towards the northern border of his patrol along Lot Street. The summer night was beautiful, with a cool breeze to waft away the mosquitoes and the pungent scent of fresh grass and the invisible and nameless wildflowers that sprang up wherever they were not discouraged. So welcoming was the evening that Cobb was in danger of forfeiting his aggrieved state. And this in spite of his aching feet and the throb of his bruised cheek and Wilkie's apostasy. Moreover, and to his unacknowledged disappointment, there had been not a single pub disturbance or domestic contretemps or attempted theft the entire time he had been tramping about the northwest sector, almost spoiling for a fight.

"WHERE IN THE WORLD IS THIS palace?" Beth said as she glanced left and right and observed only raw forest.

"We can't be too far now," Marc replied. The reins were slack in his right hand as the horse trotted at a leisurely pace along an ungravelled but well-worn path. "We're starting to go uphill. No need to worry, there's only one road in this part of the township."

Certainly the grand house of the Baldwin family had been set well away from any encroachment by the rapidly expanding city. The southern portion of this pathway, above Lot Street, had already been named Spadina Avenue, but here, beyond the city limits, the wilderness loomed as a reminder of its general hegemony in a vast province where there were still only a few hundred thousand inhabitants.

"Ah, here we are!" Beth announced.

The road had not only begun to rise, it swung sharply northwest and then straightened out to become a gravelled approach to the edifice on the hill a quarter of a mile ahead. There was just enough light at the edges of the sky for Marc and Beth to discern the white ribbon of road and the fact that the woods had been cleared away thirty feet or so on either side, with vague smudges here and there indicating that more domestic and compliant trees had already been planted. By the time Marc had urged the horse and gig up to the impressive parabola where a dozen fancy carriages and several covered coaches were debouching their passengers, the air had darkened, and two or three intrepid stars had peeped out along the southwestern horizon. Still, enough of the solstice glow of mid-July remained to throw the silhouette of Spadina House into stark relief. The effect was sudden and imposing: massive turret, belvedere, balustrade, and chimney pot in a tumble of intimidating shadow against the diffident gloaming behind it. At least the verandah, illuminated by powerful lanterns of varied hue and several torches set on the lawn below, was beckoning: its graceful stairs, carpeted for the occasion, were strewn with cut blossoms whose perfume rose upon the little breeze that had arrived, it seemed, just to perform this amiable service. Two members of the Horse Guards, borrowed from the Fort George contingent, stood resplendent and watchful at either side of the entrance.

Marc's gig had barely come to a halt before the bridle was grasped by a liveried postilion, who gave Marc a reassuring smile as he helped Beth step down.

"We're the only ones driving our own wagon," Beth said, deliberately loud.

"And I plumb fergot to bring the oats," Marc replied with a straight face.

A formidable receiving line awaited Marc and Beth in the cavernous entrance hall. Marc had coached Beth in the protocol of a formal ball, but it was the curtsy that had seemed to give her the most difficulty. Even Charlene had picked it up almost instantly, then proceeded to tease her mistress until she teetered or tottered in a fit of self-mocking laughter. Marc advanced the opinion that Beth, otherwise agile and quick, was simply temperamentally predisposed to fail at such a deferential gesture of obeisance—an opinion that earned him a glare but produced results. "Anybody can fake humbleness," Beth said after a hyperbolic dip. "And we'll see plenty of examples at Spadina House."

Their preparation for the dancing had been a lot more pleasant. Beth was a natural dancer and had participated in many a reel and country jig. Whether the more sedate minuet or quadrille could constrain her tendency to kick up her heels (and her skirt) was still a moot question when their rehearsals ended late in the afternoon. Moreover, the ball gown, supplied and made over by Mrs. Halpenny, had not been finally fitted until after supper, and so had not been permitted a trial run on the dancer herself.

At the head of the receiving line, a sturdy-looking gentleman with a serious expression that refused to cooperate with his smile greeted them. "I am Charles Buller, Lord Durham's secretary, and this is my daughter, Emily."

Marc introduced Beth and then himself, watched Beth curtsy like an angel, and let himself be passed along according to the time-honoured ritual. Luckily the line was moving briskly. Almost all of the town's elite had been invited, Tory and Reformer alike, and the guests were now pressing forward, up the front steps, fashionably late. Still, Marc was able to form a first impression of men whose names were legend in English Whig circles and who were now standing in Dr. William Baldwin's vestibule. Charles Buller, of course, was much more than a secretary: he was a known confidant and adviser to the earl. Thomas Turton, who gave Marc a polite nod before making a lingering appraisal of Mrs. Edwards, was in charge of the earl's legal affairs, but it was widely rumoured that he had been one of the copyists of the Great Reform Bill of 1832, sequestered in Lord Durham's home for the two months it had taken the earl and his three cabinet colleagues to frame those historic changes in the electoral structure of British government.

Both Marc and Beth had tried not to stare too rudely at the penultimate personage in the line, but it was difficult not to, as he was the most notorious of Lord Durham's cronies. Edward Gibbon Wakefield did not look in the least Byronic, despite the fact that, as a callow youth, he had abducted an heiress and carried her off (whether the girl was willing or otherwise had not been finally decided by the court of public opinion), before being tracked down and imprisoned for his romantic excesses. Wakefield's slim build, wispy blond hair, and tiny bespectacled eyes made him look more like a bank clerk than a Don Juan. At the present moment, as Marc well knew, Wakefield was the most knowledgeable Englishman in regard to colonial affairs. Whatever his amorous proclivities, his advice to Lord Durham during this critical period of assessment would be material and persuasive.

Suddenly they were in the presence of Lord and Lady Durham, their hosts for the evening. (The Baldwins, as Reform leaders, had graciously declined to join the receiving line in order that no political bias be perceived in what was, after all, the Durhams' gala.) Lady Durham was simply dressed, polite without condescension, and smiled genuinely, but she was unable to dispel the aura of legitimate gentry characteristic of her every gesture. Beside her, John George Lambton, the earl of Durham—Radical Jack—stood tall and imposing. Even at forty-six and after a life of constant travel and mental exertion as a landlord, mine owner, ambassador, and government minister, he was darkly handsome, with curly brown hair, thoughtful eyes alight with intelligence, and a Roman nose and sensuous lips that had set many a feminine breast aflutter. He took Beth's gloved hand and kissed it, then turned his penetrating gaze upon Marc.

"I trust your war wound is healing nicely, Lieutenant," he said, and was already leaning towards Magistrate Thorpe and his wife when Marc halted momentarily in surprise at the remark and its evident solicitude.

"Wakefield didn't give you a second glance," Marc said as he and Beth approached the ballroom and the valets who were waiting to pounce on top hat and stole. "I don't know whether to be relieved or aggrieved."

"The night's still young," Beth teased, looking around expectantly.

The ballroom before them was rapidly filling with the patricians of the city and their wives, daughters, and distant cousins from the townships. It was the largest domestic space Beth had ever seen, though Marc refrained from commenting that it was modest compared with its counterparts back home. Nonetheless, it was impressive and certainly worthy of the demi-royal personages who graced it this evening as host and hostess. Along the eastern wall, a bank of tall, elegant windows reflected the dazzle of a dozen gigantic candelabras. Opposite, a mezzanine held the twenty-piece orchestra—Toronto's finest bolstered by half a dozen players accompanying the earl—which had just struck up a lively lancers. Through several arches below it lay the cloakrooms, powder rooms, a smoker, a billiard parlour, and a lounge set up for whist or piquet.

The dancing began rather formally, for despite the short notice many of the guests had had time and foresight to secure dance cards and initiate the delicate process of filling them with names. As no program had been printed, a name opposite a number had to suffice. However, it was not long before the informality of local custom and its regrettable levelling effects began to hold sway. Brazen young Canadians barged into the protective ring of family circles to forcibly carry off the prettiest, mildly protesting member. Gentlemen of girth and standing permitted themselves to be seduced out of their dignity by giggling ingénues and an intoxicating beat. Beth and Marc waited for the minuet, easing into the pleasures of an evening that promised to be lively and prolonged. After all, it was July, the winter had been divisive and stressful, and now a sort of saviour had arrived in their midst, an Apollo come down from Olympus to restore calm and reason. When the orchestra was persuaded to strike up a Virginia reel, the room shook with the stamp of feet and the mêlée of sets being improvised or reconstituted. Dance cards were tossed aside when a caller, who materialized as if on cue, boomed out the steps and courtesies of the quintessential North American dance.

Marc lost Beth in one of the scrums of partner switching.

Sweating and thirsty, he made for the refreshment table, where he found a goblet of icy champagne and his good friend Owen Jenkin. They chatted briefly about the ceremonial arrival of Lord Durham that morning and agreed that His Lordship had no doubt calculated every gesture in the show of pomp and authority which they and five thousand others had witnessed. Any Englishman who could influence the czar of Russia as no one had before him, or leave the governor of New York awestruck in Fort Niagara, was a man who had greatness in his bones.

"We must do everything we can to make his stay here purposeful and productive," Marc said.

"I think he's managing quite nicely on his own," Owen said. "The town Tories have worked themselves into a sweet sweat over a Whig and a probable Radical being sent here to tell them what's needed to keep the peace. But look at them now: jigging like a flock of Kentuckians, and scraping and bowing like penitents before the pope."

"He's off to a good start anyway."

"I feel like a pipe. Care to join me?"

Marc looked about for Beth. The dancers were forming up in groups of four pairs for an announced quadrille. He spotted a tiny white hand fluttering across the room near the alcove where Lord Durham's party had been holding court for the past half-hour. It was Beth, about to step smartly into the opening steps of the quadrille. At her side, with an arm about her waist, stood the most notorious man in Spadina: Edward Gibbon Wakefield.

Beth smiled at her husband before being swept away.

"Let's have that pipe, Owen."

Marc followed Major Jenkin through an archway and along a broad hall that gave them access to the men's smoker. The major was in full dress uniform, but seeing his friend in the regalia he had recently given up roused no feeling in Marc of regret or loss. He was at ease with his decision, at least for the moment. They found their way through the cigar and pipe smoke to a pair of leather chairs, lit up, and leaned back in perfect contentment.

"I'm afraid to say so, Marc," Owen said at last, "but there are a good many men in this house tonight who would like to see Lord Durham's mission fail and fail badly."

"You're right, but it's a pity they can't see that things can never be the same as they were before Mackenzie and Papineau. It's not even a matter of who's right or who's wrong. The horse is out of the barn and galloping apace."

"And we could use a new horse and a new barn, eh?"

A burst of rough male laughter erupted behind them. Marc turned towards its source. An open archway led to an adjacent room, the one set up for card playing.

Owen Jenkin chuckled. "Now there are four gentlemen sharing a laugh who otherwise might not give one another the time of day."

"I don't think I recognize any of them."

"The chap with the paunch is Alasdair Hepburn, a big shot in the Commercial Bank. His whist partner, unlikely as it may seem, is Patrick O'Driscoll."

"The grand panjandrum of the Orange Lodge here in the city?"

"The same. A muckraking zealot if there ever was one. Like oil and water, those two, I should think."

"Who's the fellow with the collar?"

"That's the Reverend Temperance Finney, a Methodist ranter who should be burning his cards, not slapping them on the table."

"And that's not tea in his glass, I'll wager." Marc was enjoying himself immensely.

"His partner, the scrawny chap, is Samuel Harris, as lean and ascetic as Hepburn is paunchy and epicurean. He owns about a quarter of King Street."

"Then he'd have something in common with the other Tories."

"True: money, power, and privilege. Unfortunately for him, he's Catholic."

"Oh, dear."

"With a French wife."

"Maybe they're playing for keeps."

"Well, they look mighty chummy to me."

At this point the orchestra let out a fresh blast of danceable noise, indicating yet another shift in tempo.

"I'd better get back there and rescue my girl," Marc said.

When he re-entered the ballroom, Beth was nowhere to be found. He paced the periphery of the waltz, a European dance which pinioned couples together in an elegant but over-proximate contact. Beth could not waltz. At least he assumed she couldn't.

"I can't find her anywhere," Marc said to Owen after they had gone halfway around the dance floor.

"She's off in the powder room, I expect."

"If it's Mrs. Edwards you're looking for," said a feminine, cultured voice nearby, "she's over there under the mezzanine, conversing with my nephew."

Both men gulped hard, then snapped a pair of quick bows to Lady Durham, after which they stood speechless in the presence of Earl Grey's daughter.

"Your wife, sir, is a delight, if you'll permit me to say so."

"By all means, Your Ladyship," Marc managed to say.

"My nephew, my sister's boy, Mr. Handford Ellice, has been standing beside your good wife for the past ten minutes—talking."

"I hope she's not monopolizing his time—"

Lady Durham laughed, a melodic ripple that would have done a diva proud. "Good gracious, no. You see, Handford is painfully shy and socially rather awkward. He refused to stand in the receiving line and spent the first hour of the party in our rooms, trying to drum up the courage to make a brief appearance, lest he suffer what he takes to be the wrath of his uncle. I believe we call that being forced to choose between Scylla and Charybdis."

"Well, I'm pleased he has found someone to talk to."

"Mrs. Edwards has a way with people," Major Jenkin said with a smile.

"My word, gentlemen. Look, she's leading him towards the dance floor!"

And she was. They passed by about twenty feet away, not aware they were being watched with some amazement. Marc got his first close look at Handford Ellice. The youth was slender and no more than five foot two in height. His hair was a light shade of brown, almost blond, his features compact but well formed. The most memorable aspects of his person were the pale eyebrows, alabaster complexion, and eyes so faintly blue that he might have been an albino. About him there was an ascetic, almost haunted look as he shuffled nervously behind Beth. The orchestra struck the opening chord for a minuet, Beth drew him gently by the hand and they stood erect and poised for the dance to begin.

Lady Durham remained at Marc's side, staring in disbelief at what she was seeing. Although usually stiff and prone to embarrassing miscues, her nephew moved easily through the minuet, hardly ever taking his eyes off his partner. At times he approached gracefulness, his body caught up in the music and the blissful forgetting it can engender.

"I think you may have lost a partner for the evening," Lady

Durham said, then excused herself and hurried towards her husband, presumably to give him the happy news.

When the set was over, Beth reluctantly let go of Handford Ellice's hand, and he bowed deeply before turning and stumbling towards his aunt.

"You've made a hit with Lady Durham," Marc said when Beth came up to him and Owen, breathless and not a little excited.

"I didn't even know who he was," she said, "until he told me just at the end. I nearly fainted."

"I think it was the young man who was near fainting," Owen said.

"Perhaps he'll get up enough courage to try again," Marc said.

"I hope so. I spotted him hiding in a corner and just felt sorry for him. He's got a stammer that comes and goes, so I just kept talking a lot of nonsense until it seemed to go away. I told him that dancing would help it even more."

"Well, it certainly improved his confidence," Marc said.

"I was afraid he'd keep on drinking. Apparently that's how he copes with his shyness."

"Has he been doing so tonight?" Owen asked, suddenly concerned.

"He'd had a few glasses of champagne, but you saw him dancing out there: he was far from drunk."

"Thank God for that."

"Well, he's now under the watchful eye of his uncle," Marc said, but even as he spoke, they saw Handford Ellice shake off his aunt's hand, smile at her, and head in the direction of the smoker.

"So much for more dancing," Owen said.

"Don't worry, Owen dear," Beth said. "He told me he's been trying all night to get up the nerve to join the gentlemen playing whist. Seems he's got a great passion for the game but is too bashful to get himself invited to sit in. I think I may have helped him along a little."

"And good for you," Owen said. "I just hope you've got enough energy left to put an old soldier through his paces."

"For you, always," Beth said. She turned to Marc. "But first, I think I'm ready for something fizzy and one of those tidbits."

Left alone again, Marc glanced toward Lord Durham, standing a few steps to his right and, for once, unattended. He approached and was gratified when the earl remembered him from the receiving line. "Marc Edwards," he greeted him warmly, as the two men shook hands once again.

They exchanged niceties about Spadina House and the weather only briefly before Lord Durham asked for his views on the current political situation in the Canadas. Marc was hesitant at first, but then found himself reciting the familiar litany of farmers' grievances and frustration with a deadlocked legislature.

"How can we break that impasse?" asked Durham, perhaps testing the younger man.

"We need an elected assembly with real powers," Marc said boldly. "And ministers who are responsible to it."

"A controversial but interesting notion," was the reply.

Just then Lady Durham arrived and, with apologies, steered her husband towards a nearby group of hovering admirers.

Marc found Beth and happily partnered her for the rest of the evening's dancing. From time to time, they glimpsed the whist players, who kept their game going despite the distractions of music and food. Handford Ellis played with concentration and did not return to the dance floor. Shortly after eleven o'clock, Beth admitted to fatigue and Marc agreed they should take their leave. They said their good-byes to their hosts, Lady Durham gracious and grateful to Beth, Lord Durham smiling broadly at Marc.

•   •   •

"I COULD REACH UP AND TOUCH that big star," Beth said sleepily, her head resting on her husband's left shoulder as they sat close together in the gig on the way home, "if I had an ounce of energy in me."

"You left it all on the dance floor back there."

"You did pretty well yourself, for a man with a war wound."

They moved along in companionable silence, with only the rhythmic clack of the gig's wheels and muffled clop of the horse's hooves to interrupt their thoughts.

"You did a wonderful and generous thing tonight," Marc said, as they wheeled off Spadina Avenue, crossed Lot Street, and entered the city proper.

"You mean I survived the good intentions of the Family Compact?"

"You made young Ellice's evening. His shyness was painful to watch."

"I hope he enjoyed his whist."

"I'm sure he did. In addition to the obvious benefit, I think you may have helped to put Lord Durham's mind at ease in that regard. He's got enough worries here without that particular one adding to the list."

"Handford must've had a lonesome upbringing."

"I can imagine it—only son of a famous and ambitious father, wealthy from his business interests and highly influential with the Whig government. Do you know, they call Ellice Senior the Bear!"

They swung east onto King Street.

"By the way, there's something important I must tell you," Beth said, suddenly solemn.

Marc almost dropped the reins. Was this the news he had been hoping for? The marriage of Beth and Jesse Smallman had produced no children, but still . . .

"I think I may be starting to fit in with that crowd up there," she said, with just a hint of amusement.

Marc swallowed his disappointment and asked, "Why is that?"

"Mr. Wakefield pinched my bottom."

THREE

Cobb reached the corner of Lot and Yonge for the umpteenth time, and nodded at the nearly full moon that had risen far enough into the eastern arc of the sky to pour a mellow glow along the ungravelled road, making the shadowed ruts appear deeper and not a little sinister, and the silhouettes of the buildings and houses loom ominously at the edge of his vision. Across the road, Montgomery's Tavern was unlit and eerily silent.

A tiny, involuntary shudder rippled up his body as Cobb approached the intersection of Bay and Lot (the name of the latter, it was suggested in the right circles, to be changed to Queen Street in honour of the new sovereign). Bay Street ended here; everything north of it as far as College Street was part of the extensive university grounds—College Park, as it was locally dubbed. However, the few hundred acres of its expanse that lay just to the north and west of the Bay-Lot intersection, not a quarter mile from the majestic Osgoode Hall, had a less savoury designation: Irishtown.

Technically it was part of Wilkie's patrol, but unless called upon in some dire and self-evident emergency, no constable ventured into its grubby interior and, even then, not alone. The area was essentially a squatters' haven. Its three dozen dwellings were ramshackle affairs at best: half-log shanties, clapboard hovels, temporary lean-tos confected out of the handiest scraps and flot-sam of the town they appended, as welcome as a carbuncle on a buttock. Here the unemployed, the underemployed, and the unemployable permanently congregated and became indistin-guishable from the petty criminals, absconding spouses, and all-'round deadbeats who found temporary refuge among the maze of crooked lanes and labyrinthine walkways no respectable citizen could, or would wish to, negotiate. The stench of open sewers rose up around Irishtown as sturdy and dissuasive as a rampart.

It had been christened Irishtown some years back when a few destitute families from Connaught had camped there, but its cur-rent denizens were as polyglot as their legitimate counterparts in the town and, if the truth be known, little different in the range and persistence of their vices. However, lest a decent citizen wax sentimental about this truism, Cobb would be the first to point out that Irishtown had been the likely source of the biennial epi-demics of cholera in the early thirties. It was an indisputable fact that anyone entering the area, day or night, without a plausible reason for doing so was almost certain to be persuaded to depart posthaste, and usually physically assisted in the act.

Among the acceptable excuses for nocturnal entry—and one earnestly condemned each Sunday from multiple pulpits—was a visit to either of two well-maintained and annually repainted houses. These were, in the fiery words of Archdeacon Strachan, "houses of infamy" or, in the common parlance preferred by Cobb and his colleagues, "hooer-houses." There were, of course, a num-ber of less settled and less ostentatious bawdy shops or cathouses throughout the town. But while these came and went, flourished and withered, the unholy pair in Irishtown had stood stalwart against verbal assault and police raid. (The latter threat had been carried out only once, a few months after the constabulary was

formed in 1835. When the found-ins were discovered to be principally members of the same class who had established the new
police force to eradicate such crime, a stalemate was quickly declared and it was hands off ever since.)

But why would any respectable gentleman, born or self-
proclaimed, risk the night dangers of Irishtown for a brief and
costly romp with some mangy female of indeterminate age and
pedigree, when other, less hazardous alternatives were often
available? It was a question Cobb had asked himself once or
twice but, finding no answer, he dismissed the puzzlement as
inexplicable and got on with his life.

What he did discover, from Wilkie and at first hand on his
occasional patrols up here, was that the hazards of reaching and
returning from these dens of fleshly delight were minuscule in
comparison with those inside them. If a gentleman of obvious
prosperity or a sailor with a bulging purse lingered on the edge
of Irishtown any time after dark, he would soon be corralled by
what Wilkie termed a tracker or scout, usually a scruffy youth,
who would lead the prospective client through the shadowy maze
of lanes to the house of his choice: Madame Renée's or Madame
Charlotte's (neither woman was French, nor *madame*). A discreet
knock, whispered negotiations, and the contract was sealed. Much
later, sated and lighter in the wallet, the client would be guided
back to Lot Street, where a tracker of obsequious discretion might
well be tipped a shilling for his pains. What actually went on in
these French parlours, beyond the mundane act itself, Cobb did
not know and was unable, despite some effort, to imagine.

He surmised it must be nearly two o'clock in the morning,
as the three-quarter chime of the City Hall clock had rung some
minutes before. For the past hour or so he had paced along Newgate between Bay and John Streets, watching the gala revellers

pass by on their way to their beds or to further wassailing in im-
promptu parties at home. Most of them seemed to feel obliged to
wave at him and roar out some greeting more raucous than intel-
ligible—in derision or pity he could not determine. He declined
to return the favour.

Cobb decided to take one more stroll around the perimeter of
his patrol and then go home to the comfort of his own bed and
Dora's more than adequate bodily solace. As he moved eastward
along the southern edge of Lot Street and passed the lugubrious
silhouette of Osgoode Hall at the head of York, he spotted a few
feeble lights, bonfires most likely, flickering up into the general
gloom. A woman screamed with a sound as sharp and terrified
as a seized animal, then her cry skittered upward and became a
manic ripple of laughter. Male guffaws answered it. Finally silence,
except for the seesawing crick of peepers and the deeper boom of
bullfrogs bellowing their belligerent lust from ponds above the
shantytown. In the pauses between gusts of night breeze, mosquitoes—bred by the millions in the pools of slime between hovels—
buzzed at Cobb with evil intent.

He quickened his pace, praying that the wind would not die
and no disquieting noises would erupt from the vicinity of Newgate or Hospital Street. He had almost reached Bay when he heard
just such a noise. But it came not from the streets of his patrol to
the south. It was coming distinctly and beseechingly from his left,
from somewhere in the impenetrable darkness of Irishtown.

"Help! Help me! Somebody . . . *please!*"

Cobb turned and peered across the roadway. The voice was
female and urgent with terror. Still, Cobb could see nothing.
With his hair rising at the repeated and ever more desperate pleas
and with every nerve instantly alert, he edged across the road.
Just as he reached the far side, he spotted something white and

shimmering in the darkness ahead. There was just enough moonlight to catch its sudden flutter, stepping between the shadow of
two trees into the roadway. It was a girl, a young woman actually,
clad only in a cotton shift. Her face was as pale as her clothing.

"What's the matter?" Cobb demanded.

The woman flinched at the sight of a stranger with a club in
his right hand. As she turned to flee, Cobb grabbed her by the
arm.

"It's all right. I'm a policeman. What sort of help do you
need?"

Cobb was beginning to breathe more easily. Even in this poor
light it was plain that the woman was the inmate of one of the
brothels or at best the unlucky appendage of some tough or drunk
in Irishtown. Unless it were a clear case of attempted assault, he
would not move a step farther to the north.

"Thank God, thank God," the woman sobbed, her fear now
venting itself in tears. Cobb felt her young body rock against his,
not unpleasantly. He doubted very much whether God would be
any more likely to intervene here than the constabulary.

"Do you need a safe place to stay fer the night?" he offered
wearily, knowing that Dora never refused a woman refuge in such
circumstances. "It's the best I can do."

Controlling her sobs as best as she could, she said in a desperate rush, "You don't understand. Somethin' terrible's happened,
and Madame Renée's sent me to fetch the police. I can't go back
without you."

"And what's so terrible at Madame Renée's?"

"Someone's been murdered! There's blood all over. It's awful!
You've got to come."

Cursing his fate, Cobb knew that he no longer had any choice.
He let the terrified girl take him by the hand and draw him deep

into the noisome interior of Irishtown, where no sensible bobby ventured on his own. Fortunately, the girl seemed to know her way through the warren of huts, ruts, middens, and pathways greased with God-knows-what from coop or sty. Cobb skidded and lurched, grazed and ricocheted, arousing the suspicions of several dogs, whose jaws snapped at his boots, and one pig, who protested with a teeth-jarring squeal. The girl took no notice. She continued to pick her way with unerring dexterity, like smugglers were said to do across the deadly night moors of Devon.

Finally, exhausted and panting, they came to an abrupt stop before a dwelling that resembled an ordinary house. There was just enough moonlight to reveal a one-storey brick structure with a gabled roof, regular windows with sills and curtains, and a stout hardwood door that sported a saucy knocker on its scarlet façade.

"We're here, sir," the girl said, as soon as she was able to straighten up and breathe normally. "This is Madame Renée's."

"Then . . . we'd better . . . go in," Cobb said between gasps. Instinctively his right hand moved towards his truncheon, but he did not draw it out for fear of spooking the girl. Nevertheless, he was on alien ground and would need to remain alert. Although he prided himself on being able to smell trouble in a tavern minutes before it actually erupted, it was men he was dealing with there, men whose moods and motives he could read like a divvy. But women were a different species of humankind: unpredictable and unfathomable.

"I'm Molly," the young woman said, and to Cobb's surprise she reached up and banged the knocker rhythmically, as if tapping a code. As she did so, one of the straps on her shift slipped off her shoulder. Cobb looked away quickly, realizing with a resigned sigh that he was leaving himself vulnerable to any sort of random assault.

"Why don't you just call out?" Cobb said.

Molly gave him a puzzled look. "But you could have me in a hammerlock, couldn't you?"

A heavy bar was heard sliding behind the door, which was then eased open a crack.

"You okay, Molly?" The voice of an older woman, frightened and wary.

"I brung the constable, like you said, Mum."

"Good girl." The door swung outward. The tepid light revealed a woman in a flowered dressing gown but was not sufficient to show the features of her face. Her size and posture and the deep alto of her voice signalled unmistakably that this was the mistress of the establishment. She reached out and Molly fell into her arms, sobbing uncontrollably. "There, there, girl. You've been a great help. There's nothing more you can do now but go back to your sisters and give them what comfort you can."

Molly nodded her assent, gave the dressing gown one last clutch, then tottered into the shadows behind her mistress, who had turned just far enough to let her go by. Then the woman looked Cobb square in the eye and said, "Come in, Constable. I'm known hereabouts as Madame Renée." She ushered Cobb in as if he were perhaps one of her gentleman callers.

"I'm Cobb, ma'am. Yer Molly come out onto Lot Street babbling somethin' about a murder."

Madame Renée's large, dark eyes were luminous with tears that did little to disguise the contending emotions in them: fear, bravado, uncertainty, defiance, pain—all that complex stew of feelings and responses which Cobb associated with the female gender and which caused his head to spin and his heart to thump.

"I'm afraid so, Mr. Cobb. One of my girls. Come, I'll show you."

She glided back into the room and picked up a bright candle lantern from a fancy, draped table, the hem of her dressing gown floating across a patterned Persian carpet. Beyond the carpet, however, and two padded chairs that had seen better days, the parlour of Madame Renée's bordello, reputed to be the classier of these carnal establishments, was nondescript. Cobb caught shadowy glimpses of a pot-bellied stove in one corner, three or four hard-backed chairs of undistinguished provenance, and a severely scarred sideboard upon which decanters of wine and whiskey tilted forlornly. Somewhere nearby an incense candle wafted a thick scent into the room. Cobb was disappointed: he had expected this brand of sin to have a more sumptuous face.

Cobb followed Madame Renée through a narrow hall to a curtained-off doorway.

"I can't look in there again," she said, her voice faltering as she pushed the lantern into Cobb's hand. "Sarah was like a daughter to me."

"No need to, ma'am. That's my job," Cobb said with more confidence than he felt. He had been involved in only two murder cases since joining the force, not counting the lethal consequences of tavern brawls. Thus he had seen a number of dead bodies, but the thought of somebody deliberately murdered and a woman to boot was unnerving in the extreme. He took a deep breath, pushed the curtain aside, and went in.

He found himself in a small bedroom, furnished only with a washstand and a low-slung bed not more than a foot off the wooden floor. Above the bed, high up on the wall, was a window in which a kind of muslin screen ballooned gently, letting in a bit of the night breeze and keeping out the mosquitoes. But it was the bed itself that caught Cobb's attention and held it in a horrified gaze. The lantern trembled in his hand.

Two people lay on top of a skimpy coverlet, both naked, one of them snoring monstrously and the other very much dead. Cobb forced himself to concentrate on the gaping wound in the girl's neck as she lay motionless on her back with her legs apart and all her womanly appurtenances exposed to the lantern light. There was blood everywhere. The coverlet was soaked, as was the throw rug beside it and the bedding under the young male who lay beside the victim. In his right hand, a slim dagger glittered, gobbets of the girl's blood still wet upon its six-inch length. Cobb thanked the Lord that her eyes were closed.

He edged forward, keeping to the outside wall to avoid stepping in the blood on the rug and trying to clear the shock from his head. He was also doing his best to recall what he had learned at the side of Lieutenant Marc Edwards during his investigation of the murder at Frank's Theatre last year. Observe the scene coolly before becoming part of it, he said to himself. He stopped in the narrow space between the bed and the wall with the window in it. The cheesecloth screen covering the eye-level window looked untouched: no one had come in or gone out that way. He held the lantern high and peered across the bodies to scrutinize the blood-drenched throw rug and blood-smeared plank floor from another angle. No sign of footprints. It appeared that neither Molly nor Madame Renée had ventured into the room after coming upon the grisly sight.

While the naked man continued to snore loudly, Cobb leaned across him to examine the murdered girl, still keeping half an eye on the knife in her client's hand. Her hair, lustrous brown and unbloodied, lay demurely upon its pillow; her small rosebud lips were opened as if to register a final "oh" of surprise or regret. She wore no makeup. She didn't have to: she was naturally beautiful. And a whore.

Cobb sighed, and the man stirred, moaned, and took up snoring again. Cobb leaned farther over him and held the lantern up to examine the wound. It looked wide and deep, but it was clear she had been killed by a single thrust. Dr. Withers would be able to tell him more. Cobb forced himself to make a quick survey of the rest of the girl's body, feeling the heat in his cheeks, but there were no visible signs of any other kind of injury. He straightened up then and shone the light upon the girl's killer. He was surprised to see a fine-boned young man with a shock of ashen hair, beardless and, even in this poor light, pale-skinned. Cobb lifted the knife free of the man's fingers. They were uncallused. That, and the clothes strewn about Cobb's feet, indicated a man of means. Not unexpected, in Madame Renée's establishment. There would be no end of trouble, Cobb surmised, when the murderer was well-heeled and the victim a lowly denizen of a brothel. But at least there would be no doubt about who the killer was. Cobb would escort this gentleman to the jail himself. With no apologies.

Cobb wrapped the knife in his freshly laundered handkerchief and quietly left the room. For the moment he had decided to question the madam and Molly about the circumstances leading up to the murder. Get a clear picture of what happened as soon as you can, would be Marc Edwards's advice. And if the gentleman wished to sleep and keep himself out of the way, so much the better. Before entering the parlour, however, Cobb took a quick look at the layout of this part of the house. The bedroom behind him was one of three such cubicles exiting off a narrow hallway. He walked to the far end of it, where a water closet lay to his left. Even in the unlit corridor, he could see that there was no window in the end wall. The other two cubicles were empty, with their forlorn little cots neatly made up.

When he came back into the parlour, he saw Madame Renée sitting in one of the padded armchairs. She was holding her chin in her hands as if physically trying to still her shuddering body. Cobb had seen it before: delayed shock. Molly had come back into the room, her own tidal waves of trauma passed, and was prodding a fire into life in the stove, preparing to brew some tea. Across the room in a doorway leading to another part of the house, Cobb could see two moon faces peering out: the other girls, no doubt.

Cobb nodded to Molly to carry on, then went to the sideboard. He brought a glass of whiskey across to Madame Renée, and she accepted it gratefully.

"I'm gonna haveta ask you and yer girls some questions, when you feel up to it. I also need to have someone go up to Dr. Withers's place and lead him back here to examine the body."

Madame Renée trembled anew at the mention of the word "body."

"I treated her like my own, didn't I, Molly?"

"We all did, Mum," Molly said, plunking the tea kettle onto the hot stove. "Sarah was the sweetest girl. She wouldn't hurt a flea."

"Is there a boy we could send into town for the doctor?" Cobb asked. "And, if possible, another lad to fetch the chief constable." Cobb was beginning to worry about being the lone authority with a killer to watch over and witnesses to interrogate. God knows what other form of trouble might be lurking nearby. He couldn't be everywhere at once.

Madame Renée collected herself. "Yes. I sent our trackers home hours ago, but they just live two doors up. Carrie, dear, go up and fetch Donald and Peter." A natural air of command had come back into Madame Renée's voice.

Carrie, in a flimsy wrap, inched out of the doorway, her face glistening with tears. "Is Sarah really dead?"

"Yes, she is, Carrie. And Constable Cobb is here to help us. So be a good girl and fetch the lads. Tell them it's urgent."

Cobb reached into his pocket and pulled out a coin. "Would sixpence speed them on their way?"

"You give them that and we'll not see hide nor hair of them," Madame Renée said, a brief twinkle surfacing through her distress.

A few minutes later, when the tea had been made and Madame Renée's grief had subsided, Cobb went outside and gave two skinny, yawning boys their instructions. He slipped them each a three-penny piece, and they vanished into the darkness. As he re-entered the parlour he heard Madame Renée saying to Molly, "We're ruined, you know. We've lost Sarah and we're ruined."

While Cobb knew that Marc would have questioned the witnesses one at a time in privacy, he could not bring himself to order Molly or her mistress out of the room while he dealt with them individually. Besides, if they had wished or needed to concoct a plausible lie about what had happened, they had had plenty of opportunity to do so before his arrival. So he drew up a chair beside Madame Renée and Molly, while the others were allowed to look on. Cobb decided to start with what he assumed to be the most salient points first, then backtrack to the larger narrative of events.

"Who was the victim?" he said to Madame Renée.

"Sarah McConkey. She was one of my four girls. You've met Molly—"

"Molly Mason, I am."

"And over there is Carrie Garnet and Frieda Smiley. We work in this part of the house and live together in the adjoining section."

"Was it you, ma'am, who found Sarah like that?"

"It was Molly and me together. We were all asleep in our rooms over there—Molly was sleeping with me and Frieda and Carrie right next—"

"You left Sarah alone with a . . . customer?"

"He seemed so harmless," Madame Renée said, and faltered.

"It weren't your fault, Mum," Molly said, reaching across and giving her mistress a pat on the forearm.

"What I need to know more'n anythin' else is exactly what you saw when you opened the curtains and looked in there."

"Molly and I were asleep when Molly woke up saying she heard someone yell."

"It was a sort of shriek," Molly said with a shudder, recalling it.

"Sarah?"

"I'm sure it was the gentleman."

"Anyway, we both ran in here and then into the east bedroom," Madame Renée continued. "We were both standing in the doorway, struck dumb."

"The candle beside the bed was almost burned down, but we could still see, couldn't we, Mum?"

"I saw the blood, everywhere. I saw the wound in Sarah's neck. I knew she was dead. And that man, that horrid little man was snoring away—still drunk."

"Then he must have cried out in his sleep," Cobb said. "Sarah must've been stabbed long before that noise woke you up. It'd take some time fer all of that blood to drain outta her."

Frieda and Carrie, both very young and very frightened, emitted a joint cry of anguish. Cobb turned and apologized, "Sorry to be so blunt."

"Yes, I knew she was already dead. And I couldn't bring myself to walk through her blood, I—"

"Now, don't go upsettin' yerself so," Cobb said. "It's the man I want to know about."

"He had Sarah's knife in his hand!" Molly said.

"*Sarah's* knife?"

"She kept that little dagger under her pillow whenever she had a caller—"

"You warned her about it, didn't you, Mum?"

Madame Renée looked at Molly with a sad, grateful nod. Her eyes were full of tears. "But Sarah was a strong-willed girl," she said to Cobb.

"So you both saw the knife in his right hand, just as I did?"

"Yes, we did."

Well, that more or less clinched it. Cobb congratulated himself. Nevertheless, he felt obliged, despite the discomfiture of feminine tears and the near nakedness of the women he was questioning, to establish a chronology of events before waking the murderer and making any accusations. Piece by piece, with help from both Madame Renée and her three charges, they painted a vivid picture of what had happened before the discovery of the body. Because the brothel drew its clientele from among the prosperous and respectable in the community—merchants, bankers, councillors, army officers, and the like, if Madame were to be believed—the governor's ball had robbed them of a good night's take. Only three of their regulars had visited, elderly gentlemen too decrepit or senile to attend the gala at Spadina. Cobb was fascinated by the complex workings of a fancy brothel in the midst of a shantytown. Each of the regular callers, it seemed, had a nickname (Madame professing not to have the slightest notion of who they really were). Her trackers scouted the verges of Lot Street and, when a regular showed up, they escorted him safely to the red door. The caller would then use the brass knocker to rap out a prearranged code (frequently changed). The tracker lads had a different knock if they merely wanted to convey messages or otherwise be admitted. The parlour door, heavily barred, was the only way into the working section of the house. The windows were all high, small, and either shuttered or screened. None of the screens showed any signs of forced entry. One other door at the far west side of the house, with its own sturdy bar, led into the living quarters of the women.

About one o'clock, realizing that no one else was likely to arrive this night, Madame had sent Peter and Donald home, barred the red door, and prepared to close up shop. They had just finished a cup of tea and were walking towards their own quarters when they heard a discreet rap—of one of the regulars. They waited. The knock was repeated. Madame unbarred the door and eased it open. A pale young man, heavily cloaked, stumbled in as if he had been pushed. He was a stranger. Puzzled, for the knock had been legitimate, Madame stepped out in time to see the back of a man in a purple or black cape and top hat moving quickly into the darkness. She concluded that one of her regulars—who knew his way in without assistance—had brought along a friend, though it was curious that he himself had not stayed to introduce him. When Cobb queried Madame as to why she didn't simply toss the intruder back into the murk outside, she sighed and said that he was very young, unthreatening, and exceedingly drunk. He also waved a wad of pound notes at her, ogled the girls, and gave them all such a boyish, helpless sort of grin that they took pity on him. And none of them, it was clear, would ever forgive themselves for doing so.

Because Sarah McConkey was the only one of the girls not to have entertained a client that evening, she inherited the task of divesting the young gentleman (whom she dubbed Jocko, which seemed to amuse him) of his clothes and enticing him into bed. Madame insisted that she had remained awake in her room for half an hour or so, until she heard Jocko's drunken snores. Then she peeked in and found both of them sound asleep. She returned to her own room and lay down beside Molly. The rest he now knew.

Cobb stood up and thanked Madame. He was sure he heard footsteps approaching. It would be Dr. Angus Withers to confirm his own findings or Chief Constable Sturges to congratulate him and take the accused into custody. But before he could unbar the door, he was startled by a sound behind him and a collective gasp from the women. He swivelled around. There in the opening to the little hallway—naked, detumescent, blood-smeared, and plainly horrified—stood the murderer.

DR. ANGUS WITHERS, PHYSICIAN TO THE well-heeled and the self-important but a kindly gentleman himself, was in Sarah's cubicle examining the body. The man presumed responsible for its condition was seated on the edge of a hard chair near the stove, which was throwing off more heat than anybody but the killer required. The moment he had appeared in the parlour, Cobb—offended by the man's nakedness and spooked by the wild look in his eye—had moved decisively. Calling for a blanket to cover the wretched creature's shame, Cobb had thrown both arms around him and half-dragged him to one of the armchairs. Amid the initial shrieks of the three girls, Madame Renée was a pillar of steely determination. Whatever revulsion she may have felt for the man who had slaughtered Sarah, she kept it under control, chivvying her young charges back into their quarters and returning with another dressing gown. She tossed it at Cobb, and he wrapped it around the shivering form before him.

Cobb had waited in vain for the man to calm down, hoping to question him and even drawing out the notebook he carried to jot down items he might fail to remember. His memory, however, was usually quicker and more reliable than his handwriting, so he was content to carry information in his head and, when he returned to the station, to dictate it to Augustus French, the police clerk. But the only word the trembling fellow had uttered in the past fifteen minutes was something resembling "awful," and even that was garbled and hesitant. Madame Renée sat a few feet away, staring at him. Cobb could sense that she too was on the verge of crumbling. Dr. Withers had suggested sedatives all 'round, but Cobb had waved him to the victim's room.

As soon as the doctor disappeared down the hallway, Cobb had decided to accelerate the proceedings. He unwrapped the dagger, which he set on one of the end tables, and held it up into the candlelight before the killer. "This is what you stuck inta that poor lass's throat," he snarled.

The man had yelped, as if he too had been stabbed, leapt up, and staggered over to the chair near the stove. Without looking up, he moaned, and this time the words were clear: "I d-d-didn't mean to."

Cobb had turned away in disgust. So here they sat, the three of them, waiting for the doctor to confirm the obvious and, in Cobb's case, listening for the arrival of the chief constable. The wood in the stove crackled like gunshot.

Cobb suddenly thought of a use for his notebook. He turned to Madame Renée.

"What was the young lady's full name again?"

"Sarah McConkey."

"And the others?"

"Molly Mason, Carrie Garnet, and Frieda Smiley."

Cobb gave a little cough and said, "And your name, ma'am?"

A wee smile trembled at the corners of Madame Renée's mouth. "Norah Burgess," she said. "Just plain Norah Burgess. Madame Renée is my . . . professional appellation."

Cobb nodded sagely. "Yer sober-ket, I take it." He scribbled down all the names, content with phonetic approximations. Gussie French could tidy up the spelling, and enjoy himself in the process.

"Do you know where Sarah's from? Who her parents are?"

Norah Burgess grimaced. "I do. But I doubt they'll give a damn about what's happened here." She spat out these words, then added tonelessly, "They live on a farm out near Streetsville."

"Sarah and them didn't get along?"

"They threw her out on the street. Disowned her. It was me who took her in when no one else would. She was beautiful and sweet. They didn't deserve her."

"They'll have to be told, all the same," Cobb said gently. "Do you know where we can find them? They may want to make the arrangements."

Norah's face darkened, its pleasant, plump contours suddenly hardening. "I'm gonna give her a proper burial. Up in the town. I won't have her body dumped into some pauper's grave."

"Well, ma'am, her soul's elsewhere now."

"With God," Norah said, with a touch more bitterness than gratitude.

Cobb wasn't sure there were harems in heaven, so refrained from comment.

"We're ruined, you know, Constable. What gentleman would come here now with such a scandal about the place?" She looked around at her handiwork. "We'll have to cater to drunken sailors with the clap and no manners."

Just then Dr. Withers emerged from the bedroom. He glanced fiercely at the perpetrator of the outrage he had just scrutinized. The killer, however, remained oblivious, rocking on the edge of his chair with both arms locked around his chest and his chin on top of them, the rose-petalled dressing gown still draped preposterously over his pathetically thin body. He was white enough to intimidate a ghost.

"She was stabbed once in the throat with a thin blade," the doctor said to Cobb and Norah Burgess. Cobb indicated the bloody weapon on the end table.

"A single powerful thrust. Straight in, then twisted about. Cut the jugular in two by the looks of it. Then kept on going through the neck, severing the spine, I'd say. Certainly there was no resistance, no spasming of the body. Very likely she was in a sound sleep and died instantly." He looked at Norah Burgess. "Without pain."

"I think you oughta have a gander at the fella here who did it. I can't get a sensible word outta him."

"Shock," Withers said. "It does that to people."

"But the fella was sound asleep and snorin' like a spent horse when I got here," Cobb said. "How could he stab a helpless girl to death with such a blow and then drift off like nothin'd happened?"

"Perhaps he did it in his sleep," Withers suggested. "It wouldn't be the first time." With that he went over to the fellow, stayed the rocking, catatonic figure with one gentle hand, and very slowly lifted the chin up to expose the wan face and desperate eyes, feral with fear.

"I'm going to give you something to drink, young man: tincture of laudanum. It'll calm your nerves."

Outside the door they could hear footsteps and voices. Cobb recognized the cockney semitones of his superior: reinforcements had arrived. But most of the work here, Cobb thought to himself with restrained pride, had already been done—and done well.

"My God!" Withers cried. "I know this man."

Cobb reached for his notebook. The final piece of the puzzle was about to fall into place. There was a timely pounding on the scarlet door.

"Who is he?" Cobb asked quickly of the doctor.

"I saw him at the gala out at Spadina not three hours ago. At the whist table."

There was a flicker of recognition in the murderer's face.

Norah Burgess stood to unbar the door.

Dr. Withers drew Cobb to one side and said in a low, tremulous whisper, "This is Handford Ellice, Lord Durham's nephew."

Cobb dropped his notebook.

FOUR

Marc was taking his first sip of coffee at ten o'clock the next morning when there was a loud rap at the front door. Beth was still pleasurably abed, but Charlene scooted across the parlour to answer the knock. Seconds later she came through to the kitchen.

"It's the police," she gasped, awestruck.

Marc got up. He could hear Beth stirring behind him in their bedroom. "All of them?" he asked Charlene with a teasing smile.

"Just one. A large fella who looks like he could use a good pressin'," Charlene said, obviously relieved by her master's reaction.

"Wilkie, then."

And Constable Ewan Wilkie it was, rumpled and pale. "They routed me outta my sickbed, sir," he began without ceremony.

"What's happened to occasion such a catastrophe?"

Wilkie blinked. "There's been a murder, sir. On my patrol."

"And it concerns me somehow?"

"In a way, sir. Some bigwig stabbed a"—here he lowered his voice and whispered—"a hooer, if you'll pardon my French. In Irishtown."

"I'm sorry to hear that."

"What is it, Marc dear?" Beth had come up behind them, pulling her robe close.

Wilkie blushed and ducked sideways.

"There's been a murder," Marc said.

"And you're to go to the station and then on up to Government House," Wilkie said to the rosebush beside the stoop.

"But what is wanted of me?" Marc asked again, genuinely puzzled.

"It's His Earlship, sir."

"Lord Durham?"

"He's asked particularly fer you."

COBB AND SARGE—AS CHIEF CONSTABLE WILFRID Sturges was affectionately called when he was out of earshot—were waiting for Marc at the police quarters: two cramped rooms at the rear of the Court House and directly across from the jail adjacent. Gussie French, the desiccated clerk, was seated behind the constables scribbling furiously at official-looking papers.

"Thank the Lord you've come," Sturges greeted him.

He and Cobb appeared to have been up all night.

"What on earth's happened?"

For the next fifteen minutes Cobb, with occasional grunts or sighs of agreement from his chief, poured out the sad narrative of the night's events. As he had just finished dictating the details to Gussie French, who would affix them to documents for the magistrate upstairs, Cobb had little difficulty in recounting the brutal murder of Sarah McConkey, despite several unintentional yawns. He especially emphasized the indisputable fact that there were three witnesses, including himself, who saw the blackguard covered in the girl's blood and with a gory knife in his hand. The suspect, though disoriented and evidently not recovered from the drunken stupor in which he had committed the insane act, had not formally denied his guilt, though he was going to be interrogated this morning at Government House, where he was temporarily incarcerated. Cobb also mentioned that no one other than the four women could have entered that part of the brothel during the probable time of the murder. He then summarized the doctor's preliminary findings.

"That's quite a story," Marc said at last. "But what has it got to do with Lord Durham or me?"

Cobb and Sarge had decided not to reveal the identity of the accused until after Marc had had time to absorb the details of the crime, and Wilkie, of course, had no idea what was going on.

"You tell him," Sarge sighed heavily. He motioned Gussie into the adjoining room and closed the door on him. "We're keepin' the fella's name between us—fer the time bein'."

"The guy we're certain done it is Handford Ellice," Cobb said, sotto voce.

"Sweet Jesus." Marc was incredulous.

"There's a cab out back," Sarge said. "It'll take you straight up to Government House."

"I'll go, of course," Marc said. "But I still don't see how I can be of much help. I've never met Handford Ellice and I've had barely a single conversation with His Lordship."

Sarge cleared his throat. "When I broke the news to 'im an hour ago, he was flabbergasted. He claimed it were impossible that his nephew could do such an 'orrible thing."

"Quite a natural reaction, I'd say."

Cobb looked sorrowfully at Marc. "The poor fool thinks his nephew's innocent. He won't accept the facts we give him."

"And?"

"He asked me, point-blank," Sarge said warily, "if there was anybody in town who knew how to conduct a proper investigation."

It was Marc's turn to sigh. "And you suggested me."

"No," Cobb said. "I did."

WHILE COBB WENT HOME TO CATCH a few hours' sleep, Marc was whisked up to Government House at the corner of King and Simcoe. He had spent a number of months here after his arrival three years ago as a newly commissioned officer in the 23rd, commanding the lieutenant-governor's guard. He knew the grounds and the sprawling residence well. But it had been some time since he had been asked here on official business. The corporal at the door ushered him into Lieutenant-Governor Arthur's office, where, to his surprise, he was suddenly alone and face-to-face with Lord Durham.

"Thank you for coming at such short notice," Durham said. Only the shadows under his eyes betrayed that he might have felt fatigued and perhaps even alarmed. The intelligent dark eyes and handsome, confident face met Marc's gaze unflinchingly across the expansive desk. "Please, sit down. My own feet are a little weary after last evening's pleasant exercise."

"Thank you, sir. I came as soon as I heard, and it goes without saying that I will do all I can to be of service."

Durham folded himself into a padded chair. Then, as Marc did likewise, Lord Melbourne's envoy to the Canadas stared at some papers on the desk for a full minute. Marc waited patiently.

"Let me begin, Mr. Edwards, by saying that since your name was mentioned by the constable this morning, I have made discreet inquiries about you and your—exploits, shall we call them—here in the colonies."

Marc felt himself colouring. "And you've learned that I have been a lifelong Tory, I daresay."

Durham seemed amused despite the obvious stress he was suffering. "*Were* a Tory is the word around here."

"Ah. I suspect the reputation of my wife has preceded me."

"Please, believe me, sir, when I say that I care little what politics you subscribe to. Your record of service as an officer and your conduct of several murder investigations are exemplary. I am confident, then, that should you agree to assist me in this sordid affair, you will serve without fear or favour."

Marc nodded in mute acceptance of the compliment. "How do you think I may be of assistance? I believe the police have briefed you thoroughly on the events in Irishtown and your nephew's unfortunate involvement."

"They have done so, and I'd like you to assure them that I have no doubts about their integrity or their efforts. However, since I believe my wife's nephew to be incapable of such a crime, I feel I must have a more thorough and perhaps dispassionate investigation by someone more . . . experienced."

Marc did not respond right away. He was searching Durham's face for some hint of ambiguity in his last statement.

Durham gave Marc a wan smile. "You think I meant that you were somehow to find a route around the truth?" he inquired.

"Such an interpretation did occur to me, Your Lordship. With all due respect."

"And I am pleased that you are so frank. We'll need to be ruthlessly honest with each other if we are to get to the bottom of the matter." He leaned across the desk as he must have done countless times in the cabinet room when he wished to hammer home a point to his less talented colleagues. "I want the truth,

Mr. Edwards. And when you find it, I will be the first person to endorse it and make it public."

"Then I will be pleased to help you, sir."

Durham leaned back and took a deep breath. "Good. Now we can get down to business. I expect that you too have been fully briefed by the chief constable."

"I have. Though I must admit that at first I was as shocked and baffled as you must have been when you arrived here this morning and found your nephew under house arrest. It can't be more than ten or eleven hours since Beth and I watched Mr. Ellice enjoy himself at Spadina. That he could have got all the way from there to a brothel in Irishtown and committed a murder in so short a time seems incredible."

"That was precisely my reaction."

"Has Lady Durham been told?"

Durham sighed. "Governor Arthur has kindly driven out to break the news to her, accompanied by Dr. Withers."

"But from Cobb's report—and I can personally vouch for his honesty and impartiality—it is clear that somehow your nephew did reach the brothel around one o'clock. He was found there and brought directly here. And was examined there and again here by Dr. Withers."

"I am not disputing the incontrovertible."

"I realize that, sir. But so many of the facts appear to have only one interpretation."

"You sound like the Duke of Wellington annunciating absolute truth."

Marc risked a smile and got one back. "It was Cobb who found the knife in Mr. Ellice's hand and him lying bloodied and asleep beside the corpse."

"I know, and the house apparently impregnable to intruders with murder on their mind. But how many a man has thought his own home to be burglar-proof and paid the price?"

Marc thought for a moment before saying, "It is conceivable that any one of the other four women could have committed the murder or unbarred the door to allow an accomplice entry."

"Exactly. There must be an alternative explanation. I need to know that these women have been properly questioned and assessed. If you can find no plausible motive as to why one of them should kill one of their own and are convinced of their veracity, then I will accept your word on it."

It was Marc's turn to take a deep breath. "It is an awesome responsibility that you are placing on my shoulders, sir."

"I've been told they are very broad shoulders."

At this point there came a discreet tap at the door and Sir George's batman whisked in with a pot of hot coffee and biscuits.

Marc sipped gratefully at his coffee, thinking rapidly. "I believe I know how much Lady Durham must love her sister's son, and how much hope she has allowed herself in regard to the benefits for him of this foreign journey, as well as the possible distractions it might cause for you in your work here. She spoke to me about Handford early last evening and later on confided in Mrs. Edwards."

"And you are wondering if my certainty about Handford's innocence is simply based on my loyalty to my wife and perhaps some intimate but misguided knowledge of the lad's character?"

"Something like that, sir." Marc decided he wouldn't want to be a Tory facing Lord Durham across the floor of the upper chamber at Westminster.

"I tell you what. Why don't you go back to his room and see him for yourself. Then come back and tell me what you think."

• • •

HANDFORD ELLICE WAS SITTING UP IN bed, propped up by pillows twice his size. A full breakfast, untouched, rested on a table beside him. He seemed more like a consumptive Keats than a lusting Byron. But then Marc knew from his previous investigations that murderers rarely looked the part. Marc introduced himself but got no response.

"Your uncle has asked me to take charge of the inquiry into the death of Sarah McConkey earlier this morning. Would you be willing to answer a few brief questions?"

Ellice was listening, but he kept his gaze glued to the hands in his lap.

"Your uncle is convinced of your innocence and wants me to help prove it."

Ellice nodded and peered up. His eyes were red and swollen. Blue veins throbbed at his temples. His lips were gray, his expression lifeless.

"You met my wife at the ball last night."

"Mrs. Edwards?" he responded, showing the first signs of real engagement.

"Yes. I saw you dancing with her. You seemed to be enjoying yourself."

"I d-d-don't dance." The head went back to its drooping. "I don't d-do anything."

"That's not so. You were seen at the whist tables later on. Beth tells me that you are an avid player."

"She was k-kind."

"Do you remember how you got from Spadina House to Madame Renée's way up north of the city?"

A shake of the head.

"I'm sure you didn't walk."

"Rode in a c-coach."

"Whose coach?"

"Man and a l-lady."

"Did they tell you their names?"

"M-m-may have. I don't remember."

"Perhaps when you've had a chance to rest and—"

"I was drunk!" The intended venom of this admission was cut off by a sob.

"But you must have walked through Irishtown. Did this couple let you off there? Did someone then take you to the brothel?"

"A n-nice gentleman."

"Why would you leave your aunt and uncle and go to a strange house in town after midnight? Especially when I'm told you are too shy even to dance."

"Don't know." The lower jaw shook as if it had become unhinged.

Marc waited.

"I wanted a w-w-woman."

"And the nice gentleman promised you one?"

A slow, sad nod.

"Would you recognize him if you saw him again?"

"Don't remember."

"Do you recall arriving at Madame Renée's? Meeting Sarah and going into a room with her?"

"I was confused, thought she was Mrs. Edwards . . ."

"You were found naked beside Sarah McConkey with her dagger in your hand. Surely you remember getting into bed with a young woman?"

Ellice kept his head down and brought his hands up over his eyes as if to blot out the horror of some image there. Marc realized what a horror it must have been to awake in that room in those circumstances.

"Do you remember making love to her?"

The head came up and the face with it, anguished and shamed. "I don't know. I c-can't remember!"

"WELL?" DURHAM ASKED WHEN MARC HAD returned to the office.

"I find it difficult to believe that your nephew could have committed the murder. I think it more plausible that he was so far intoxicated as to be barely mobile and far too disoriented to have rummaged around for a knife said to be under the girl's pillow and then driven it with deadly force and unerring accuracy through her throat and spine. I can see no motive nor any latent hostility or repressed rage in the young man. He appears abnormally passive."

"Then how do you intend to proceed? The resources of the government are at your disposal."

Marc had already been thinking about that. "The only way we can exculpate your nephew is to find the guilty party. I shall go out and interview the women at Madame Renée's—without revealing your nephew's name, of course. There has to be something Cobb has missed. If so, I'll find it."

"You believe, then, that this could well be the result of a dispute among the inmates of that brothel?"

"That's the most obvious place to begin. Four of them were in the house when the stabbing occurred."

Durham looked thoughtful. "That's true. But if one or more *was* responsible, we may never be able to prove it—if they stick together, as they well might, having a fortuitous scapegoat handy."

"Yes. I don't suppose I could appeal to their patriotism."

"And the rack went out with the Inquisition."

"I think we should try to track down the couple who gave Mr. Ellice a lift into town. Where they dropped him off could be important. They may also have seen who collared him and led him off to Irishtown. In the least they'll be able to vouch for the state of his insobriety. Surely someone at the gala, one of the whist players or a valet or coachman, must have seen your nephew leave and with whom."

"There's no need for you or Cobb to go out to Spadina. I'll put Wakefield onto it. He'll know by this evening every move that Handford made up to the point of his leaving, whom he talked to, and what was said. The walls, and servants, have ears at such functions."

"That would be very helpful, sir. But even if we find out who took him to Madame Renée's—and it appears to have been one of her regulars—we're still left with the business of explaining subsequent events inside the house. Madame Renée told Cobb that she saw the man leave right after dumping the young man on her doorstep."

"True, but I am thinking now of something related to motive." Durham drummed his fingers on the desk and glanced across at Marc as if making up his mind whether or not to continue. At last he said, "There are many people in this city who would like nothing more than to see my mission here fail."

"Almost every Tory, I should imagine, sir, and a few of the less temperate Reformers."

"To that end, a major personal distraction would be a heaven-sent gift, don't you think?"

"You suspect that one of your opponents here might have taken advantage of Handford's near-comatose state and naiveté and deliberately lured him to that brothel?"

"It is a possibility you must keep in mind."

"But no one could foresee the death of the girl in his bed."

"I agree. But the mere scandal of my wife's favourite nephew being found in a squalid house of ill repute would have been enough. I'm sure you're aware that my mission here was almost aborted because I chose to bring along two trusted associates, Thomas Turton and Edward Wakefield."

Marc nodded. "Yes, I see. Both were embroiled in scandals when they were younger men. And Prime Minister Melbourne has enemies within his own caucus waiting to pounce."

"Who are also my enemies, who would stoop to anything to have me brought to heel and disgraced."

"In that case, the damage may already have been done."

"Possibly. That is why Handford must not only be cleared but, if true, be seen as the victim of a heinous plot."

"How long have I got to do all this?"

"Three days at the most. I must be back in Quebec City by the beginning of next week, which means leaving here by Friday noon. As you can see, I've already had to reschedule my planned meetings this morning to free up time for this conference. I am prepared to deal with any personal consequences from a perceived scandal when I get back to London, even if it means resigning my ministry. But these provinces are not yet wholly free of military conflict and they have no future unless I can provide one for them. Few men in the Whig government care a fig for what happens in British North America. And the Radicals, who would like to have me lead a political coup, will pay lip service to my recommendations only as long as it suits their immediate purpose."

"But what will you do if I fail?"

"That's just it, Mr. Edwards. I find myself on the horns of a terrible dilemma. How can I leave Handford here in a jail cell to await trial and certain conviction in the fall assizes, while I go off to Quebec to broker a just peace? And how could I ask my wife to leave her nephew in a strange country to hang alone for a crime he most assuredly did not commit? Even if I were cruel and heartless and felt no affection for Lady Durham, I could not work fruitfully in such stressful circumstances."

"But you are supreme governor of all the provinces with absolute authority."

Durham smiled grimly. "Believe me, my power has been well hedged by the cabinet, for which I am, despite much chaffing, very grateful. Moreover, if I did use my executive authority to unduly influence the legitimate efforts of the police and the independent courts, my enemies would have a free-for-all with my reputation and vaunted probity. Besides, is it not just that sort of arbitrary action I am here to bring an end to?"

Marc got up. "What you're saying, Your Lordship, is that I must not fail."

"Something like that."

The fact that the future of the Canadas might be at stake was, mercifully, not revisited.

FIVE

That afternoon, with a sense of urgency that they had only three days to absolve Handford Ellice of Sarah McConkey's murder, Marc and Cobb walked briskly to Lot Street and peered across at the ramshackle suburb of Irishtown. The shanties themselves did not begin for thirty or forty yards beyond the northern edge of the street, where a ragged copse of alder and hawthorn provided an inadequate screen for them and their unfortunate inhabitants. It was certainly less intimidating in the daytime, Cobb thought, than in the dead of night. In a year or two the severed lots on the north side of Lot Street would be cleared, and legitimate houses or businesses built on them. What would happen then to the squatters on the bleak acres behind was a question no one in authority was willing to discuss in public.

"How do we get in?" Marc wondered aloud. He could see nothing resembling a road.

"At night the sailors, low-lifes, and men of proberty slink along here until a tracker or scout hails 'em."

"And then?"

"They get led by the baton to some house of ill repute, dependin' on which vice they're interested in or can afford."

"So that's how young Ellice and the blackguard who led him this far found their way to Madame Renée's?"

"Her real name's Norah Burgess, though that wouldn't do fer the con-see-urge of a fancy hooer-house," Cobb said, starting across the street. "But Ellice wasn't taken there in the usual way. That's just one of the queer things about this business."

They had reached a scraggly clutch of hawthorn trees, their bright pink blooms just beginning to shrivel and tarnish.

"As you said earlier," Cobb continued, "one of them gents from the ball must've lured the silly fella from Spadina down to here. Then, accordin' to the Burgess woman, the gent must've known the way to her place in the dark, 'cause he come right to her door, give the secret knock only her regulars know, shoved the lad inta the parlour, and skedaddled."

Cobb pointed to a gap between two trees and, ducking to avoid the thorns, led Marc onto a narrow path that meandered through the scrub ahead of them.

Marc picked up the narrative. "My guess is that this gentleman did not want to be recognized last night—not even by the madam or one of her trackers. That suggests to me that we are investigating something more complex and sinister than a prank or a piece of mischief designed to embarrass Lord Durham before he begins his work here."

"Well, we shouldn't go jumpin' to conclusives, Major."

Marc smiled at being reminded of one of his own homilies, however mangled.

They were now out of the bush and into the shantytown proper. While Marc stared in disbelief—he had seen worse slums in London but did not expect to encounter such communities here—Cobb was again struck by how much less intimidating and how much sadder the place was in the revealing light of afternoon.

They had come out onto a wide pathway that, while it curved about carelessly, was nevertheless a street of sorts—with makeshift huts and jerry-built shacks arrayed on either side, each with a flimsy and stinking outhouse tucked in behind. Where there was glass in a window, it was invariably broken. Most of the dwellings simply had gaps in the side walls to let air in and the stench out. A few were clad in oiled paper in faint hope of stemming the tide of blood-sucking mosquitoes in the night. Middens and festering garbage pits lay in squalid view between or in front of the hovels, where dogs, pigs, and rats contended for a meal.

Nonetheless, children, oblivious to the rags their unwashed little bodies were clothed in, sprinted along the roadway, kicking a ball or darting among the houses in the squealing pursuit-and-retreat of an age-old game of tag. One tilting, barn-board cabin sported a set of red-checked curtains that lifted and fell in the soft breeze. But any trees or shrubs that had once been native here had long since been hacked down and used for firewood. The city council had given up trying to discourage the poaching of hardwood from the university parkland to the north and west of Irishtown—the sheriff having more vital concerns since the Rebellion in December—so the sun blazed down upon the inhabitants here without interruption or pity. The squall of exhausted and overheated babies mingled with the happier shouts of the children outdoors. So far they had seen no adults but were certain that every step they took was observed.

"You lookin' fer somebody?" A scruffy lad of twelve or thirteen had stepped out onto the path in front of them, not belligerent but wary.

"Madame Renée's place," Marc said.

"They don't work in the daytime." He was speaking to Marc but his gaze was fixed on Cobb's truncheon.

"We wish to speak with Madame Renée."

The boy looked puzzled.

"You're one of her trackers, ain't ya?" Cobb said. "Peter or Donald."

"Who wants ta know?"

The scarlet of Cobb's nose brightened alarmingly. "The police," he barked.

Marc put out a restraining hand. "We're here to find out who killed Sarah McConkey. Please show us where we need to go." He held out a penny. "Is this your usual fee, Donald?"

"Peter," the boy answered, and latched on to the penny before it dissolved. "Come with me."

"You'll spoil the little bugger," Cobb chided, but he followed Marc and Peter without further comment.

After a left and a right turn, of sorts, they came upon the sturdy brick dwelling that Cobb had visited last night, a structure replete with screened windows, a chimney, and what appeared to be a cistern along the far west wall.

"Sarah was the nicest girl I ever met," Peter said. "But we already know who stabbed her—some toff from the town."

Bad news travels faster than good, Cobb thought.

"Do I just knock or do I need the secret code?" Marc said as one man to another.

Peter grinned, exposing a one-inch gap in the teeth of his upper jaw. "Lemme do it."

He gave an intricate sequence of taps with the knocker on the scarlet door. It was almost a minute before it opened reluctantly, like an arthritic hand.

"BUT I BEEN OVER ALL THIS last night," said Norah Burgess, a.k.a. Madame Renée. "Can't your man remember the colour of his hat?" She glared at Cobb, who was seated on one of the hard chairs across the room. Cobb glared back but said nothing.

"Constable Cobb has made a full report, in writing and again to me in person. I'd just like you to go over the events of last night, painful as they must be, in the hope that you might recall some detail or other you may have overlooked in the stress and turmoil of the situation."

"Well, sir, there was plenty of both, and neither me nor my girls has slept more'n an hour since."

Norah Burgess had little need to make this point: one look at her devastated face was enough. Her green eyes were bloodshot, the lids swollen and raw from weeping, the indigo pouches below proof of sleeplessness. She had thrown on an ordinary flowered housedress in obvious haste, and her hair, normally a kind of frizzy, pinkish halo that gave her plain features a natural attractiveness, lay upon her scalp in unkempt, greasy coils.

Her girls, younger and more resilient, had fared better. Their hollow-eyed, tear-stained faces were certain signs of their own grief and anxiety, but their youthfulness and bodily good health (too much of it exposed, perhaps) simply made such distress seem eccentric and temporary. Molly Mason, Carrie Garnet, and Frieda Smiley were draped about their mistress on the arms and back of the padded chair below the parlour window in a variety of wanton poses. Marc had seated himself directly across from them on a hard chair. Cobb was beside him but had angled his chair so that his gaze caught Norah Burgess's profile and managed to take in as little as possible of the obtrusive female flesh around her. Marc, however, felt he must size up the four women carefully and dispassionately, for all of them were critical witnesses at best, and at worst one or more might be implicated in conspiracy and murder.

"We ain't got nothin' to hide, have we, Mum?" Molly said with a trembling lower lip.

"That fella seemed like a nice young gentleman, but I hope they hang him twice!" said Frieda from her perch on the other arm.

"Poor Sarah. The doctor come this mornin' and carted her off to cut her up," Carrie said, so vehemently that she slipped from the back of the chair and inadvertently advertised more of her leg and less of her slip.

"There, there, Carrie. The doctor is gonna do no such thing," Norah soothed.

Cobb tipped up onto his feet. "I better have a look at the other half of the house. We need to check all the windows and the other door to make sure nobody snuck in whilst you ladies were asleep."

"Good idea, Cobb," Marc said.

"You go with him, Carrie," her mistress said, and no one contradicted her.

Blushing furiously, Cobb followed Carrie into the domestic part of the house. Marc noticed that the door between the parlour and the hall leading to the private bedrooms was sturdy and equipped with a bar on the inner side.

"Tell me, Miss Burgess, do you bar that door after, um, business hours?" he said.

"Yes, we do. But I didn't last night because 'business,' as you term it, was still being done in Sarah's cubicle over there. And please address me as Mrs. Burgess. I was married once, but the bastard ran off and left me nothing but his name."

"I see. Well, then, Mrs. Burgess, I have some questions for you and your employees that Constable Cobb may not have thought to ask. But first I would like to go over what happened last night, starting with the early part of the evening."

"As you wish," Mrs. Burgess replied with a resigned sigh. As she began, Molly and Frieda reached out and put a hand tenderly on each of her plump arms, an apparent gesture of affection and mutual support.

For the next quarter-hour the events of the previous evening were detailed for Marc, and they jibed in every important respect with the account given him by Cobb. And while Mrs. Burgess bore the burden of the sad narrative, Frieda and Molly chipped in spontaneously with minor additions and several emendations: "Oh, Mr. Whiskers had on his yellow vest, didn't he, Molly?" or, "I don't think it was me, Mum, who said we better answer the knock after midnight, it was Frieda, I'm sure." At which accusation Frieda burst into tears and was instantly comforted by Molly and her mistress. The critical points were retold much as Cobb had said: the house had closed for the night; the clock on the sideboard had chimed one o'clock; Mrs. Burgess and the four girls were about to enter their rooms when the knock of a "regular" was heard, loud and insistent. Mrs. Burgess opened to it and was nearly bowled over by Handford Ellice ("the pale gentleman" subsequently dubbed Jocko) stumbling inside, aided by a push perhaps from a black-caped gentleman who melted into the darkness before he could be identified.

"Are you asking me to believe that you had no idea who this gentleman might have been? One of your regulars? Surely his height and bulk and posture would have given you some indication."

"You may choose to believe what you wish, sir. I am telling you what actually happened." Mrs. Burgess drew a deep breath, inflating her considerable bosom in the process. "And since I do not inquire after the names of our callers—we know them solely by the nicknames the girls give them—I might tell you only that it could have been Fluffy or Tumbles. But I cannot do even that. The parlour here was unlit. The moon was down in the west. I had one candle that was jarred out when the pale gentleman almost knocked me over. I cannot say more."

The story continued without interruption on Marc's part to the point where Sarah, whose turn it was, took Jocko's money and led him into her cubicle, after which Mrs. Burgess and Molly retired to one of the bedrooms in the domestic wing, and Frieda and Carrie to the one next to it. The door adjoining the two halves of the house was left open so that any "nonsense" in Sarah's cubicle could be heard and dealt with. The outside parlour door was barred. After a while, perhaps half an hour later, Mrs. Burgess came out of her room, noted that Frieda and Carrie were asleep, tiptoed to where Sarah was entertaining the young man, and saw that they were naked and fast asleep. The heavy snoring from Jocko suggested that he was in a deep, drunken stupor. He had arrived drunk, of course, and nearly incoherent (they hadn't realized that he stammered), which had prompted a short debate among the women as to whether they should accommodate him or pitch him outside to fend for himself. But he had waved a lot of money at them, appeared harmless, and Sarah had been willing to do her share during an evening when business had been scarce because of the gala. At this detail, Mrs. Burgess came close to losing control, but when the two girls leaned down to console her, she shook them off gently.

Marc was inclined to accept the story as true thus far. He had been alert throughout for any sign of a rehearsed version. But the interjections by Molly and Frieda, and the occasional fuzziness in Mrs. Burgess's recollection, seemed too natural to have been preplanned. Moreover, the trauma and sheer horror of the murder, whatever their involvement, had left them exhausted, so that any act they might have felt compelled to put on would have been nigh impossible to carry out. The second thing Marc was watching carefully for was any evidence of tension or conflict among the members of the household. It had occurred to him that, even though he had no firsthand experience of how brothels were run—he had begged off the many excursions to the local dens arranged by his fellow officers—there were bound to be petty jealousies and perhaps powerful enmities aroused whenever a group of people were cooped up for long periods of time (the barracks being but one example). Clients would naturally prefer one girl to another, prompting rivalries or aggrievement over a fair division of spoils. And surely the madam, invariably an older woman and authority figure, would have ambivalent and conflicting emotions regarding her charges, complicated by the presence of competition from neighbouring establishments.

Marc was aware that Cobb, who could be heard outside tapping and probing the windows, felt the murder to be the result of a domestic dispute, and if he were right, then motive could be the key to solving it. But there was clear evidence of mutual affection between Mrs. Burgess and the other three girls. It was conceivable, of course, that they all had some reason to hate Sarah and had colluded to get rid of her and blame a nameless client. He would have to keep an open mind about that. Still, he was bothered by the fact that neither Mrs. Burgess nor her three surviving girls fitted the stereotypical view of madam and whore, relayed to him in suffocating detail by his fellow officers eager to broadcast their exploits. What he had expected to find here were women of varying age, coarse demeanour, lathered with makeup and perfumed to camouflage their rapidly decaying bodies, and conveying in every word and gesture a sense of defeat, resignation, ennui, and hopelessness. But Carrie, Molly, and Frieda were of an age, perhaps twenty or a bit more. They looked as if they could have been cousins, sharing a slim build, heart-shaped faces, light complexion (Scots or Irish), and curly brown hair. Moreover, the best adjective Marc could think of to describe them would be "wholesome." For here in the bland daylight, without makeup or corsets or coiffed tresses or lurid frocks, they looked healthy and guileless. And, Cobb had assured him, Sarah was of similar age and robustness, despite the shocking state of her body in death.

Nor did their mistress, Madame Renée, fit the received notions of a woman in her profession. First of all, she had been quick to drop the façade of "Madame Renée" and encourage the use of her real name. Secondly, she did not give the appearance of having worked in the trade herself, an almost universal prerequisite for the job of madam. While showing the world the effects of middle age (she looked about forty)—plumpness of flesh with unmistakable sagging of chin, forearm, and, no doubt, breast—she too wore no makeup, nor were there any signs that she regularly used it beyond some lip rouge and a pat of powder on the cheeks. She didn't need it because while she was, and always had been, plain of feature, her eyes and range of expression radiated a personality to be reckoned with: shrewdness, detached humour, toughness, and strong feeling, for and against, Marc thought. Whenever she was interrupted by Frieda or Molly, she showed no irritation but merely paused, listened, and then carried on. Marc surmised that she governed with a productive mix of strict authority and genuine affection. At least, this seemed to be the case so far. There was still a ways to go.

Cobb and Carrie came back into the room. "All the windows are the same: high and narrow. And they got them cloth screens nailed onto them from the inside. No sign of any of 'em being tampered with."

"I've told you, sirs, that no one entered this house after the pale gentleman."

"It would seem unlikely, I agree," Marc said, "even though you all say you went sound asleep after Mrs. Burgess here assumed that Sarah was safe for the night."

The girls readily agreed.

"Sarah didn't like to be woke up and moved once she nodded off with her last caller," Carrie said, back on her perch with one pretty knee boldly exposed.

"'Course, we never let a caller stay the night," Frieda said.

"That's right, Mr. Edwards. I have a hard-and-fast rule about that. I roust them out at two o'clock whatever they might wish or whatever money they're prepared to offer me. Peter and Donald are always ready to escort them back to Lot Street and their wives' cold beds."

"Which rule you violated last night."

Mrs. Burgess slumped in her chair. When she looked up, her eyes were swimming. "Why do you think I been up all night? It's the worst mistake of my life. But as I told Constable Cobb, we all thought the fellow was harmless and too drunk to do much. We felt sorry for him, if the truth be known. I never seen a young man look so desperate, so pleading—more in need of mothering than whoring."

"That was my opinion of him, too," Marc said.

"You knew him, then?" Mrs. Burgess asked. "Nobody's yet told us who he was or how he happened to come here with one of our regulars."

Marc hesitated before deciding how to answer. "I'm not at liberty to tell you his name, but he's a gentleman about twenty years old, and is one of the party who arrived with Lord and Lady Durham."

Mrs. Burgess's face went even paler than it already was. The girls sucked in their breath.

"You mean to say he's connected to one of the bigwigs the girls saw coming across the bay yesterday like Jesus walking on water?"

"I'm afraid so. You'll understand why Lord Durham has asked me to make the most thorough investigation of the facts and—"

"—and pin the blame on one of us!" There was both defiance and apprehension in the glower she turned upon Marc.

Two of the girls began to weep, but Mrs. Burgess raised a restraining hand and they blubbered to a stop.

"Not so," Marc said. "I have carried out four previous investigations in the province, three of them under the aegis of a governor. In each instance I got to the truth, even when it proved to be unwelcome news. I have sworn to Lord Durham that I will do so here, and he has agreed to abide by my findings whatever they may be."

Mrs. Burgess gave him a long, searching appraisal. Finally she said, "Well, as I have no say in the matter, I'll take you at your word. For now."

"Thank you. Now, back to the facts of last night. All of you claim to have fallen into a deep sleep about one-thirty or so. I don't think the exact time is as important here as the precise sequence of events. All was well, you told Mr. Cobb, until you, Molly, were wakened by a scream of some sort."

"It was a kind of shriek," Molly said. "But it wasn't Sarah. It was definitely a man's voice, though I remember thinkin' it was like a little boy screechin' at somethin' he seen in a nightmare, or somethin' like that."

"I believe we may assume for the moment that the pale gentleman had woken up and witnessed the young lady dead and bloody beside him."

"Please, sir—"

"I will not ask you or Molly to describe again the horror of
that scene," Marc said quickly. "Constable Cobb's description and
Dr. Withers's report are all that we require on that score. There
were no footprints or other smears in the blood on the floor or
mat, so we're satisfied you two didn't dash in there and tamper,
however innocently, with any aspect of that grisly tableau."

"I sent Molly out for help right off, then sat out here waiting,
and keeping an ear and eye out for Jocko—the pale gentleman—
and the knife in his hand."

"Did you have a weapon to defend yourself, had he wakened
and attacked you?" Marc asked, and saw Cobb nod knowingly. It
seemed a weak part of Mrs. Burgess's story.

"I had that poker over there by the stove," she said evenly. "It
was pitch-dark in here, though Sarah's bedside candle may still
have been going. I planned to stand by the archway over there and
crown him if he appeared belligerent."

"And of course he would scarcely know where he was."

"But he never come out, did he? And I had no intention of
looking again on poor Sarah—"

"Naturally," Marc agreed with a sympathetic nod. "And Constable Cobb's description of that awful scene is very near to your
own. But I am still a bit puzzled as to how or why the young
gentleman cried out, apparently fifteen or twenty minutes after
he had viciously stabbed her, and then dropped off to sleep again
while she bled all over him and the—"

Carrie's sob stopped Marc's comment, and she ran crying uncontrollably into the other wing of the house.

"I'm sorry," Marc said.

"You better go after her, Frieda, luv," Mrs. Burgess said, pointedly ignoring Marc and his seemingly gratuitous brutality. Frieda,

about to emulate Carrie, stumbled out of the room. Her mistress then turned a baleful eye on the investigators, and said, seething, "The man was drunk. Drunks do unexplainable things. It is not up to me to account for his motives. I found him with Sarah's dagger in his right hand and my darling's throat cut and her lifeblood drained away."

"I suppose somebody could've taken the knife outta Sarah's neck and put it in the gentleman's hand," Cobb said in an offhand tone.

"They'd've been covered in blood and left their footprints in it." Mrs. Burgess had braced herself to recall the details: her hands gripped the arms of her chair and there was a restrained tremor in her throat.

"But I managed to edge my way around the other side between the bed and the wall," Cobb said, "and reached the gentleman without any trouble. There wasn't no blood over there."

Mrs. Burgess thought before responding to Cobb. "Yes, a person could do that, even a portly person like yourself. But could you reach across Jocko and pull the dagger out of Sarah's neck or stick it in the fellow's right hand without touching the blood on him or the bed?"

Cobb was taken aback. "I suppose not," he said at last.

"And if I had stabbed the girl I treated like my own daughter and then reached over to plant the dagger on Jocko, would I not be covered in blood?"

"I see what you're saying," Marc said.

"And the chief constable himself and the doctor took lanterns and searched high and low for any signs of blood in here, in our bedrooms, or anywhere else in the house."

"That's true," Cobb said. "And when I went back into the other side of the house with Carrie a minute ago, I looked again, and Carrie helped me search the drawers and hampers for bloody clothes. And it ain't easy to scrub bloodstains outta softwood floors."

"Good work, Cobb. I'll do the same just to be absolutely sure." Marc turned back to Mrs. Burgess. "Let's move now to your sleeping arrangements. You told Mr. Cobb that you and Molly slept in one room and Carrie and Frieda in another. Was this usual?"

"The girls sleep together in pairs, as they please on a given night. I have my own room, but Sarah often sleeps in her, ah, workplace, as she did last night, and if I think she might be doing that, I crawl in with Molly—"

"I get nightmares if I sleep alone," Molly said, "don't I, Mum?"

"I understand," Marc said, smiling at Molly. "But you must see that if all four of you were fast asleep shortly after one-thirty when Mrs. Burgess decided Sarah was all right on her own, then in theory, any one of you could have feigned sleep, waited her chance, slipped into that room, and stabbed her."

Mrs. Burgess gave Marc a grim smile. "But such a person must have left the dagger there in her neck or else be covered in blood—which she would have no chance to clean off or disguise. Molly woke up well before two o'clock, raised the alarm, and Constable Cobb was here fifteen minutes after that. When could the killer have hidden her clothes and washed the blood off in the dark without leaving a speck anywhere outside that dreadful room? And then crawled back into bed with one of us?"

That stopped the flow of conversation for half a minute. Cobb coughed. Carrie and Frieda, red-eyed, came back and sat beside the woman they called Mum.

"What does the pale gentleman have to say for himself?" Mrs. Burgess said.

"He's too upset and confused to say much."

"Maybe he hasn't got much *to* say."

"We don't need any opinions from the likes of you," Cobb said.

Marc gave Cobb a reproving glance. He leaned back and said conversationally, "Could you tell me about Sarah, Mrs. Burgess? Perhaps knowing more about her might help us get to the truth, whatever it is."

Mrs. Burgess softened visibly. "The truth is, Mr. Edwards, whatever you think of the business I'm in, Madame Renée's is a special kind of pleasure place for gentlemen. I took my life's savings and had this house built exactly as you now see it. I even have a deed for an acre of property around it, so many of the houses you see about are squatting on my land, with my blessing. I decided from the outset that I would hand-pick three girls and train them in my own way. Only respectable customers are allowed in. We have codes of entry, as you now know, and our own trackers. We have strict rules of conduct, which I enforce."

"With yer poker?" Cobb asked, mainly to stanch this flow of self-justifying drivel.

"Our gentlemen callers know that their identities are safe with me. They also know my girls are healthy and free from disease. They get checked over by Dr. Pogue twice a month. They've got their own accounts at the Commercial Bank in the city."

"All this is quite admirable," Marc said, "but where does Sarah fit in? She makes four girls."

"Sarah was found by a tracker one night last November up on Lot Street. She had been thrown out of her family's home for being pregnant. We learned she had been a servant for a few weeks in some fancy home in town—she never would say where—and there's little doubt her employer or one of his sons got her in the family way and then gave her the sack. But I can't understand how her own flesh and blood could turn on such a sweet-natured and innocent girl. But they did. She was brought here that night—I found her on the doorstep—and I took her in. What else could I do?"

"Mum has a soft heart," Molly said.

"But surely if she were with child, she would not be suitable for your enterprise," Marc said tactfully.

"That is correct. I took Sarah in out of charity. She was grateful, and she carried her weight here by cleaning, doing the girls' laundry, and helping me."

"We loved her, didn't we, Carrie?" Frieda said.

"She was like a cuddly pet, she was," Molly said.

"I can't believe she's gone," Carrie said.

"Well, girls," Mrs. Burgess said, "she's gonna have a proper funeral. And I ain't having her buried up in Potter's Field. We're all going to Gunther the undertaker this afternoon and make the arrangements."

This remark seemed to cheer the girls a little, as it was meant to. Cobb began to feel that they were going around in circles. He yawned conspicuously.

"When did Sarah have her baby?" Marc asked.

"Now that's a sad story in itself," Mrs. Burgess said. "She wasn't due till this month, but in April she was doing an errand for me in town when her cramps started coming. Someone ran for the midwife. The babe was born dead, in a barn somewhere. The midwife took it away. Some kindly folks looked after her for three days. Then she came back to us, looking just awful."

"We was frantic, sir," Molly said. "We tried to ask about her in town, but most folks refuse to talk to us."

"And we have to be careful *who* we talk to," Frieda said.

"I figured she'd tried to go back home to her parents near Streetsville," Mrs. Burgess added. "Thank goodness she come back to us."

"That was in April?" Marc queried. "So when did Sarah become part of the, uh, business?"

"As soon as she recovered her strength, which wasn't long. She'd begged to be part of it soon after she got here, but I said no and that was it. But she had nowhere to go after she lost the baby, and by then she was part of the family."

"Just like a sister," Frieda added, beginning to sniffle again.

"She fitted right in, didn't she, Molly?" Carrie said.

"Some of the gentlemen asked specially fer her," Molly said, as if that was a feat to boast about.

Marc looked at Sarah's benefactress: "Could she not have tried to work at something else?"

"Something respectable, Mr. Edwards?"

"I was thinking of something less hazardous, Mrs. Burgess," Marc said.

The madam's head dropped.

"Why do you need to know so much about Sarah anyways?" Molly asked, stroking the back of her mistress's neck.

"Well, it's occurred to me that Sarah's suddenly joining the enterprise and, from what I gather now, becoming a favourite among your regulars, might have occasioned some resentment among you girls."

This remark was greeted by puzzled silence. The three girls looked at one another, and Molly spoke for the other two: "There was none of that."

Marc was inclined to agree but pressed on. "There is also the possibility that one of the rival businesses nearby might, out of envy or competitiveness, wish to ruin you, and how better than to hire some cutthroat to murder your star performer. Surely any sort of scandal here would scare off your special clientele."

"I'll admit there is no love lost between me and Madame

Charlotte," Mrs. Burgess said, "but a murder down here in Irish-town can do nobody any good. We'd all suffer. As we're going to do soon. Besides, I've told you that no one else got in here after midnight except the pale gentleman, and there's no way anyone could have got into this house once the doors were barred."

"Except through the booby-hatch," Carrie blurted, then slapped three fingers across her lips.

Marc sat bolt upright. "Are you saying that there is another way into this house?"

Mrs. Burgess blushed, started to look daggers at Carrie, then turned to Marc and said with a sigh, "I'm afraid so."

SIX

I t's right down here." Mrs. Burgess directed Marc and Cobb along the narrow hallway that led to the three cubicles and water closet. (It *was* a cistern Marc had noted on the outside wall.) The curtains were tightly drawn across the doorway to the murder scene; Marc noticed Mrs. Burgess shudder as they passed it. Once at the end of the hall, she stood to one side and pointed at the lower wall. Marc squatted down with Cobb peering over his right shoulder. The outline of a small door, hinged on top like a hatch, was just visible, but he could see no latch or handle. He pushed at the door but it did not move.

"It opens only with a key," Mrs. Burgess said. "You can get in or out by kneeling down and squeezing through."

"But why on earth would you put a door like this right next to the rooms where your girls work and sometimes fall asleep?"

"It's really an escape hatch. I had it put in when the house was first built. I wanted a secret door so if there was trouble in the parlour or these rooms, one of us could slip away and get help."

When Marc looked skeptical, she said pointedly, "You'd be surprised how folks around here help one another out. We have to; nobody else will."

Marc stood up and stared at the end wall. Unless a direct light were thrown on it—even in the afternoon the windowless hallway was gloomy—the hatch was barely detectable. Which would explain why neither Cobb nor Sturges had spotted it last night. And Carrie, for whatever reason, had chosen not to point it out when she accompanied Cobb on his inspection of the windows earlier.

"There's no knob inside or outside," Mrs. Burgess said. "You need a key to unlatch the lock and to pull the door open." With that, she reached down into her ample cleavage and drew out a large key on a thin gold chain. She knelt down, inserted it in the keyhole close to the floor, and, using it as a knob, eased the hatch upward. Then she locked it again and returned the key to its bower.

"But how would one of the girls be able to use this as an escape route? Do they all have keys?"

"Of course not. That would be foolhardy. I had the locksmith on King Street make only two keys for this lock. I keep one around my neck. The other is tucked behind that picture on the wall there."

Marc looked at the dusty, framed engraving of an English racehorse hanging on the wall well above the hatch.

"Only my girls and I know it's there."

"Well, we'd better check to make sure, don't you think?" Marc asked patiently.

With a resigned gesture, Mrs. Burgess lifted the picture off its hook and turned it over in both hands. A small groove had been carved into the bottom slat of the frame to accommodate the key.

But the key was not in it.

ONCE AGAIN THEY WERE BACK IN the parlour, and ready for another go-round. And this time there was a different kind of tension in the air.

While the three girls sat somewhat stiffly around Mrs. Burgess and exchanged furtive glances, Marc began. "It now appears that one of your customers may have stolen the escape-door key and used it to slip unnoticed into the hallway, murder Sarah McConkey, and get away into the night."

Mrs. Burgess sat tight-lipped. Clearly she had been shaken by the discovery of the missing key. Marc could almost hear the wheels turning in her head.

"Do you have any idea who might have taken it or when?"

Mrs. Burgess shook her head.

"When did you last check to see if it was still in place?"

"I do so every few days," she said with some of her former defiance. "The safety of my girls is uppermost in my mind. It was there two days ago."

"Did any of you girls see anyone who might have taken it in the past two days?"

They too shook their heads.

Finally it was Molly who spoke, looking not at Marc but at her mistress. "It could've been Michael, couldn't it, Mum?"

"Michael?" Marc exclaimed. "Who in hell is Michael?"

Mrs. Burgess reddened. "I suppose I must tell you. I didn't see how it was of any importance earlier."

"Tell me what?"

"About Michael Badger. He's our bruiser. But I sent him packing yesterday morning."

This announcement elicited cries of surprise from the girls and a gaggle of questions. Once they were calmed enough to listen to a rational explanation, Marc and Cobb leaned forward with fresh anticipation to hear what the mistress of the house had to say now.

"Please continue," Marc prompted, gently but firmly.

"Michael's the young man who's been acting as our bruiser off and on since last fall."

"A bruiser's usually a big fella who keeps the customers from flippin' their wigs or bustin' their flies," Cobb explained to Marc. "Most of the cathouses and some of the rougher waterin' holes keep one or two on a leash."

"And Badger was this sort of protector?" Marc asked.

"Yes," Mrs. Burgess said. "Not that we needed much, mind. You've probably been wondering why I spent good money to buy land here and build an expensive residence for the trade."

"That question had entered my mind."

"Well, the answer is simple. It's safer in here than in the town. We haven't got any policemen or sheriff to protect us in here, but we look out for one another. We got rules and we got people who will help see that they're followed."

"Why the bruiser, then?"

"All of our callers are gentlemen, so we have little trouble there. But whenever a ship arrives or some hooligan's just come into cash from thieving or gambling, sailors and the like come pounding on our doors and cursing at our windows, annoyed when they can't get in and threatening to wreak havoc. So, whenever we suspect there might be that sort of trouble, I send for Michael and he comes for the duration."

"And he was intimidating enough to scare off any trouble-makers?"

The girls whooped at this, and for the first time Marc caught a glimpse of the happier, youthful side of their personalities that had been cowed by grief and fear.

"He was a big fella?" Cobb asked, which excited more giggles.

"Michael Badger is as tall as Mr. Edwards and a foot broader in the shoulders," Mrs. Burgess said. "And he's got a shock of orange hair as wild and shaggy as a lion's mane. One look at him and they'd run like rabbits."

"Were you not worried that he'd intimidate your clients or pose a danger to the girls here?"

This comment induced more tittering.

"In here, Michael was a softie, wasn't he, Mum?" Molly said.

Mrs. Burgess paused before saying, "I gave him strict instructions about his duties and deportment when I first took him on. I realized that the girls might be a temptation to him, so I specifically warned him that they were off limits. If he was desperate for a woman, I told him he could go on up to Madame Charlotte's and I'd pay the fare. I offered him a wage he couldn't hope to make anywhere else in the city."

"So he abided by your rules?" It was hard to imagine anyone not doing so, Marc thought.

"He teased us a bit, that was all," Carrie said.

"He did make us laugh, didn't he, Mum?"

"Oh, how he could tell a story," Molly added.

"He sounds like the perfect employee," Marc said. "So tell us, Mrs. Burgess, why you summarily dismissed him yesterday morning and failed to inform your girls."

"I would have told them, of course, in good time and in my own way." She turned slightly to the women. "You didn't know it, but that fun-loving, likeable bear of a man was a gambler and, when it came to money, a bit of a wastrel."

Mrs. Burgess dismissed their quick protests. "I know this for a fact, for he used his good nature to prey upon mine. Very foolishly, I loaned him money."

"You didn't!" Molly cried, as if that possibility was unthinkable.

"Not a lot. At least not all at once. But he pleaded with me, saying he'd lost his wages and more at that dive, the Tinker's Dam, and the men up there were threatening to break his legs."

"The Tinker's Dam is the sinkhole of Toronto," Cobb said with disgust.

"So it is," Mrs. Burgess agreed. "At first I merely gave Michael advances on his wages. I called him in several times when he wasn't really needed and we spent the evening tripping over him. But soon it became clear to me that he could never work off his debt."

"So you decided to have it out with him yesterday?" Marc said.

Mrs. Burgess sighed. "Yes, I did." She looked at Molly next to her. "I'm sorry, luv, but I had no choice. He owed me thirty dollars. I told him he had to pay me what he owed within a week or leave my employ."

"How did he respond?"

Tears filled Mrs. Burgess's eyes. "He laughed in my face. He said he owed more than that to the gamblers at the Tinker's Dam. So what else was I to do? He hadn't shown up when we needed him on Saturday and here he was on Monday morning asking for money again. I ordered him off the property. I told him I was going to put the word out in Irishtown, so he knew I meant business."

There was a collective gasp from the girls.

"What do you mean?" Marc asked.

"He would be persona non grata in Irishtown. If he was to put his big toe anywhere on our territory, a scout or tracker would know, and if he was fool enough to keep on coming, he'd be lucky to escape with his skull in one piece."

"So you effectively banished him?"

"I did, and he knew it."

"So he cleared out. And all this happened yesterday morning?"

"Yes. The girls were still in town shopping after the ceremonies."

Marc hesitated before saying, "You do realize, Mrs. Burgess, that Michael Badger is the person most likely to have reason and opportunity to remove the key to the hatch from behind the picture?"

Mrs. Burgess paled. "He did go into one of the rooms back there to collect his belongings, but—"

"But he may have become a desperate man, willing to attempt deeds quite out of keeping with his character."

The girls cried out in disbelief and anguish.

"I think we have to entertain the unpalatable possibility that Michael Badger came through the escape hatch sometime last night."

IT WAS LATE AFTERNOON WHEN MARC and Cobb wended their way back through the maze of Irishtown towards Lot Street. They had done all they could at Madame Renée's. Mrs. Burgess and the girls, weary and wrung out as they were, were allowed to visit the undertaker to make arrangements for Sarah McConkey's funeral on Thursday, the day after tomorrow.

When they had departed, Marc and Cobb, using lanterns, went over every inch of the sprawling house in search of bloodstains or evidence of recent attempts to scrub them away. They found nothing. They reluctantly concluded that none of the victim's blood—and pints of it had been spilled in that horrific room—had been carried outside of it, except for the bloody footprints made by Handford Ellice when he'd staggered naked into the hallway. Cobb had immediately carried him to a chair and ordered Mrs. Burgess to fetch a blanket or robe for him. Thereafter he had lurched over to another chair by the stove until the blood dried on him and Dr. Withers arrived. Then, under the doctor's instructions, the distraught Mr. Ellice had been washed by one of the girls and put back into his clothes, unbloodied on the far side of the bed. As the women had made no effort to clean up the parlour before Marc's arrival, Ellice's progress from the bed to the hall doorway and thence to the chair were still evident, and un-problematic. Assuming Ellice was somehow innocent, it was the blood from the killer's hands or clothing that they were hoping to find elsewhere in the house. In particular, they examined the area around the hatch but discovered no traces.

Then they moved outside and walked all the way around the house. It had not rained for four or five days, and so no telltale footprints were visible in the dusty soil under the windows or near the hatch. A scrawny bush meant to camouflage the latter's pres-ence had been defoliated by marauding ragamuffins, so the hatch would have been no secret among the inhabitants of Irishtown. Whether that was of any significance remained to be seen.

"Well, Cobb, what do you make of this business so far?"

More delighted to be asked than he was willing to let on, Cobb said, "I don't rightly know the ins and outs of it yet, but I'd put my money on some kinda feud among the low-lifes in there. Somebody snuck in, or else one of them girlies did it outta jeal-ousy."

"Unfortunately, it's those ins and outs that matter. When we know how and why, we'll have no trouble deciding who."

"You think that Badger fella used the key and got in there and back out real quick and quiet?"

"It's the most probable possibility," Marc said, recalling his Aristotle.

"Lookin' fer money or somethin' he could nick and sell?"

"Perhaps. But my hunch right now, given what we have learned thus far, is that it's more sinister than simple robbery or revenge, both of which motives may certainly be attributed to Michael Badger."

"You ain't thinkin' conspiracy again, are ya?" Cobb asked, making the word rhyme with "piracy."

Marc smiled, not sure after having known Cobb for two years now whether his solecisms were deliberate, naive, or a bit of both. "I am indeed."

They came out onto Lot Street and headed east towards Yonge, the smell of Barnett's tannery ripe in their nostrils.

"I am willing to entertain the hypothesis that Badger had good reason to steal that key and return to the house last night, in spite of the evident risks, to burgle and perhaps do something to damage the reputation of the brothel. But I cannot see a gambler, petty criminal, and deceiver like Badger viciously stabbing one of the girls, whom we are told he treated as if they were his sisters. It makes no sense. His immediate need was money in order to avoid reprisals from the gamblers at the Tinker's Dam. There must have been a stronger motive."

Marc walked along for minute, deep in thought.

Cobb said, "I'd better go up there and check out that story."

"Yes. We need more facts. I also hope to learn from Lord Durham when I report to him this evening exactly when and how Handford Ellice left Spadina. At the moment we have only the women's word that the sequence of events began shortly after one o'clock."

"Is that important?"

"I didn't think so at first, but if Ellice left the gala at, say, eleven o'clock, and got to the brothel before midnight, then the women would have had time to rig their little exculpatory drama at leisure. But if he arrived at, say, one-fifteen, as they claim, and you arrived just after two, then their story gains credibility."

"You still figure Badger was involved somehow?"

"I'm saying that if he did actually commit the murder, he

would have had some reason beyond petty revenge or simple robbery. He apparently needed cash, a lot of it, but certainly more
than he was likely to find lying about the brothel. Where could he
get that kind of money?"

Thinking out loud, Marc continued, the rush of his words
matching a military stride that left Cobb puffing in his wake.
"Yesterday morning he was caught unawares by Mrs. Burgess's
ultimatum. Let's say that someone from the city who wished to
scupper Lord Durham's mission had been dangling monetary bait
before him in anticipation of doing just that. At first he had refused, out of perverse loyalty to the woman he was fleecing or out
of simple discretion. Suddenly he is desperate for money, fearing
perhaps for his own life. So he decides to take on the nefarious
task.

"His co-conspirator—the man behind the plan—is embold-
ened to implement a scheme he has been contemplating for some
time. He will know all about the troubled nephew from his counterparts among the Tories in Quebec. He will know that the sexual
scandals still clinging to Edward Wakefield and Thomas Turton
will make Lord Durham vulnerable to any further disgrace of that
sort. He helps get young Ellice drunk, lures him away from the
gala, and leads him directly to that scarlet door. Badger is hiding
nearby.

"At the right moment—he'll know the routine of the house—
he sneaks in through the booby-hatch, as Miss Garnet called it.
Perhaps he was meant merely to injure Sarah—it could have been
any one of the girls, remember, as he couldn't know whose turn it
would be—but some fit of rage at Mrs. Burgess grips him as he
slips the knife out from the hiding place he knows well, and he
drives it into the helpless victim's neck, killing her instantly."

Cobb did not offer a comment on this sustained peroration

until they had turned south on Yonge Street. "I c'n follow all that, Major, but there's just a coupla things I don't see yet."

"Oh?"

"How would some fancy-pants toff get to know and conspire with the likes of Michael Badger?"

"Quite easily. We know that Ellice's escort used the code when knocking to gain admittance. He was or had been a regular. As such, he may have had plenty of opportunity to get to know the bruiser of Madame Renée's and sound him out about his plan to sabotage Lord Durham's vital work here in the Canadas."

"That's possible, Major, but a bit far-fletched fer my likin'."

"You're willing to accept that it is pure coincidence that Handford Ellice has become the target of someone's malice?"

"Seems to me the girl Sarah was the target."

"Of course. But why put the knife in Ellice's hand? Surely being found beside a prostitute with a dagger still in her throat would have been sufficient to implicate him."

"Though Ellice probably would've blamed one of the inmates or else skedaddled without anybody knowin' who he was."

"Exactly. The frame-up had to be foolproof, didn't it? He had to be found comatose with the bloody weapon in his hand. Somebody wanted Ellice to be charged, in the least, with felonious assault, and to be put in jail here to await trial. As he is likely to be very soon. See what a bind that puts His Lordship in? With that knife in his grip, Ellice could not claim to be a victim of circumstances, however sordid."

"I agree, but that just makes my second question all the harder to answer."

"I forgot you had another doubt."

"How did that knife get into the lad's hand, the right hand that was next to the girl, without the true murderer gettin' blood on himself and trackin' it to the hatch or inta the ladies' half of the house? Doc Withers told me the knife cut through the big vein in Sarah's throat. He said the blood wouldn't spurt, but kinda gush—like a pig's throat when it's first slit. If the killer pulled out the knife and then had to reach across the body in the dark to find the lad's right hand, he'd get blood on him, wouldn't he?"

"True, but he could have pulled it out and edged around to the other side of the bed, as you did apparently, then reach over from that side to plant the knife."

"But you ferget, I had a lantern. There was only a stub of candle in the room. You figure the killer, with Ellice breathin' there three feet away, is gonna go stumblin' around in the dark—without gettin' *some* blood on him or rousin' the lad?"

"I think you're likely correct in that assumption. That's a part of the mystery I can't quite work out yet. But as soon as Ellice is recovered from his shock, he may be able to shed light on it."

"There's another likelihood you gotta consider, Major."

"And what is that, pray tell?"

"That Mr. Ellice did it himself."

FOOT-WEARY AS HE WAS AFTER A night patrol, four hours' restless sleep, and an emotionally charged interrogation, Cobb dutifully turned into the police quarters at the rear of the Court House on the corner of King and Church Streets. It was near suppertime and Gussie French was just about to tidy his desk when he looked up to see Cobb enter. He groaned.

"Get yer quill quilled, Gussie," Cobb said. "We got work to do."

French slumped unhappily over his desk while Cobb dictated a summary of what he and Marc thought they had learned, minus any high-blown theories. To further irritate the clerk, Cobb pulled out his notebook and pretended to be reading from it. Cobb had long ago gauged the velocity of Gussie's pen over paper to the second, and hence was able to dictate just fast enough to infuriate him without actually bringing the business to an ink-blotted halt. Cobb's words reached the page in a barely legible scrawl.

Cobb finished at last, snapped his blank notebook shut, then whirled and walked out, leaving the door open long enough to permit a platoon of flies easy entrance. Behind him he heard a series of slapping sounds, the clatter of falling objects, and a string of vituperative oaths. Cobb whistled all the way home.

Cobb's house was situated near the edge of town on Parliament Street just below King. From his back yard he could see the smokestacks of the brewery and distillery down by the Don River and watch the slow churning of the gigantic Dutch windmill on its promontory above the lake. Dora, bless her, kept a neat cottage inside and out. Cobb paused to admire the unknown flowering shrubs beside the front walk ("I don't haveta know their names to like their looks," he had argued on more than one occasion). He could hear his son, Fabian, hoeing in the vegetable garden out back. Fabian must be ten years old by now, or was it still nine? Feeling enervated but otherwise at peace with the warm spring evening and an honest day's work behind him, Cobb entered his castle and called out for Dora.

Delia popped her pretty blond head out of the kitchen doorway, wiping her hands on her apron.

"Where's Missus Cobb?" he demanded, suddenly irritable.

"Mom's gone off on a call. I've got supper here whenever you're ready." Like her mother, eleven-year-old Delia had learned to ignore his mood if acknowledging it would inconvenience her. It was maddening.

"Why must women do their whatchamacallems at suppertime?

Yer mother's place is here. In her home. Lookin' after her children."

"It's venison stew," Delia warbled, and ducked back into the kitchen.

Cobb realized that he wanted to unburden himself at the end of a day like the one he had just endured. But even if Dora had been home, he knew that he would have been allowed to do so only if she'd granted him special dispensation. For they had a code, strictly adhered to, never to burden the other with sad tales from their different but equally troublous professions—unless by mutual consent. While Cobb assented to this arrangement (he had been given little choice), he felt it to be inherently unfair, for he bridled and blushed and squirmed at any description of matters to do with female plumbing, while she could be quite unmoved by accounts of the fistfights and blasphemies of drunks.

The aroma of venison stew seduced him into the kitchen.

"How old are you, lass?" he asked Delia, who kept on humming.

MARC FARED BETTER AT BRIAR COTTAGE. He had sent Beth a brief note from Government House at noon explaining the assignment he had been given, so she was primed and eager to hear what had happened to young Handford Ellice. Since it was she who had encouraged Ellice to come out of his introverted shell to dance and to join the whist players in the card room, she now felt somewhat responsible for the subsequent tragic events. Over supper, Marc gave Beth chapter and verse. He did not have to censor his narrative, for Beth had seen more of this world and suffered for it than most men in the province. Nor would she thank him for any such misguided expurgation.

When Marc had finished, he sat back, paused, and asked, "Well, what do you make of all this?"

"What you mean is, do I think the boy did it."

Marc smiled. "More or less. Lord Durham is certain he didn't. And when I talked briefly with Ellice this morning, I found him confused and frightened. I think he was so drunk he can't remember much, and even when the shock wears off, I doubt he'll be of any help. His fear may come from the thought that he could have done it. Cobb mentioned that Ellice seemed to mumble 'I didn't mean to' when first questioned, though he was so dazed that Cobb didn't set much store by it."

"We can often blot out unpleasant memories," Beth said. "For weeks after I found Jesse dead in the barn, I had no memory of that dreadful image. I knew he had gone, but I didn't know how or where. Then it came to me, in bits and pieces, in my dreams. Finally I began to believe my dreams, in the daylight."

"So you think there's a chance that young Ellice might eventually recover any images or actions he is now repressing?"

"Possibly."

"I've got to locate Badger. He might hold the answers to all my questions. In the meantime, though, I need to find an explanation for how the knife got into Ellice's hand."

"Cobb'll find Badger if he's still in the city."

"God, I hope so. We've only got until Thursday night to identify the killer. Lord and Lady Durham leave on a steamer for Kingston at noon on Friday."

"Will you interview Handford again tonight?"

"If Lord Durham permits it, yes."

"I'll wait up for you."

Charlene then joined them, and the talk turned domestic. Marc had decided to wait until morning to write up the notes he liked to make as an aide-mémoire.

"So, did you two ladies spend the day recuperating after the excitements of yesterday?" Marc said, winking at Charlene.

"Actually," Beth said, "we walked down to King Street and had a long look at the shops."

"You're going to sell them, then?"

Beth had inherited adjoining shops on King near Bay from her former father-in-law, Joshua Smallman, who had run a dry-goods store in one of them. There Beth and Aunt Catherine had launched their millinery and dress shop.

"I've been thinking about it. Mr. Ormsby next door came out when he saw us and told me he was pulling out next month and moving to Brantford to live with his daughter."

"So both shops will be empty?"

"Yes."

Beth was anticipating a further response, but Marc merely yawned.

"You'd better have a nap before you go up to see His Lordship," Beth said.

"You'll wake me up at seven-thirty?"

"I will. Now go."

At the bedroom door Beth placed a hand on Marc's shoulder and said quietly, "You don't suppose Lord Durham wants you to find a scapegoat for this murder, do you?"

"His Lordship is a man of honour," Marc said, a touch too emphatically. "He's no Tory, darling."

"But he is a lord, isn't he?"

SEVEN

I t was nearly eight o'clock in the evening when Marc walked down the tree-lined lane that led to Government House. Just as the chimney pots of the great house came into view, an open carriage drawn by two stout horses clattered past him. He recognized fleetingly the familiar profiles of John Strachan, the rector of St. James; Sir Allan MacNab, hero of the Yonge Street rout and the burning of the *Caroline*; and Ogle Gowan, grand master of the Loyal Orange Lodge. The Tory contingent had been having their say before the Queen's envoy, no doubt, pressing for the preservation of their accumulated entitlements. No one waved.

When the orderly showed Marc into the office, Lord Durham was slumped in his chair behind the desk, around which were arrayed half a dozen ladder-backed chairs, now empty. Durham looked ill. For a second Marc was alarmed, but as soon as His Lordship recognized his new visitor, he pulled himself to his full height, smiled, and said with genuine warmth, "Ah, Mr. Edwards. I am happy to see your face. Do sit down."

Marc wasn't sure whether it was his arrival or the Family Compact's departure that prompted the shift in mood, but he welcomed it. Fatigued as they both must be after a long night and a troubling day, they had matters to discuss that transcended personal weariness or private pain.

"Thank you, sir," Marc said, taking a seat across from the earl.

"Please, tell me everything you've discovered, in your own way. I'll just listen."

"I will do that, sir. But first I must ask after the health of young Mr. Ellice."

Durham frowned. "He's been sedated most of the day. Dosed with laudanum. He's been more or less in a delirium since you left him, spouting a lot of nonsense. Lady Durham feels he may be going mad."

"Good God. What sort of nonsense?"

"Well, most of it's gibberish, but Lady Durham has heard him say several times that he's stabbed Mrs. Edwards and he's desperately sorry."

"Beth?"

"Yes, your wife, who was so kind to him last evening. You do know how pleased and hopeful we were when we saw him dancing and when he left our side later to join the gentlemen in the card room. If some monarchs are said to have the common touch, then surely Mrs. Edwards has the noble version of that talent."

"She has a way with people."

"But then this nightmare dashed our hopes. Lady Durham is distraught, and I rely upon her for support and advice. While I don't profess to be close to Handford—he's been uncommunicative all his life—my firstborn son, as you may know, died tragically young. And I have since lost two of my daughters. So I know what it is to be a parent or guardian and lose someone precious and irreplaceable."

"Well, sir, I intend to find the real killer. That will be a start in helping Mr. Ellice recover. Perhaps then he could be sent home to recuperate."

"You are right, of course. But I was hoping, as you may be, that Handford could provide us with material assistance in the investigation. Yet so far he seems to have confused Mrs. Edwards with this . . ."

"Sarah McConkey, the murdered girl."

"Yes. I'm afraid he thinks not only that he may have committed murder, but also that he has destroyed a woman who befriended him."

"Be assured, sir, that I lend no credence to what Mr. Ellice may say in a delirium or as a result of delayed shock."

"Your discretion is appreciated. Now, please tell me what you've discovered at the crime scene."

For the next twenty minutes Marc talked and Durham listened. Marc recounted what he assumed to be the established facts in the case, avoiding all speculation and theorizing. He told Durham that it appeared Ellice had been deliberately lured away from Spadina about midnight, probably by one of the whist players, driven to Lot Street, escorted to Madame Renée's, taken to bed by Sarah McConkey, and subsequently discovered asleep beside her bloody corpse with the murder weapon in his hand. Marc then reviewed the interrogation of the four women, the revelation of the escape hatch and the missing key, and the madam's dismissal of Michael Badger.

When Marc had finished, Durham sat back wearily and asked, "How far can we trust anything these prostitutes say?"

"I believe we have to be skeptical of anything they tell us. The denizens of Irishtown don't exactly revere authority of any kind. What Cobb and I have endeavoured to do is to look for inconsistencies and to tally their claims against those incontrovertible facts we do know. For instance, none of the victim's blood left the bedroom except for that on the bare feet of your nephew. Cobb himself saw the dagger in the young man's hand, with no evidence that anyone else had entered the room after the stabbing to stage a false scene. It's conceivable that all four women were in on it together, but we have found no plausible motive yet for such an assumption, nor do we have a rational explanation for how they might have managed it."

"I see."

"So it is important in that regard to verify the timeline. We need to know for sure when Mr. Ellice left Spadina and, if possible, whom he left with."

Durham smiled. "I can help you there. As I mentioned this morning, I ordered Wakefield to question the servants carefully about what they observed last evening. Mr. Wakefield is both persuasive and thorough."

Marc's heart leapt. "He found out who lured Mr. Ellice away?"

"Not quite. But here is what he believes to be a reliable account of what happened. It was about ten-thirty when Handford left us to try his luck at whist. He was observed to join one of the tables and keep to it for the remainder of the evening. One of the four gentlemen already there would give up his seat for fifteen minutes or so—putting in a token appearance with his wife in the ballroom, no doubt—then return and take the seat of another, who left in turn, and so on."

"I think I know the four gentlemen in question," Marc said, to Durham's surprise.

"You do?"

Marc named the foursome that he and Owen had observed from their vantage-point in the smoker: the Reverend Temperance Finney, Alasdair Hepburn, Patrick O'Driscoll, and Samuel Harris.

"Precisely. And you know these gentlemen?"

"Good Tories all," Marc said. "Finney is a fire-and-brimstone Methodist, Hepburn runs the Commercial Bank, O'Driscoll is second-in-command of the Orange Lodge, and Samuel Harris is a wealthy landowner in town and an importer of dry goods."

"You suspect there may have been some skullduggery in that card room?"

"It's possible. Though I think that whatever happened there was partly improvised. But before I bore you with my theories, please tell me more of what actually happened."

"Several times Handford accompanied one or another of the gentlemen to the bar for a drink before Handford was sent back to rejoin the whist. All this was apparently convivial. Nonetheless, one of the servants was alarmed at Handford's state of inebriation and went looking for my valet. He couldn't find him, and when he returned to his post, Handford was gone—to his quarters, the man assumed."

"Did he leave the whist table alone?"

"Yes."

"Not with one of the players?"

"No. They were there until nearly midnight."

Marc's hopes sank. They had to find the culprit who drove Ellice into town.

"But he was spotted leaving the grounds." Durham smiled at the effect this revelation had. "At precisely ten minutes past midnight, in one of the carriages, accompanied by a gentleman and possibly his lady."

"Then it could have been one of the whist players after all. Do we know who?"

"Alas, no. Two different stableboys saw Handford stagger into the carriage, but neither can recall whose carriage it was—only that it was likely a barouche. It was dark and several other carriages were leaving about the same time."

"Damn. Most of the guests came in barouches."

"Wakefield will continue the investigation out at Spadina. It's still possible that someone will recall something of significance."

"I hope so. But this new information is helpful. It tallies with the account of events given by the women at Madame Renée's, and makes it almost impossible to believe that they had time to perpetrate the crime as a group and cover their tracks. And it suggests that Mr. Ellice was plied with drink—possibly even drugged—and may have been seduced into accompanying one of the whist players."

"Those conclusions, however tentative, sound reasonable to me."

"If true, it narrows our search to four men, not the dozens now scattered across three counties."

"Though it is not inconceivable that a fifth conspirator may have been engaged to do the transporting."

"Perhaps, but I now have four people to interrogate that I didn't have half an hour ago."

Durham looked at Marc as if unsure how he should broach the point he felt obliged to make. "I think we have to be extremely tactful in how we go about interrogating prominent citizens about a murder, especially those not known to be Whig sympathizers."

"But I—"

"And that is why I invited you to lead the investigation rather than leaving it to the local authorities."

"Thank you, sir."

Durham dredged up a smile and said, "Now, I sense you're keen to begin theorizing."

Marc smiled back. "Yes, sir, I am." And with that, he

sketched out his hypothesis—now reinforced by Wakefield's report from Spadina—that the murder was the result of a conspiracy to derail His Lordship's mission and its perceived pro-Reform bias. One or more of the whist players—Finney, Hepburn, O'Driscoll, Harris—had arranged to get Ellice drunk and lure him to a brothel. Hiding close by was a recruited thug, who knew the routine of the house and possessed a key to its hidden entrance, not six feet from the door to the victim's room. When the house was quiet, said thug slipped in, slunk into the cubicle where Sarah McConkey and Ellice were asleep (his snores audible through the netted opening of the window), and created mayhem.

"Surely the slaughter of an innocent girl—fallen soul though she was—seems a bit extravagant for the purpose of embroiling my family in a scandal," Durham ventured.

"I agree, sir. As I mentioned earlier, Badger had a personal grudge in addition to his need for money, but even so, I don't believe he was paid to kill anyone. When we apprehend him—"

"If we do—"

"If we do, then I'll bet we find that he was hired to beat up the girl, perhaps knocking her unconscious, then scoot back out the hatch before the women were wakened and came running in. That would be enough to compromise your nephew, especially if the respectable citizen who set this up informed the police or encouraged Mrs. Burgess to make a complaint. Or perhaps Badger was meant to break Mr. Ellice's leg or otherwise incapacitate him so he would be found there in disgrace."

Durham looked skeptical. "Would he be able to do any of this and get away?"

"I believe so, for two reasons. First, he was a professional bruiser. He made his living by intimidating rowdies and beating people up.

He'd have little trouble silencing Sarah while he clubbed her unconscious or smashing a leg with a brick, and then retreating through
an unlocked escape hatch only steps away."

"And all this to sabotage my mission?"

Marc grimaced. "I'm afraid so. Remember, we just fought
a bloody civil war over the fate of these provinces, and publicly
hanged several of the rebels. Even as we speak, our borders are
being threatened by Yankee fanatics."

Durham nodded in sad agreement, then said, "Well, it's a
plausible theory. But as I see it, we need to find two men before
we can take it one premise further: Michael Badger and the man
who took him to the brothel."

"Cobb is heading to the Tinker's Dam tonight to look for
Badger and check out Mrs. Burgess's characterization of him as a
reckless gambler and deadbeat."

"Meanwhile, I've prepared the ground for you and me both to
assess the character of the whist players."

"You have?"

"After Wakefield's report, I anticipated that we might need to
examine these men, even if only to eliminate them from our suspicions. You said you've read the characters and relationships among
the women of the brothel during your time there this afternoon.
Well, I have invited Finney, Hepburn, O'Driscoll, and Harris to
meet with me here at ten o'clock tomorrow morning, ostensibly to
have them offer advice to me and to be privy to some of my current thinking on potential solutions for the political problems in
Upper Canada."

"But won't they be suspicious, especially if more than one is in
on the game?"

Durham gave Marc a look that he must have used a hundred
times in cabinet meetings just before revealing some particularly

subtle piece of political deception. "I've also invited Robert Baldwin, son of the squire of Spadina and lifelong Reformer, to provide diversion and ballast."

"But you said 'both' of us."

"I did. You will bring your notebook and sit in a corner with Charles Buller, as my recording secretaries."

"Two secretaries?"

"It'll reinforce the importance I attach to their every word, eh?"

Marc was impressed. "So you'll get to look these chaps in the eye while I observe unnoticed from the side?"

"Exactly. Moreover, I intend to invent some pretext for asking, casually you understand, about certain events in the card room last evening. We'll test their responses and go from there."

"I'll be here, with notebook, before ten."

"Good. I feel we've made real progress in just a few hours."

"Thank you. Oh, one last matter: was there any further information from Dr. Withers about Sarah?"

"He submitted a copy of the written report prepared for Chief Sturges. There's nothing new. She was stabbed once and fatally. There were no other wounds or even bruises. Interestingly enough, according to Withers, she had not been . . . engaged, shall we say, during the evening. Poor Handford was so inebriated he must have doffed his clothes and then collapsed on the bed and fallen asleep."

"It does sound as if he might have been drugged."

Durham sighed. "You may be right. If so, your conspiracy theory gains credibility."

Marc wished now he had checked the decanters on the sideboard at Madame Renée's. It would be far too late to do so now.

More likely, though, any drugging had taken place out at Spadina or en route to the brothel.

"Dr. Withers released the girl's body to Mrs. Burgess and the undertaker late this afternoon. Apparently her own family has publicly disowned her."

"Sadly, I believe that is so," Marc said, "though I intend to verify it."

Marc rose and the two men shook hands.

Outside it was now dark. Marc walked briskly towards Sherbourne Street and home. One of the cabs that had just started to patrol King Street slowed expectantly, but Marc waved it on. He was far too agitated to ride in style. He was not only in the midst of a murder investigation that might heavily influence the future of Upper Canada, he was about to be allowed entry to the inner sanctum of high-level politics. At ten o'clock tomorrow he would be privileged to watch one of the most brilliant public men of the post-war period in action.

SOMEONE WAS JABBING COBB IN THE ribs with a truncheon. But whenever he tried reaching for his own trusty instrument of justice, his arm froze in mid-reach and his ribs took another wincing blow. Cold panic twisted in his gut . . .

"Dad! Wake up!"

Groggily, Cobb forced his eyelids open.

"You said to wake you up before dark, but we couldn't get you to budge!"

Delia and Fabian stood beside his prone figure with expressions of bewilderment and irritation.

"Mom ain't home, so it was only us," Delia said, more in the way of defence than apology.

"It was Delia's idea to use the soup ladle on your chest," Fabian said.

"Missus Cobb's been out all night?" Cobb sat up, trying to shake off the lethargy of deep and illicit sleep.

The children laughed. "It's not morning, Dad. It's about nine o'clock at night. We've been trying to wake you up for almost an hour."

"Jumpin' Jesus!"

The children recoiled, not so much at the expletive as at the daunting sight of their father clad only in cotton drawers that did little to prevent his paunch from greeting the world raw and unmitigated.

"Fetch my clothes! I gotta be up to Lot Street before dark!"

"It's too late for that," Fabian said.

COBB FOUND CONSTABLE ROSSITER AT HIS customary post, a nameless dive on Yonge Street near Lot. Rossiter had the northeast patrol and the distinction of policing the worst den of thieves and miscreants in the city. Where Irishtown was an unintentional slum inhabited mainly by fatherless families, the unemployed, and sundry others left stranded and friendless by mainstream society, it was blackguards and outright felons who populated the shacks and hovels grouped around the Tinker's Dam along a straggling lane that ran off the corner of Lot and Jarvis. Cobb never went there alone at night, though he had often been compelled to join Rossiter (and once, a sheriff's deputized posse) in search of men wanted for serious crimes. If they didn't turn up their quarry on the initial sweep, there was no hope of getting anything truthful or helpful from the rest of the population.

Rossiter was not happy about having his backgammon inter-rupted but agreed to come when informed that this case was so important that Chief Sturges himself had offered to cover Cobb's southeast patrol until it was solved. It was pitch-black by the time they turned onto the lane that led to the Tinker's Dam. Rossiter had brought along a lantern, but Cobb refused to let him light it.

"We'll nip along in the moonlight," Cobb said. "Our only chance of catchin' the bugger is to surprise him in the back room where there's usually heavy bettin' on the dice."

"If they ain't off in the fields watchin' a cockfight," Rossiter said.

They made their way cautiously along the lane, hands on truncheons just in case they were mistaken for ordinary citizens who had wandered in unawares. But no one accosted them. Several dogs barked ferociously from nearby outposts but chose discretion over valour. Up ahead a barn-like blotch of shadow against the moonlight, low from the east, signalled their proximity to the Tinker's Dam. At the same time the burst of laughter and umbrage from its open doors and paneless windows struck the constables like the wall of a tidal wave.

"Well, they sure as hell won't hear us comin'," Rossiter said.

"You go 'round back," Cobb directed. "There's a door that opens up from the root cellar. Stand there with yer club at half-mast and rap the bugger on the noggin when he comes out. I'm goin' in a-hollerin' his name, and he'll make like a ferret in a burrow."

"Jesus, Cobb, be careful. They got knives in there, and pistols too."

Cobb waved him to his post, then strode into the mêlée with his truncheon cocked. No one noticed. The light tossed up by the candles was uncertain and more camouflaging than revealing. The noise level among the tipplers—crowded half a dozen to a table-cum-tree stump or sandwiched along the raw plank that served as a bar and separated the throng from the barrels of whiskey behind

it—was so deafening that Cobb could not detect his own bel-
lowed threat: "Police! We're here to arrest Michael Badger! Give
him up now!"

Cobb prodded his way through the stench and smoke, but
there was so much incidental elbowing going on that no one
particularly noticed a jab from a constable's truncheon. "Michael
Badger! You're under arrest!"

"What kinda whiskey did ya say?" the bartender shouted next
to his ear.

Exasperated, Cobb pushed towards the door to the gambling
den. Suddenly a large and very ugly man lurched in front of him.
"Where the fuck do ya think yer goin'?"

"In there, to arrest Michael Badger." Cobb raised his stick and
pointed it at a spot below the man's chin.

"Michael Badger ain't in there, so bugger off!"

"I think I'll just see fer myself."

"I'd advise against it, Consta—"

No further syllable emerged because Cobb's truncheon had
poked its snout well into the bruiser's voice box and sent him
gagging against the bar. Cobb pushed open the door and stepped
brazenly into the gambling den. "Where's Michael Badger?" he
boomed.

A dozen men, crouched in a circle around a pair of dice and
wads of wagered dollars, looked up, their eyes removed from the
tumbling and fickle bones for the first time in an hour. They froze
in place there, as if the mental effort and emotional anguish demanded by the game had left them disoriented and momentarily
petrified. Finally, one of them, whom Cobb recognized as Burly
Bettman, stood up and declared, "That son-of-a-bitch deadbeat
ain't here, and if he was, I'd rip off his legs and bash his brains out
with 'em."

Bettman either owned the Tinker's Dam or had it by squatter's rights.

"Badger owes ya money, I take it," Cobb said.

"More'n thirty bucks. The stupid bugger don't know when to quit."

"When did you see him last?"

"He was in here Saird'y night. Tried ta sucker me inta double or nothin'. I told him ta pay up by last night or I'd double the debt and then take it outta his hide slice by slice."

"Okay, you fellas c'n go back to losin' yer shirts," Cobb said. "But I'd check them funny dice if I was you."

Cobb went looking for Rossiter. He found him beside the cellar door, standing over a prone figure lying motionless in the grass.

"What the hell—"

"You said to conk the bugger," Rossiter protested.

"Yeah, and I told ya Badger was six feet tall with a bushel of orange hair. This guy's five feet and bald. I hope ya haven't killed him."

"But he come bustin' up outta that doorway like he'd seen a ghost."

A sudden groan suggested that the victim was still alive. Cobb bent down and turned him face up. "Christ! It's Nestor Peck, one of my snitches."

"So it is," Rossiter said, more surprised than concerned.

"He must've heard my voice in the barroom and skedaddled. The last person he'd want to be seen with in this territory is a constable."

"We just gonna leave him here?" Rossiter said, stifling a yawn.

"Yeah. You hit him in the one spot he can't be hurt. But I gotta see him and my other snitches first thing in the mornin' to put the word out about Badger. If he's been holin' up in one of these shacks around here, he's long gone by now. His name's mud in these parts, and pretty soon he's gonna have the whole town snappin' at his arse."

Nestor groaned again and tried to open his eyes.

"We better get a move on," Cobb said.

Rossiter agreed.

COBB STAGGERED INTO HIS PARLOUR, FLOPPED into an easy chair, and let his boots drop off. "Missus Cobb!" he shouted.

Dora came in from the kitchen, an apron tied around her nightdress. Her parabolic curves consumed the doorway. "Shoutin' may get you respect in the dives you free-kwent, but it don't travel far in this place."

"I was just askin' if you was home, luv."

"Askers don't beller."

"Glad ya got home just the same."

"Darn glad to be home. I've had one helluva day."

"Don't tell me about it, please."

"I wasn't plannin' to."

"The kids got me supper. They're gettin' better at it—"

"Is that a complaint, Mister Cobb?"

Just then Delia called from the kitchen.

"What the heck's she doin' up?" Cobb said, happy to redirect the conversation.

"School's out and it's summer, ya old fart. They ain't little kids no more."

"Ya mean ta say Fabian's still outside?"

"Yer deed-duction is ah-cute tonight, constable."

"He's playing hide-and-go-seek with the boys," Delia said from the kitchen doorway, her tone part reproof and part envy.

As if on cue, the front door was flung open and ten-year-old Fabian stumbled into the room, flushed and excited.

"What's happened?" Dora said.

"We saw a bogeyman!" Fabian said, his pale eyes delightedly wide and eager to calculate their effect of his words on the elders.

"Don't be daft," Cobb said.

"But we did, Dad. Butch and me were hiding in the bushes up near King Street when this monster pops up out of nowhere and roars at us."

"Just some tramp," Cobb said, glancing at Dora but not ready yet to risk a wink.

"You probably scared him more'n he scared you," Dora said.

"This wasn't any normal mortal," said Fabian, who had begun reading his grandfather's *Shakespeare* and dazzling his classmates with unsolicited bursts of pentameter. "He was as big and ugly as Caliban!"

"Now, Fabian—"

"And there was a fiery halo 'round his head!"

Cobb went suddenly still. "When you say big, you mean tall, eh?"

"Tallest man I ever saw, honest."

"Jesus!" Cobb cried. "It's him!"

"Mister Cobb, watch yer—"

But Cobb was already scrambling for the door. "Which way did he go?" he said to Fabian, who was on his heels.

"Butch and me let out a yell and the creature turned and run off."

"But where?" Cobb gasped, tripping on the steps and teetering forward onto the stone walk.

"Straight up King Street. We could see his halo bobbing away."

"Heading up King towards the river?"

"And running like he had the devil up his backside!"

Cobb was about to reprimand his son for using such an unsa-voury image but instead found himself yelling, "Jesus Christ and Christendom!"

Fabian began to laugh. He couldn't help it: his father was hop-ping about in his stocking feet and pulling thistles out of their soles.

Back in the parlour—fuming and mortified—Cobb informed Dora that the bogeyman was undoubtedly a fugitive he'd been tracking and, alas, was now heading for the Kingston Road and townships east. He began pulling his boots on over his swollen and prickled feet.

"You're not goin' out again?" Dora said. "You'll drop dead of exertion!"

"I've gotta find Sarge and wake him up. We're gonna need the troops to catch this bugger tonight."

"What's goin' on?" Dora asked, alarmed. "We gonna have an-other rebellion?"

Cobb stood up on his tender appendages. "We might be— Ow!"

"You gonna shoot him, Dad?" Delia asked, wondrously scan-dalized.

"I'd like to, luv."

Moments later, Constable Horatio Cobb was hurrying gin-gerly through the dark streets of his city, looking once more to his duty.

EIGHT

When Marc arrived home from Government House, he found Beth tucked up in bed, reading. Her father, a Congregational minister from Pennsylvania, had bequeathed her an impressive library of books, most of which she had read more than once. She looked up, smiled, then giggled.

"Do I look that bad?" Marc said, sitting down beside her.

"Not you," she replied, leaning over to be kissed. "Mr. Pickwick."

"Ah, you've started in on Uncle Frederick's collection, then?"

"Mr. Dickens is a lot more amusing than Blackstone's *Commentaries* or Phillips' *Evidence*."

"Uncle Frederick sent those for my edification, not entertainment."

"This Dickens fella doesn't have a lot of respect for barristers."

"Who does?"

She waited till he had undressed and slipped in beside her before she asked, "Well, are you going tell me about it?"

"Yes, but in the morning when my mind wakes up."

He reached over and placed a warm hand on her belly.

She shook her head gently, but her smile seemed to say "soon."

•   •   •

MARC SLIPPED OUT OF BED AND into his study before seven the next morning. He wanted to write down what he had learned at Government House while it was still fresh. Outside his window, bobolinks and meadowlarks warbled the fields and gardens awake. About eight o'clock Charlene tapped on the door and brought in tea and toast. A little later he heard the two women preparing breakfast in the kitchen, chatting amiably as they did so. How far such easy domesticity seemed from the sordid and sad scene at Madame Renée's: a girl's blood spilled wantonly and death sudden and undeserved.

When Charlene tapped next, Marc assumed it was the call to breakfast proper. He was surprised when she announced that Constable Cobb had arrived. They had planned to meet at the police station at nine-thirty. He hurried out to the parlour, where Cobb stood fiddling with his truncheon and looking everywhere but at the women of the house.

Without ceremony he announced, "I got some news, Major."

Cobb then sketched out for Marc the events up at the Tinker's Dam and the almost certain sighting of the red-headed giant thereafter. Chief Constable Sturges had trotted up to Government House, roused Sir George Arthur from a warm bed, and persuaded him to dispatch a mounted troop to the Kingston Road in search of Badger.

Marc seemed more interested in the Tinker's Dam than in the imminent capture of their key witness. "That was very good work up there last night," he said. "You know, of course, what it means?"

"Yeah, we didn't catch the bugger." Cobb blushed, then glanced towards the kitchen where the two women had discreetly retired.

"It means two things. First, Badger turns out to be a reckless gambler in trouble with the toughs of the town, who was facing a deadline for repayment of his debts to them, which in turn means that Mrs. Burgess's account of him and his recent behaviour has been essentially substantiated. So far we haven't caught her or her girls in a single lie. For instance, I learned from Lord Durham last evening that the timeline of their story jibes with what Wakefield discovered at Spadina."

Marc brought Cobb up to speed on that subject.

"You mentioned two things," Cobb reminded Marc.

"The second is that we now have a chronological account of the entire evening, from the moment Ellice entered the whist game until you found him with a bloody dagger in his hand sometime after two in the morning."

"And?" Cobb seemed more bemused by all this than impressed.

"We have ipso facto both the perpetrator of the deed, Badger, and his motives, money and revenge, along with a fair idea of who might have supplied him the blood money and escorted Ellice to the brothel: one or more of the whist players. And we can easily infer what their motive was."

"And you're gonna see these gents at ten o'clock?"

"Precisely."

They agreed to meet at the Cock and Bull at one. Cobb turned to go.

"What are you going to do this morning?" Marc asked at the door.

"I'm gonna dig up my snitches and put the word out on this Badger fella, in case he tries to sneak back into town. But with that head o' hair and that size, he won't be able to find a hidey-hole anywheres in this county."

Cobb neglected to mention that he had other investigative plans of his own. The Major wasn't the only one who could concoct a theory.

MARC SAT DOWN TO A HEARTY English breakfast. While Charlene was clearing up, Marc and Beth sat in the parlour discussing his visit to Government House the previous night. When he had completed his summary and followed up with his conspiracy theory, Beth nodded politely, then remarked, "I'm worried about that poor young man."

"We all are, darling. That's why we're desperate to find the real killer."

"He sounds like he's about to lose his mind."

"I think Lord Durham feels the same."

"Then it won't matter much who killed Sarah McConkey, will it?"

"No, but—"

"I feel I'm partly to blame for what happened. If I hadn't got him to dance and start feeling comfortable with himself, he never would've gone into that card room and—"

"Beth, you must not blame yourself for this tragedy. Not in the least way. Handford Ellice is a grown man. He made the decision to go with a stranger to look for a woman."

Beth let the admonition pass. "You said he's hallucinating about stabbing me?"

"Yes, that's what His Lordship told me. More exactly, he said that his nephew repeatedly fantasized pulling the knife out of your neck."

Beth thought about that, then said, "I think they're pouring too much laudanum into the boy. He's got to come back to reality, not escape it by being drugged silly."

"You may be right, but—"

"He needs to see me, in the flesh and alive."

"You're not thinking of going up there!"

"No, I'm not thinking about it at all. I've made up my mind to go."

After much further debate with no change in outcome, Marc agreed to prepare the way for Beth to visit Handford Ellice that afternoon on condition that she not try to tell Dr. Withers how to practise medicine. He took her nod for consent.

THE COLLOQUY WITH THE EARL OF Durham, Her Majesty's High Commissioner to British North America, took place in a comfortable meeting room in the east wing of Government House. Padded chairs surrounded a rectangular table of polished oak. A warm breeze billowed the curtains on the mullioned windows open now to the benevolent weather. Lord Durham sat at one end of the table, resplendent in his formal morning clothes and smiling at his guests, though a tightness at the edges of the mouth betrayed the tension he was feeling. The Tory gentlemen sat in pairs along either side, looking a bit nervous in the presence of such power and privilege but nonetheless confident in their cause and its ultimate preponderance. At the other end sat Robert Baldwin, son of Dr. William Baldwin of Spadina, and still a Reformer, if a somewhat tarnished one after his ambiguous role in the Rebellion. His expression was unreadable.

In one corner of the room, well away from the table, sat Charles Buller and Marc Edwards, pens poised. The only person in the room requiring an introduction was Marc. And Lord Durham proceeded to do that as the first order of business, having noted the puzzled and not unsuspicious glances of his Tory guests.

"I have asked one of your own to take notes and prepare minutes of our meeting in addition to my own secretary, Mr. Buller.

This is Mr. Marc Edwards, formerly Lieutenant Edwards of the 23rd Regiment of Foot, now a permanent resident of the city and"—he paused until all eyes had returned to him and added—"a heroic combatant at St. Denis."

While Marc was continually embarrassed by such references, he understood precisely why the wily earl had mentioned it. The Tory gentlemen—or whist players, as Marc thought of them—visibly relaxed and thereafter paid no attention to him.

Lord Durham opened the dialogue.

"Let me begin, gentlemen, by saying that there is not much about the conflicting political positions in Upper Canada that I do not know at secondhand. I have read every *Report on Grievances*, every written submission made to Parliament over the past three years, and a number of critical dispatches shown to me by the colonial secretary, Lord Glenelg. I have spoken at length with that distinguished gentleman and with his successor-designate, Lord John Russell. I have brought with me Edward Wakefield, the public servant who knows more about the colonies and colonial policy than any other man in England, in order to benefit from his advice. But there is no substitute for firsthand experience, for being able to listen to the very people whose lives are entangled in the issues and who reside in the disputed terrain, as it were."

There was a murmur of assent here, and Marc noticed the whist players lean forward perceptibly, abandoning the detached air they had been feigning.

"However, what I need most at this point in my odyssey of reconciliation and reconstruction is not so much a reiteration of long-entrenched views and positions—though I promise to attend to these if you feel you have a particularly cogent or fresh perspective on them—as to hear your response to the proposals which I have been formulating as potential solutions to the province's difficulties and the political stalemate it finds itself in."

"I don't know about your proposals, sir," said the Reverend Finney, suddenly raising his voice as if he had begun his complaint in mid-paragraph, "but I wish to comment on the regrettable acts which you've already committed and which can't be undone."

"Of course. Such heartfelt comments may be valuable," Durham replied diplomatically, "in assisting me to mend my ways in the future. What decisions are you referring to?"

"The surprisingly lenient treatment of the French rebels for one."

"You mean the fact that I didn't hang them one and all?"

"Hanging's too good for them. They're convicted murderers. They torched houses and barns. They bankrupted honest English citizens!"

"That is true."

"Up here we did our duty, we strung up Matthews and Lount as soon as we decently could: an eye for an eye. And I'll tell you, sir, the sight of them two blackguards dangling from a gibbet beside the Court House soon put a stop to any further shenanigans."

"Let me try and explain, then." Durham looked at the other Tories, who were bobbing their chins in support of Finney. Robert Baldwin sat expressionless, like the good barrister he was. "The first thing I felt obliged to do—"

"Was dismiss the duly appointed Executive Council!" broke in Patrick O'Driscoll. "Do you realize what sort of precedent that may have set?"

"I did, and I do, sir. But I believe I was responding to the previous point, which usually takes precedence."

"I hope, Your Lordship, that you will not take umbrage at the strength of our expression here this morning, for we have been bottling up our opinions and views for some months. The tone may be somewhat vehement, but its tenor is notwithstanding solemn and important." The voice of reason belonged to Alasdair Hepburn, banker.

"Vehemence and passion are not unwelcome here. I have been accused of those vices myself inside and outside of the Privy Council. So, to return to my original point. My first obligation in regard to the hundreds of rebels jailed without benefit of habeas corpus was to sort out the wheat from the chaff."

"A murderer is a murderer!" Finney huffed.

"There was murder and arson on both sides. The situation demanded that I distinguish the political and military leaders of the revolt from those who were low-level participants in what was, after all, a civil strife, and from those who merely sympathized and hoped. This was done on the basis of forensic evidence and proper judicial procedure, which are, along with habeas corpus, the cornerstones of British freedom and social order."

Baldwin nodded.

"Once I was certain that men like Papineau and Nelson were indeed the instigators and leaders of the uprising, I put them on trial and saw them properly convicted."

"Then slapped their behinds and told them to be good little boys!" Finney blustered.

"I banished them for life, by special ordinance, and exiled them to Bermuda. The punishment, however it may be viewed, has proven to be as practicable as I had hoped. Moderates among the English faction and the new leaders emerging from the French community—like Louis LaFontaine—have supported my decision. It was clear and harsh enough to be seen as punitive and efficacious, and yet not so draconian as to be perceived as vindictive."

"Vengeance is mine, saith the Lord," Baldwin murmured, and got several rude looks for his pains.

"With that legal issue resolved and the regular courts restored," Durham continued, "I could then, and only then, proceed to political matters."

"By sacking the entire legitimate council and appointing your own Special Council to rule as you liked!" O'Driscoll charged again.

"Under the terms of my commission," Durham said quietly, "I can more or less rule as I like, without benefit of any council. However, that has not been the route I have taken, as your presence here this morning illustrates."

Samuel Harris now spoke for the first time. "Let me congratulate Your Lordship on the speed with which you released the impounded monies back into circulation. It's all very well to babble on about politics, but a country's well-being is primarily dependent upon its economic health and its mercantile ingenuity."

"Well said," Hepburn added for good measure.

"That is true, sir, and as a lifelong Whig I am a proponent of open trade and low tariffs and a minimum of political supervision of the economy. But my reading of your troubles is that it is the political deadlock that has stultified economic growth: race against race in Quebec and Tory against Reformer here in Upper Canada."

"But that's where you're wrong!" O'Driscoll cried, his black eyes burning. "For ten years now it's been loyalist against traitor, monarchist against republican, men of means and respectability against upstarts and Yankee infiltrators and all those Papists we've let in to pollute our soil!"

Hepburn cleared his throat. "Please, Mr. O'Driscoll, remember that this is not about religion but about loyalties and probity."

Harris, who had reddened, glared at O'Driscoll.

"I'm sorry, Sam, but I'm just so Goddamned angry—"

"And so are many hundreds of others," Durham soothed. "I have been sent here to help assuage that anger, to provide some framework within which the native intelligence of all concerned citizens can be encouraged to flourish and henceforth produce local decisions by democratic means."

"But even as we speak," Harris said in his modest dry-goods voice, "members of the Hunters' Lodges in New York and Ohio are denouncing us and gathering forces to invade and 'liberate' us. And as long as they do so, normal cross-border trade will remain at a standstill."

"And thousands of farmers are fleeing to Iowa," Baldwin countered, "honest men who have been branded traitors and hounded out of the province, selling their farms for a song—"

"And withdrawing their savings from my bank," Hepburn added with a wry glance at Baldwin, as if to assure him that the banking community was not behind the exodus. Then he turned to Lord Durham. "But you already know all of this. We would be most interested in hearing what solutions you are contemplating in order to comment on them from our various perspectives."

Marc thought that the bank business must have thrived heretofore, for Alasdair Hepburn had obviously spent much time at a well-stocked trencher with vintage wines and Portuguese sherry to wash it down. His face, once handsome, was bloated and shot through with tiny, throbbing veins. He thought also that Hepburn, like the others, was being somewhat disingenuous, for the outlines of Durham's "solution" were widely rumoured and already being debated in the local press. Still, Durham himself had made no public pronouncements on the subject.

"I'd be pleased to," Durham said. "But I must first emphasize in the strongest possible terms that I will not make any final decisions until I return to London early next year. On the other hand, if I don't offer potential solutions for serious debate and considered response while I'm in situ, then I might as well have stayed at home."

"We're all ears," O'Driscoll said.

"My view so far is that the conflict in Quebec is racially based. The political, religious, and social differences between French and English are wide enough to be insurmountable in the short term and problematic in the long term. In Upper Canada the conflict is political—pure and simple."

"I wouldn't call it simple!" Finney said. "Nor is it unrelated to religion. I suppose Strachan was in here last evening bending your ear about the Clergy Reserves and the divine right of the Church of England."

"I can't deny it," Durham said with a rare smile. "But even the Clergy Reserves question is political. For example, if political power and will were not gridlocked between the governor with his appointed bodies and the elected assembly, then some compromise solution with the support of at least a decent majority of the populace would have been long ago worked out."

"You're not seriously suggesting that the authority of the governor or his royal prerogative be subject to the passing whim of the rabble in the assembly?" O'Driscoll fumed.

Assemblyman Baldwin coughed discreetly.

"Let His Lordship speak," Hepburn said sharply.

"I won't be silenced!"

That must have been some card game, Marc thought.

"As I was saying," Durham continued, "I view the issue here as political, with entrenched positions taken up by the established elite on the one hand and the self-made men and prosperous farmers on the other. If I had merely to propose a solution for Upper Canada, my task would be straightforward. I would recommend responsible government along the British model."

"I knew it!" cried Finney, slapping the table as he did his pulpit on Sundays.

"I don't see any point in remaining—" O'Driscoll began, starting to rise.

"But, of course, I do not have that luxury," Durham said, unfazed, and O'Driscoll sat down again. "A rebellious or disaffected Quebec, sharing the St. Lawrence River and a border with the rapacious republic to the south, will guarantee the economic collapse of this province regardless of its political structure. So I am compelled to work out a single, overarching set of solutions involving both the Canadas."

"But I don't see the problem," O'Driscoll said. "We've defeated the French. The so-called patriots abroad will be crushed before the new year. What does it matter if the French are disaffected? They forfeited their right to have any say when they took up arms against the monarch."

"And someday they'll thank us for freeing them from the pope," Finney added with the conviction of the righteous.

"But the French are the vast majority in that province," Durham said. "They aren't likely to commit mass suicide just to please us."

"If the provinces were united, however," Hepburn ventured, "we English would soon be the majority."

"That's the conclusion I've been moving towards these past few weeks," Durham said without particular emphasis.

Harris spoke next. "You figure the French will be outmanoeuvred by the English in a single parliament?"

Marc suddenly recalled that Harris was not only Catholic but was married to a woman from Quebec.

"I wouldn't characterize it in quite those terms," Durham said, and continued in a much more solemn tone: "My considered opinion is that the Quebec French are principally a rural people, an unsophisticated peasantry under the thumb of their priests and unable to liberate themselves from a medieval and pernicious seigneurial system. The landed aristocracy is minuscule in number, there is an impoverished middle class, and no universal and secular school system. In brief, Quebec is as different from Upper Canada as it is possible to be. My plan on first arriving here was to create a federated state composed of all five provinces—"

"That's preposterous!" O'Driscoll scoffed. "We can't get two provinces to agree, how could you persuade five of them?"

"Exactly what I concluded when I saw that Quebec's conflicts were unresolvable in and of themselves. So I started thinking about my fallback scheme: a union of the two Canadas with a single parliament. In this scheme the British citizens would very nearly equal the French. With the genius of the British political system before them and secure in the protection of British jurisprudence and due process, along with the satisfactions of economic growth and prosperity, the French will, over time, accept and eventually prefer your way of life."

"You're suggesting that the French race is inferior?" Harris said, his voice raised for the first time.

"In the particular context and way that I just outlined, yes. As a Whig who is occasionally accused of being a Radical, I believe that political freedom is the first necessity of man. Independence of mind and enlightened self-interest will inexorably lead to the greatest good for the greatest number. They are also most conducive to personal well-being and self-esteem. So in that context and in their current circumstances, yes, the Quebec people are ipso facto inferior."

"But surely you're being naive or feckless," Finney said, "if you expect three hundred thousand Norman peasants who've been here for two hundred years to turn into little Geordies in a generation. And don't go underestimating the pope."

O'Driscoll grunted his agreement.

"Let me explain more fully," Durham said. "I don't for a moment think that the French will abandon their religion or the customs of two centuries. Nor do I envision the English doing so, who are now in charge here and hanging on to their Englishness like a drowning sailor clinging to the last oar." Durham ignored the multiple harrumphs. "That phenomenon is at the root of your problem. What is perfectly plain to any objective outsider is the degree to which the general populace of Upper Canada, despite its mix of British and American stock, has become neither."

"Nonsense, sir! You're uttering pure, republican propaganda," O'Driscoll fumed again.

"Well, why don't you look at what's around you. In two generations most of you native-born have lost your accents without adopting the American twang. You have no effective established church."

This drew alleluias from Methodist Finney and Presbyterian O'Driscoll.

"You have no entrenched, hereditary aristocracy. Here, a gentleman may soil his hands with labour and still call himself a gentleman. Despite the desperate efforts of the Family Compact to stay the drift towards equality, the levelling of the classes has proceeded apace—not towards the lowest common denominator but, from what I've seen, towards the middle. I fought for five years to have Britain's rotten boroughs eliminated and its cities represented in Parliament after one hundred and forty years of disenfranchisement. I failed to have the secret ballot made part of the Reform Bill, so at home seats in the Commons are still routinely purchased for five thousand pounds by both Whigs and Tories. Here there are no such rotten boroughs. Ridings are created rationally. The property qualification for the franchise is more generous. In my judgement, the broadly based ownership of property—the preponderance of yeoman farmers, so to speak—combined with an advancing and rational political system and freedom from the disease of inherited entitlement is rapidly producing an indigenous British North American culture."

"What are you saying, then?" Hepburn asked, mystified.

"I'm saying that if we can find a productive political structure, all the other parts are already in place for these provinces to become uniquely something of their own. A hundred years from now, it will not matter whether your ancestors were Norman or Viking or Celt. But this ideal cannot even be whispered aloud until a productive political arrangement is created."

Which, Marc thought, might well depend on his finding Sarah McConkey's killer.

"Let's get back to the notion of a union," Hepburn said helpfully.

"Surely as victors we would have a majority in any unified assembly," O'Driscoll declared.

"I think the best we can do, given the larger population of Quebec, is guarantee equal representation."

"But the capital would have to be here, well away from the evil influences down there," Finney said. "And only English ought to be spoken in the legislature."

"I agree, but once the parliament is functioning, these questions will become a matter for the house itself to decide."

"I can't see Sir Allan MacNab or John Strachan sitting in the same chamber with men who have taken up the sword," Finney opined.

"The whole idea is unnecessary," O'Driscoll said.

"You have a scheme of your own?" Durham asked, leaning forward.

"Yes. It is not mine but rather one that has wide support in the current assembly and is endorsed by many of the community leaders."

"Then perhaps I heard it proposed last evening," Durham said dryly.

"The solution we offer is straightforward," O'Driscoll continued, and Marc noted the nods of assent from the other three whist players. "Upper Canada is to annex that part of Quebec that includes the island of Montreal. That will bring into the new state the mercantile and financial powers of the English minority there, leaving the French with the rest of the province, with their rural economy and ancient capital. They will be governed by the Queen's envoy and his appointed executive, though it would seem prudent in the long run to leave them to their own quaint ways and devices. In the meantime an expanded Upper Canada can get on with the business of prospering and maintaining its British and nonrepublican character."

"With a conservative assembly as you have now," Durham said, straight-faced, "and a strong lieutenant-governor like Sir George Arthur."

"You see our point precisely," Harris said, missing Durham's entirely. "My dear wife is from Quebec, but even she realizes that without economic prosperity and a strong monarchist hand at the tiller, no race or religion is secure from the twin tyrannies of poverty and secular republicanism. Since the French in Quebec have found our ways intolerable, why not give them back their farms and parishes, and leave them to fend for themselves. Any of them who wish to better their lot by joining the nineteenth century may emigrate here, and be welcomed."

"Are you saying, then, that you find any suggestion for a unified Canadian province or an equitable federated state intolerable?" Durham said, surveying the assembled grandees.

"We are," Finney said. "We do not wish to share power with the French in an elected assembly unless the balance is weighted in our favour. And we don't envision a governor appointing them to his Executive Council or acknowledging their eccentric whims."

"Nor do we wish any form of responsible government that would curtail the governor's absolute right to choose his own advisers and execute the Queen's will," O'Driscoll added, as if that salient point had been overlooked.

"We haven't heard from you, Mr. Baldwin," Durham said.

"I've been listening, Your Lordship," Robert Baldwin said. "My views are well known: without genuine responsible government, whether we are placed in a united legislature with the French or not, none of the issues that prompted the revolt will be resolved."

"Poppycock!" O'Driscoll snorted. "Responsible government is the one concession that must never—*never*—be made! It is a direct threat to the monarchy."

"It'll turn this province into a republic with all the horrors we've watched with dismay in the United States," Finney added.

"There'll be anarchy in the streets," Harris averred. "Commerce will grind to a halt. We'll be ruled by the rabble!"

"I take your point, gentlemen," Durham said. "But I should mention that despite the warnings given me by Sir John Colborne and Sir George Arthur that my life was certain to be in danger, Lady Durham and I travelled to New York State and found the natives both civilized and uninterested in regicide."

"Do not make light of our concern, sir," O'Driscoll said darkly.

"I believe you had not finished your commentary, Mr. Baldwin. Would you be so good as to resume?"

"What I wished to add to my initial comment," Baldwin said, "is a warning to Your Lordship not to expect all the English and the French to line up with their own kind. The Rouge party in Quebec has more in common with English Reformers like me than with the Bleus, who speak their language. Nor are they likely to fade away in the near or distant future."

O'Driscoll was about to disagree when Charles Buller interjected from his corner, "Time to break, milord?"

"Ah, so it is," Durham said affably. "We shall resume after the luncheon that Sir George has laid on for us in his quarters. Mr. Buller will show you to your places. Thank you for your contributions thus far. After noon I'd like to focus on specific issues like the Clergy Reserves, the university question, the banking system, and the state of the public service."

As the others dutifully followed Charles Buller towards the other section of Government House, Durham lingered in the foyer to talk to Marc.

"Well, there they are," he said. "They seem to be united chiefly by their adherence to the extreme solution, as I term it: enlightened partition or divide and abandon."

"That could well be the grounds for a conspiracy against you,"

Marc said. "It's the one plan you would never endorse. That and their implacable opposition to responsible government." Marc didn't add that he believed the chances of Lord Melbourne's administration's approving the latter recommendation were slight.

"If you had to choose one of them as the instigator and perhaps as the nemesis of my nephew, whom would you select?"

Marc did not hesitate: "Alasdair Hepburn."

"But he spoke little and acted as a moderating influence."

"That's precisely why I suspect him. He seemed capable of subtlety."

Durham smiled broadly. "He was my choice, too—for the same reason."

"How do you propose to raise the topic of your nephew and their time with him in the card room on Monday?"

"Ah. Over port and cigars I shall mention that Handford, who has been 'ill' since the gala, is worried that he has lost a monogrammed, silver snuffbox given him by Lady Durham, and thinks that one of the whist-playing gentlemen may have picked it up by mistake. This will give me the opportunity to ask each of them when and where they last saw Handford and when and how they left that room. They don't know that Wakefield has already mapped their movements for us."

"You hope to catch them in an inconsistency?"

"In a lie, you mean. Indeed. And while I'm entertaining them and continuing our dialogue, I'd like you to visit each of their residences with a view to interrogating their wives."

"Their wives?"

"Yes. Each of them brought a spouse to Spadina, which means that each of them either left with said spouse or made alternative arrangements."

"I see. If Mr. Ellice rode in one of their carriages, then one of the wives is bound to know."

"Or will remember being asked to arrange a ride with others while our villain went off with Handford on his own."

"The trick will be to question them without letting them know about the murder and Mr. Ellice's involvement. I take it that no word has yet leaked out?"

"Not yet. Only Withers, Sir George, Cobb, and Sturges are in the know, besides Lady Durham and us. I'm leaving it to you to find a way to approach the wives without giving the show away."

"I'll start immediately."

He thanked Durham for the rare privilege of sitting in on one of his colloquies, then whirled and left Government House.

By the time he reached the King Street exit, he had already thought of a plan to win the confidence of the whist players' long-suffering wives.

NINE

Cobb had contacted the last of his snitches by eleven o'clock and then stopped for refreshment at the Cock and Bull. The tapster there mentioned that Nestor Peck would not likely be available for a day or two as he had been spotted staggering in last night with a bump on his noggin "the size of his brain."

"That tiny, eh?" Cobb replied, and ordered another flagon. With both his thirst and his curiosity sated, he set out for Irishtown and some real investigating.

While too polite to say so, he felt deep down that Marc Edwards was out of his depth in a place like Irishtown. The people there were con artists and natural liars: without such finely tuned capacities they would not survive a month. A part of Cobb admired them, especially the ones who were supporting a family by eking out a livelihood in the only ways left to them by the ruling clique, the grasping merchants, the hypocritical church, and the customary cruelties of fate. But someone at Madame Renée's had stepped over the line. A young woman had been brutally murdered with "all her sins upon her head." And a very important person had been implicated.

What Cobb was thinking as he picked his way along the hawthorn path towards the shanties of Irishtown was that he had to

catch Mrs. Burgess or one of the girls in a lie or a patent contra-
diction. Once one lie was exposed, others would soon fly up into
the light. But so far the women's story tallied with everything else
they had learned about the events of Monday night. Five minutes
later, with his generous nose twitching at the cumulative stenches
along the way, he reached Madame Renée's.

The shutters were closed over the windows. Cobb padded all
the way around the house. It was sealed up like Pharaoh's tomb.
Either the women were out or still abed. Well, either suited his
purpose. Glancing several times up and down the seemingly deserted pathway that served as a thoroughfare, he drew out of his
jacket pocket a cumbersome key. It was a skeleton key that Sarge
had issued to him and the other three constables when the force
was inaugurated in 1835. What he was expected to do with it he
was never quite sure. This would be its maiden run. He moved
adroitly to the rear of the house once more but was brought up
short when he encountered a pair of young ruffians wrestling in
the dirt beside the scruffy bush in front of the escape hatch.

"Get outta here, you scamps, before I kick yer arses inta yer
teeth!" he hissed, hesitant to deploy his fearsome stentorian tones.

The boys stopped instantly, untangled their limbs slowly, sat
back on their haunches, and stared at the intruder as if he were
some freak of nature materialized out of the dust, like Adam.

"That yer real nose, buster?"

"Does it glow in the dark?"

"Let's hear ya honk it!"

Cobb glowered and put one hand on the butt of his truncheon. Laughing in mock fright, the boys scampered off.

Cobb had to stand perfectly still for a full five minutes to determine whether the ruckus the boys had raised would disturb the
women inside or attract attention from neighbouring abodes. But

all was quiet, so he proceeded to squat down before the hatch. He eased the skeleton key silently into the opening of the lock. Then infinitely slowly he turned it to the left. There was a sharp click. He held his breath. Then he pushed the hatch inward about an inch. Satisfied, he closed and relocked it.

It was just as he had thought. This lock was simple enough to be opened by a run-of-the-mill skeleton key. And that meant that almost anyone in Irishtown who knew about the hatch (who wouldn't? was an easier question) and possessed such a key (anyone who cared to buy or steal one) would have access to the inner sanctum of Madame Renée's. And that meant finding someone with both a key and a grudge.

Cobb had already worked out the answer to the latter part of the equation: Madame Charlotte, the competition. To Cobb it seemed inconceivable that two such houses of prostitution, whatever their particular intentions and clientele, would not be rivals. From that premise it was logical that if Madame Charlotte wished to do harm to Madame Renée's business, all she had to do was hire the nearest hungry thug, supply him with a key, and send him on his way. She may even have suborned Badger himself, who already had a key. Whatever the details—and Cobb intended to get to them—the crime was connected to rivalries and animosities entirely within the boundaries of Irishtown. Whistling softly, he walked a hundred yards up the road to the rambling clapboard house of Madame Charlotte. It too was shuttered and barred. But this time Cobb took out his truncheon and rapped smartly on the paint-peeled door.

Soon after, Cobb sat in the parlour of the brothel on a stiff chair watching the two women across from him, both seated on a battered settee embroidered with roses and a number of random, greasy petals whose provenance Cobb cared not to reflect upon.

The contrast between this room and its counterpart at Madame Renée's was striking. Here, not a stick of furniture or wall surface had escaped being stained, gouged, or otherwise abused. Putrid pools of spilled wine—neat or regurgitated—festered here and there on the softwood floor, whose boards had not been swept or scrubbed since leaving the mill. Cobb couldn't decide which was worse: the stink or the frantic perfumes used to subdue it. Undaunted, he soldiered on.

"I'm here to question you concernin' an incident at Madame Renée's on Monday evenin'," he said, trying for the exact pitch between authoritative and invitational that the Major used in these situations.

"That slut!"

This assessment was offered by Marybelle, the only one of the inmates who was not "indisposed," according to Madame Charlotte. Marybelle was perched on the edge of the settee, clad only in a floppy robe and a jangle of hair curlers that looked as if they were trying to escape. She was of indeterminate age but undoubtedly well travelled. She had made a half-hearted attempt to remove the caked powder, waxy lip rouge, and brow-black from her evening face, but had managed only to smear them together. With her dark pop-eyes and sagging chin, she reminded Cobb of a circus clown who'd put his makeup on without benefit of a mirror. Her voice scraped at the air like a rusted handsaw.

"Ya mean the murder, don't ya?" Madame Charlotte demanded, staring at Cobb with bold, hardened eyes. Unlike her "girl," Charlotte was dressed for the day or night in a brash, flouncy frock sporting bluebirds and some sort of exotic fruit and cut low enough to display her well-upholstered breastworks. Her considerable makeup had been applied with a trowel and worked to perfection: vermilion lips, rouged cheeks, kohl-sculpted eyelids and brows, topped by a powdered wig that one of Shakespeare's boy-women might have blushed to wear.

"So you've heard what happened?" Cobb said.

"Nothin's kept secret in Irishtown for more'n ten minutes!" Marybelle rasped.

"I was speakin' to Madame Charlotte."

Madame Charlotte frowned. "The name is Char-*lotte*," she said with proud emphasis on the ultimate syllable. "And, yeah, we saw the body bein' carted off yesterday mornin'."

"Poor Sarah got herself topped, in her own bed!" There was more mockery in Marybelle's voice than sorrow.

"By some nob, we hear," Charlotte said. "Which means nothin'll be done about it, so why're you here disrupturin' an honest woman and her business? It don't look good to have the law lurkin' about in daylight."

"P'raps he's come fer a good time," Marybelle cackled.

This time it was Charlotte who laughed.

"If you know what's good fer you, Madam *Char-a-lot*, you'll answer my questions and answer them truthful, or I'll bring the sheriff down here with a dozen torches to rid the town of—"

"All right, all right, there's no need to get testy. We ain't got nothin' to hide, have we, Marybelle?"

"I ain't ever been accused of hidin' much," Marybelle giggled grotesquely, and to demonstrate her point she let the robe drift open to expose the tops and inner curves of her breasts.

"Someone broke into Madame Renée's about one-thirty Tuesday mornin' and stabbed Sarah McConkey to death," Cobb said.

"They couldn't've got through them oak doors," Charlotte said. "Norah seals that place up tighter'n a heifer's cunt."

"I don't believe the intruder used either door," Cobb said carefully.

"Ya mean the little hatch?" Marybelle blurted, and got a warning glance from her mistress.

"Ah, so you know about that, do ya?" Cobb said, pleased with his probing thus far.

"Everybody that lives within three hundred yards of the place knows about the booby-hatch," Charlotte said levelly. "Just ask."

"But you'd need a key to get in, wouldn't you?" Cobb said quickly.

"The way I hear it," Charlotte said just as quickly, "that little hatch was fer gettin' out, not in."

"Maybe so, but we think it was used by the killer."

"So what's this got to do with us anyways? I was here Monday night and Tuesday mornin' pullin' sailors offa my girls when their time was up. You figure I sneaked out and headed down to Madam Pompadour's?"

"I'm not accusin' you of anythin', madam."

"If I'd've kilt anybody down there it would've been the fat hooer who runs the place."

Cobb pounced. "So you two aren't friendly?"

"You could say that."

"You believe her business is hurtin' yer own?"

This remark produced prodigious mirth in both women, which triggered much jiggling of exposed and under-rigged flesh. Cobb felt himself redden.

"I'm not fond of Norah Burgess, but I ain't jealous. Here, we cater to real, honest-to-goodness men: sailors and lumberjacks and teamsters who don't powder their hair or perfume their pricks."

"And Madame Renée takes care of the other kind?"

"Poofs and nobs and old fellas who can't get it up but enjoy watchin'." Charlotte spat out the next words: "The perversions that go on down there'd make Marybelle blush, and she ain't done that since the midwife whacked her backside."

"So you're sayin' you'd have no reason to hire some tough or bruiser to break in down there and stir up trouble—maybe damage or beat up the star performer?"

Charlotte guffawed so gustily her dentures popped halfway out of her mouth. "Sarah McConkey a star performer? That little slut wasn't here six weeks before she got herself knocked up! She didn't know one hole from another!"

As the women howled at this witticism, Cobb's puzzlement deepened. Without forethought he asked, "Sarah McConkey worked here?"

"'Course she did. Everybody in Irishtown knows that."

"'Least them that poked her," Marybelle added. "Couldn't've been more'n a hundred, could it, Char?"

But the look on Cobb's face immediately dampened their mirth and Charlotte required no prompting. She told the tale of Sarah McConkey straight out. According to her, Sarah had been spotted by one of the madam's scouts, alone and desperate on Lot Street, in late September. When brought to the brothel to be fed and coddled ("I spoil my girls rotten!") Sarah informed Charlotte that she had left her home in Streetsville earlier in the month because her father had insisted she marry a religious zealot, who happened incidentally to be old and ugly. ("Them religious buggers is the randiest," Marybelle added here, "they get so pent up!") Sarah then found work as a housemaid in the home of some city preacher but, she claimed, he made advances and his wife kicked her out bag and baggage, accusing her of being a harlot. Distraught and friendless, she ended up at Madam Charlotte's. So grateful was Sarah that after a week of recuperation she consented to earn her daily bread as her sisters in the house did.

However, she was only a "working girl" for a month or so, for the "silly fool" got herself pregnant. When Madame was considerate enough to arrange for the routine ("but ruinously expensive!") abortion, Sarah balked, for which transgression she was once again tossed out on her ear. This time she was undeniably a harlot.

"We heard from the grapevine that she went back home, but her father closed the door in her face and disowned her. She was on her way back here, we was told, when one of that bitch Burgess's scouts picked her up and took her to Renée's. They pampered her there fer the whole winter, till she popped the poor dead babe a few weeks ago."

Charlotte sat back, hitched up her breasts, and said scornfully, "So there's yer star attraction at Madam Snooty's cunny-crib. A common tart!"

Ideas were bouncing around Cobb's head with alarming speed. Sarah McConkey had worked in this hellhole for over a month before she was dismissed and ended up a few days later at Madame Renée's. Everyone in Irishtown would have been aware of her stint at Madame Charlotte's. Why, then, had Mrs. Burgess and all three of her girls lied to him and Marc? They had made it sound as if Sarah had come straight to them from her job in the city. Well, Cobb would soon find out why. And where there was one lie, surely there were others.

"But I still don't see what any of this has got to do with us," Charlotte said.

"Nothin', likely, but you been helpful just the same." Cobb suddenly realized that Sarah may not have gone home when she left here. She may have gone straight to Mrs. Burgess. Which meant what? That the enmity between the two women may have had something to do with business after all. Sarah had been young and pretty, perhaps a rare find for Charlotte, with potential for expanding her horizons and hopes, only to have them dashed when Sarah was lured away to the competition. Maybe he should ride out to Streetsville and find out. Cobb's heart began to pound and the tip of his nose throbbed: this detection game was exhilarating, and he was getting good at it.

"Ya sure ya don't wanta stay a bit and divulge yerself?" Marybelle was saying. She let her legs sag apart. "That's a mighty truncheon ya got stickin' up outta yer belt."

Cobb looked furiously away and jumped up.

"Won't ya stay fer a cup o' tea?" Madame Charlotte inquired sweetly, as if she were superintending an at-home.

"And a bit o' crumpet?"

His proboscis aflame, Cobb stumbled to the door, regained his balance and some of his dignity, and was almost outside when he thought of a critical question. With his entire face now throbbing like a boil, he turned around and said sharply, "What was the name of the preacher Sarah worked for?"

Charlotte looked at Marybelle for confirmation. "Some fire-and-brimstone howler with a crazy name—Finley . . . Findlay . . . somethin' like that."

"Finney?" Cobb prompted, as his heart skipped a beat.

"Yeah, that's it. The Reverend Temperance Finney."

Marybelle howled with intemperate laughter.

WAS IT POSSIBLE THAT A RESPECTABLE Methodist minister had got himself entangled with his housemaid? And if so, had he decided to disentangle himself for good? Could he be the direct connection between the whist players and Madame Renée's? This was all too much for Cobb. He began to wish the Major were here. Still, he had caught Mrs. Burgess in a lie. That was a tangible fact—unless of course Charlotte was lying. My God, this investigating game was taxing on the brain!

Cobb just managed to sidestep a heap of fresh, festering garbage, but in doing so he bumped into one of the local urchins.

"Watch where you're goin', fatso!"

Cobb had the miscreant by the scruff and dangling helplessly before he could blink twice. "Why you little fart, for tuppence I'd wring yer neck and toss ya to the rats."

"Lemme go!"

Cobb dropped the lad, a sturdy fellow of thirteen or fourteen, but kept a grip on his tattered jersey. "Say, ain't you Peter, one of them trackers?"

"Donald," the boy whined. "And I ain't done nothin'!"

"I doubt that, but what I want you to tell me is this: do you work fer both the madams?"

"What's in it fer me?" Donald said, avarice nudging out fear.

"A broken arse if ya don't answer and a penny if ya do."

Donald pretended to mull the offer over before saying, "I useta work fer them both, but Miz Burgess pays me better not to."

"Did you bring sailors to Sarah when she worked fer Madame Charlotte?" Cobb was secretly pleased with this bit of misdirection.

"'Course I did. But that was a whiles back."

"Last fall perhaps?"

"Before the snow come."

"Here's yer penny, don't spend it—"

But Donald didn't tarry long enough to hear Cobb's fatherly advice.

Well, well, Cobb thought. So here was a tangible fact indeed. Sarah McConkey had worked for Charlotte before moving to fancier quarters. If he could confront Mrs. Burgess and her girls with their dishonesty, who knew what else might then spill out?

As he was plotting an approach to such a confrontation—a peremptory pounding on the scarlet door or a discreet rap—he noticed out of the corner of his eye something pink and fluttery behind Madame Renée's place. He marched around behind the house and almost hanged himself on a clothesline.

"Jesus! Where'd this come from?" he cried, pulling something sheer and silky and illicit from his face.

"Don't throw them knickers on the ground! I just washed them!"

Mrs. Burgess stood a few feet away beside a basket of freshly laundered underclothes so multicoloured and exotic that Cobb could not have put a name to one of them. A clothesline had been strung up from a nail on the wall to a pole that had been inserted into the ground since Cobb's visit half an hour ago.

"Put them in this!" she commanded, pointing to the basket.

The slithery underpants stuck to Cobb's fingers like taffy, but he finally shook them free and watched them float onto their companion frillies.

This was not how Cobb had planned the confrontation.

"Can't you people leave us alone," Mrs. Burgess said. "We need time to mourn little Sarah and prepare for her funeral tomorrow."

From inside the house came the sounds of furious scrubbing: the girls trying to expunge bloodstains, perhaps?

"I'm sorry, ma'am," Cobb mumbled, but it was not clear whether he was referring to the abused panties or his thoughtless entrance. "Fer yer loss," he added, noting the dark patches under her swollen eyes. She had aged ten years in a day.

"Thank you." For a moment she seemed to have forgotten her

laundry and just stood still, waiting for Cobb to say something or merely drift away.

"I need to ask you one more important question, ma'am. And I'm sorry but it can't really wait."

Mrs. Burgess braced herself, but she seemed more resigned than anxious.

"Why did you and yer girls not tell us that Sarah McConkey worked fer Madame Charlotte before comin' to your place?" The question was as direct and blunt as Cobb could make it in these circumstances and ought to have rocked even a tough old bird like Madame Renée back on her heels.

"Oh, that," she said, unperturbed. "I didn't see how it could've mattered. I told you when and how Sarah come to us. She was found wandering and delirious on Lot Street, pregnant and alone. We took her in. And all this happened last fall."

Cobb blinked and tried to regain the high ground. "But we asked you to tell us all about Sarah so we could decide what facts were important and what facts weren't. You and yer girls knew she'd lived and worked at Charlotte's place. You deliberately chose not to tell us. I wanta know why."

"Then I'll tell you, Constable, and then you can leave me to my laundry." She looked him boldly in the eye. "There were two reasons. First, when Sarah lost her baby and begged to join the business, we didn't want our gentlemen callers to know that she'd spent a frightful and torturous month in Charlotte's sinkhole. Sarah was young and free from disease and very attractive to our kind of visitor."

Cobb's distaste for such detail must have shown on his face, for Mrs. Burgess smiled grimly and said, "I apologize for my frank language, but you asked for the truth."

"You ain't embarrassin' me," Cobb said, but his nose belied the disclaimer.

"The girls and I made a pact never to speak of Sarah's former employment."

"But lots of folks knew about it. I can't believe you people don't gossip."

"We use no last names in our business. You and Mr. Edwards alone know the surnames of my girls. I have tried to be wholly truthful with you, except for Sarah's working up there."

"You said ya had two reasons fer lyin'."

"For omitting part of the truth," she corrected. "The second reason was that Sarah herself asked us to keep it a secret. You see, she was saving her money and planning someday to move back into respectable society, probably in another town. She was a very independent young woman—as her papa discovered when he tried to force her into a marriage she found repugnant."

"And you didn't object to her talkin' about runnin' off? It's hard ta believe you'd actually help her leave yer business."

Mrs. Burgess sighed, looked almost wistful. "She wasn't the first girl to have a dream like that."

"So you figured it would all peter out?"

"It always does."

Cobb suddenly thought of something neither he nor Marc had thought to ask yesterday, and he silently congratulated himself even as he said, "Was her money stolen after she was killed?"

Mrs. Burgess took umbrage at this veiled accusation. "I keep a tally of what my girls earn each week, I'll have you know, and every Friday I walk them up to the bank on Church Street. I stand at the door while they go in and deposit their earnings. I have no way of touching that money."

"And you went there last Friday?"

"We did. You can ask them at the bank. We're usually noticed."

"I will do that." Afraid that he was being bested in this exchange, he looked stern and said sharply, "So you're tellin' me yer girls are all gettin' rich?"

"I am not telling you any such thing. Before we go to the bank, we promenade along King Street."

"And visit the shops."

"Yes. Whatever's left goes in the bank. And some of that gets mailed home."

"So Sarah really didn't have a lot of savin's?"

"Sarah was not like the other girls—yet. Almost all of her earnings went into the bank. But she'd only been working for two months."

Cobb felt deflated. Mrs. Burgess's explanation seemed not only plausible but downright convincing. Still, he could relay all he'd discovered to the Major: perhaps he had overlooked some telling detail that Marc would tease out.

"I'll let ya get back to yer washin'," he said, then added, "Where're ya plannin' to hold the service?"

"In the old Mechanics' Institute hall on John Street at ten o'clock. We've found a minister who hasn't forgotten who Christ was."

Chastened, Cobb made his way back to Lot Street and his rendezvous with Marc Edwards.

TEN

Over lunch and a flagon of ale at the Cock and Bull, Marc and Cobb exchanged detailed accounts of their morning's work. Marc was obviously pleased and impressed with Cobb's efforts at the two brothels.

"What d'ya make of this business of Sarah bein' at Madame Charlotte's?" Cobb said, between bites.

"I agree with your initial assessment, Cobb. But I think I'll refrain from further speculation on the matter until I've had a chance to talk with the girl's parents. Then I believe we'll have the full story of Sarah's sad odyssey."

"Whatever you say."

"Now, what do *you* make of the whist players?"

Cobb, at a loss to see any import in the self-interested complaints of the whist players up at Government House, said so.

"I didn't expect to learn anything directly incriminating," Marc said, brushing pie crumbs off his lower lip. "But both Lord Durham and I wanted to get acquainted with them personally— His Lordship is a keen judge of character—and develop a sense of whether their opposition to his mission here is serious enough, and similar enough in kind, to allow them to be considered co-conspirators."

Cobb washed down a helping of oysters with a satisfying swig of ale. "And what do you figure after all that palaver?"

"In terms of their disagreement with Durham's known position on key issues, yes, they might, despite being radically different characters, decide to band together to sidetrack the mission. It's hard to see such diverse personalities getting together merely to play whist."

"Might, you say?"

"Well, that's something we'll need proof for. When we find Badger and unmask the person who led Ellice to the brothel, we'll have all the proof we need."

"When."

"My, you're laconic this afternoon."

"I'm feelin' quite fine, thank you, but I'd feel a whole lot better if we could dig up a few more facts."

"Spoken like a true investigator." Marc drained his ale. "And this afternoon may well see that happen."

Cobb looked regretfully at his empty flagon. "What're you plannin' to do?"

"While His Lordship keeps the whist players occupied, we're going to visit their homes. I will question their wives and you will go to the stables and question any men or boys who might have been on carriage duty Monday night."

Cobb's skepticism was visible. "We're just gonna sashay up to these pillars of the community and ask them if their hubbies took young Ellice to a cathouse to get his ashes hauled?"

Marc smiled. "I see now why you were such a success up in Irishtown this morning. But I have worked out a ruse for us to use when we approach these people. We will tell them that some valuable jewellery was stolen from Lord Durham's chamber on

Monday during the gala. An investigation yesterday revealed that one of the guests was apparently an interloper—"

"A gate-crasher, ya mean?"

"Exactly. Moreover, this person, whom nobody seemed to know, was seen lurking near the doors to the north wing where the Durhams are domiciled, and then again later he was seen being invited into one of the fancier barouches—hitching a ride to the city, presumably with the stolen goods. We, of course, are trying to trace this felon and need to know which of the respectable guests was kind enough to give him a lift, et cetera. Naturally, the description we have of him is that he was young, slim, not tall, and apparently shy—as he would be if he were hiding his identity. If you'll give me a description of the clothes Ellice tossed beside Sarah's bed, we'll add them to our portrait of this mysterious jewel thief."

"I c'n do that," Cobb said, "but I can't go usin' all of them Shakespeare words with stable hands!"

"True, but the essential question to put, after feeding them our little story, is whether anyone like that rode back in their master's carriage. I'll do the same with the wives, and try to prompt them to admit to any sort of unexpected rearrangements in their travel plans that night after the ball."

"Sounds like a good plan," Cobb said, "if it really was one of them whist players, of course."

They were about to leave when Nestor Peck, Cobb's most obsequious snitch, angled up to their table. He was sporting a bump as big as a crane's egg on the right side of his head.

"You been fallin' down steps again, Nestor?" Cobb asked.

"Some yegg clunked me up at the Tinker's Dam," Nestor whined. "I need a whiskey real bad, Mr. Cobb."

"You got anythin' to trade fer it?"

"Yup." He waited until Cobb's chin bob signalled a deal, then whispered, "Badger was seen headin' east along the Kingston Road."

"We know that." Though it was nice to have his son's sighting confirmed.

"Way past Scaddings Bridge."

Cobb dropped a coin on the table.

"Keep yer head down, Nestor," he said.

BETH EDWARDS ENJOYED THE HALF-HOUR WALK along fashion-able King Street to Government House at the corner of King and Simcoe. The day was glorious. The sun shone resolutely as it had for the past week, leaving the rutted and indifferently gravelled street dry and passable. The good weather had enticed more than the usual number of shoppers to the chic array of stores between Church and Bay that catered to those who had cash to spend or credit to demand.

What attracted her more than the gaudy bow windows of the jewellers, booteries, and haberdasheries, however, were the quaint and the idiosyncratic among the merchant class, a reminder that commerce and individuality could remain wary bedfellows. Diagonally across from the Court House, for example, stood the Checkered Store, a wooden edifice painted in red-and-white squares, tempting customers to come in and play checkers. Next to it sat Rogers's fur and hat store, announcing its proprietor's In-dian heritage via a life-size sign depicting an aboriginal voyageur limned by local artist Paul Kane. Just visible down West Market Lane was the whimsical invitation of McIlmurray's clock-repair shop: a golden lion whose forefeet sprouted watches instead of paws.

Approaching the corner of Yonge and King, Beth could never quite suppress the chill that seized her as she walked through the shadow cast by the imposing, three-storey grandeur of the Commercial Bank. The chill eased nicely, though, as soon as she neared the twin shops that once were the dry-goods emporium of her father-in-law, Joshua Smallman. Now hers, they invited her to pause and ponder what might have been. Mr. Ormsby, who rented one of the shops but would soon be gone, came out and chatted amiably with Beth for several minutes.

With just the tiniest shiver of regret, Beth continued on towards Government House. Unlike most of the ladies today, she carried no parasol to keep the sun off her face, only a straw bonnet that she wore in the garden every morning. Beyond Bay Street, the boardwalk ended: the town council, as deadlocked and divisive as the other political bodies in the province, refused monies either to extend the walk or to keep the existing one in repair. She was forced to compete with horses, mules, and aggressive teamsters for walking space. Eddies of dust whorled about her feet, and she was glad she had decided to wear a short frock that settled comfortably at her ankle-tops.

After crossing Simcoe she came to the gates that presaged the long driveway up to Government House, nestled in its six acres of parkland. It was a pleasant, shady stroll along the tree-lined way and, although anxious about what was facing her up at the house, she was in no particular hurry. A sociable being, she had out of necessity lived much of her adult life alone and had learned to enjoy her own company. In a few minutes she rounded a bend and caught a glimpse of the great building, its chimney pots tickling the fluffy cloud above them and its myriad glass windows shimmering in the early-afternoon heat. To her immediate right she spotted a small, shrub-enclosed garden with stone benches around a reflecting pool. She decided to pause for a moment to catch her breath and decide how best to approach Lord and Lady Durham about the mission she had in mind regarding their nephew.

She was just about to sit down when she noticed a tall, formally attired gentleman standing with his back turned to her, hands clasped behind him, staring into the trees. The rustle of her dress or scrape of her boot must have alerted him, for he turned quickly around, looked puzzled for a second only, then smiled broadly. She recognized him right away.

"Good afternoon, Mrs. Edwards," Durham greeted her with a bow.

"You remember me, then?" Beth said, taken aback. "Your Lordship."

"A change of dress and a little daylight have not been sufficient to render you unmemorable."

"I was coming to see you, sir, or Lady Durham, if she's here."

"I know. We've been expecting you. I am, alas, about to be closeted with four gentlemen who collectively have not half the charm or charity you have brought with you to Government House."

"I'd like to talk to Mr. Ellice. I thought I might be able to help."

Durham held out his arm. "Here, I'll take you straight in to my lady."

MRS. FINNEY DREW THE FIRST LOT. As Cobb sauntered down towards the barn and two rustic fellows lounging next to it, Marc knocked at the door of the fine, clapboard residence of the dissenting minister. A slovenly, overweight housemaid with unkempt hair gave Marc a gap-toothed smile, blushed, and led him into a pleasant sitting room, where Mrs. Finney was biding her time between knitting and stroking a black tabby.

"*Mister* Edwards?" she said with some surprise when Marc introduced himself. "But I understood—"

"I've retired from active service, ma'am."

"But you did do some brave thing or other at some French village or other last—"

"I did."

"Then good for you. I hate the French."

It took all of Marc's tact and most of his aplomb to keep his temper and spin his cover story for this exceedingly plain and aggressively prejudiced woman. But he did so.

"A common thief, you say, pretending to be one of us? How shocking! First the horrid revolt and now this. What is the world coming to?"

Marc was amused by the wife of a Methodist pastor herself pretending to be part of the aristocracy, but then, as he himself knew, such distinctions were relative, not absolute.

"You can imagine, ma'am, how important it is for the reputation of our city that we recover Lady Durham's jewels. Moreover, our inquiries have to be utterly discreet."

Mrs. Finney bobbed her chin, much in the manner she was accustomed to doing whenever the Reverend Finney paused pregnantly in a sermon. "But how can we help?" she said. "I don't recall seeing anybody I didn't know or recognize."

"Well, as I mentioned, the thief seems to have hitched a ride back to the city with one of the unsuspecting parties respectable enough to be travelling in a barouche." That many of these extravagances, like the Finneys', had been rented needed not be emphasized here: flattery would suffice. "I trust that you and Mr. Finney returned with the same members of your party who rode out with you?"

There was no hesitation. "Yes, the three Carters and Temperance and I went out and came back together. You may wish to check with them, of course. They live at number twenty-six George Street."

"There'll be no need for that, ma'am. The word of a minister's wife is good enough for me," Marc said, though he had every intention of double-checking every claim made. He rose and bowed.

"I could give you a cup of tea, if you'd like?" she offered belatedly.

"Thank you, but I must continue these inquiries."

Mrs. Finney understood perfectly: she would have to be content with the gossipy tidbits supplied thus far.

At the door, Marc said without preamble, "Did you employ a young woman here last fall by the name of Sarah McConkey?"

Mrs. Finney froze in her tracks. A deep scowl suddenly gave some character to her bland, undistinguished features. "Why do you utter the name of that Jezebel in my home?" she hissed.

Marc winced, recovered, and said, working out the lie as he went along, "I apologize, ma'am, but the chief constable has asked me to look into the disappearance of a girl by that name. It seems that her parents, good Christian people, have not been able to locate her here in the city. And until now, the police have been of little help. But just this morning one of our informants revealed that she had been seen working here last fall. I thought that, while I was here on the more important matter, I should try to verify the informant's story. Last fall is a long time back, but it might help if you had any idea where she might have gone after leaving your employ."

"She didn't leave our employ, sir!" The scowl had intensified. "We tossed her out onto the street, which is where women like her belong!"

"She offended you in some way?"

"In every way, sir. She was a lewd and grasping hussy!"

"Those are strong words about a young woman from a decent family who'd only been in the city for a few weeks and entirely in your employ."

"They aren't strong enough! She flaunted her flesh before my fourteen-year-old son, tempting him beyond endurance. She was caught kissing the hired man! We'd had enough by then, so out she went. I feel sorry for her parents, but I can't spare one ounce of pity for such a creature."

Marc thanked her for her frankness, bowed, and left. On the gravel driveway, he met Cobb coming up from the barn. Marc summarized his conversation with Mrs. Finney, to the constable's considerable amusement. Cobb then told him that one of the stablemen, a fellow he knew personally, corroborated Mrs. Finney's account of their trip back from Spadina on Monday. But when Marc suggested that they return to the barn to question both men about Sarah's troubled tenure there last September, Cobb stayed him.

"Them fellas just started workin' here at Christmastime," Cobb said. "Before they come on steady, they told me—when we got to chin-waggin'—that the Finneys were so hard to get along with that half a dozen men had come and gone before them. If work wasn't so scarce since the uprisin', they said they'd be packin' it in, too."

"That's too bad," Marc said. "However, we're gradually filling in the brief life story of Sarah McConkey, post-Streetsville."

"Sounds like she took a fancy to men right off."

"Perhaps," Marc said, but did not elaborate. Instead, he pointed Cobb in the direction of the Carters' residence, the family Mrs. Finney claimed rode with her and Finney on Monday. It never hurt to triple-check.

• • •

LADY DURHAM SHOWED BETH INTO THE sickroom. Word had been put out that Handford Ellice had fallen ill with a fever after the ball, an affliction general and vague enough to cover the symptoms of his condition. He had been moved to Government House to be near Sir George's personal physician, Angus Withers. But Lord Durham's executive powers could extend only so far and for so long. If the real killer could not be found by Friday morning or if Ellice did not recover his wits quickly enough to help himself, he would have to be formally charged and led in chains to the Toronto jail—with dire and irreversible consequences for Durham and possibly for the province.

Beth was aware of all this as she slipped quietly to the side of the bed where Ellice was dozing, propped up against several capacious pillows. His skin was not merely albino-white, it was almost translucent: in the sunlight it would have glowed pink. Lady Durham stationed herself near the door, out of her nephew's line of sight, and waited.

Beth reached across and took Ellice's right hand in hers. She squeezed it several times. Some minutes later, he groaned and opened his eyes. They were glassy from the belladonna or laudanum, and, seeing Beth, they grew round with terror. He gasped for some word to stay whatever nightmare vision he was experiencing but succeeded only in prompting a sequence of stunted coughs.

Beth squeezed his hand tightly. "It's Mrs. Edwards, Handford. I'm alive and unharmed and here beside you."

The young man's entire body was trembling uncontrollably, but he could not will himself to close his eyes. Lady Durham started forward but stopped when Beth held up her free hand. Gradually the tremoring slowed and the rictus of terror that had gripped and distorted his features began to subside. Finally Ellice was able to give the hand that held his a single squeeze.

"Yes, it is me," Beth whispered. "The woman you danced with at the ball."

Ellice nodded his head warily.

"You've been sick for two days, but Dr. Withers says you're going to be fine soon."

"I'm so glad you've come," he said, shaping one word at a time and forcing his breath to give weight to each.

Lady Durham gave a sharp cry from her station by the door— of joy and relief.

IT DID NOT TAKE LONG FOR Marc to learn that the O'Driscolls and Harrises had ridden home with the same friends who accompanied them out to Spadina and the Governor's Ball. The respective wives were quick to express their willingness to help, the Whiggery of the lord and lady being overlooked in the interests of common decency and respect for high office. But alas they were even quicker to deny any knowledge of the dastardly interloper and purloiner of pearls. Each had ridden with one other couple, and Marc, growing frustrated, had lengthened this futile line of inquiry considerably by traipsing eight or nine blocks to cross-check their claims and those of Mrs. Finney. Nor had Cobb any better luck. In the end, Marc had to conclude that Handford Ellice had not, on the face of it, been ferried to the city by Finneys, O'Driscolls, or Harrises. Foot-weary and not overly optimistic, Cobb and Marc trudged back up towards the substantial estate of Alasdair Hepburn on Hospital Street, not a block and a half south of the entrance to Irishtown.

"I can't see why any of those women would have reason to

lie," Marc said glumly. "And if they did, the friends accompanying them would have to be in on it."

"I don't see any of them whist fellers lettin' their wives in on any conspiracy," Cobb added unhelpfully.

"You're right. That's why His Lordship and I decided to approach them with our phony story about a jewel robbery: we felt sure the women would tell us what was what on Monday evening."

They turned off Yonge onto Hospital.

"You're thinkin' it may've been the Reverend Temper-rants who pestered Sarah McConkey, ain't ya?"

"The thought has crossed my mind," Marc said. "Mrs. Finney was so adamant about blaming the girl, who, after all, had not had much time to be corrupted by the iniquities of the city. I began to wonder if she were not protesting too much."

"And if Finney was taken with Sarah and his old lady tossed her out, then he still might have a hankerin' fer her."

"Possibly. I don't see him pursuing her into Irishtown, but his knowing her would give him some potential connection to Madame Renée's and, not impossibly, to Michael Badger."

"It may be all we got, Major. I don't expect we'll have any more luck here at Hepburn's. And unless I know the stableman myself, I wouldn't trust a word any of 'em utter. Most wouldn't trade the truth fer a sofa chair in heaven!"

"I didn't tell you, Cobb, but of the four whist players, both Lord Durham and I decided Hepburn was the most likely candidate to orchestrate any conspiracy."

"And I'd agree with ya: nobody beats bankers at that sort of thing."

The Hepburns occupied a fine brick and stone house located on the north side of Hospital Street. Built in the Georgian style, it boasted extensive barns and stables out behind; inside an enclosed paddock, several well-bred horses gleamed and pranced. Cobb headed directly for it.

A tall, middle-aged woman with masculine features and auburn hair pulled tightly into a bun showed Marc into a richly furnished sitting room complete with Turkish sofas, Persian rugs an inch deep, and high, spacious Italianate windows. Mrs. Matilda Hepburn was seated on one of the sofas, and from the cut of her dress and the flowered bonnet beside her, she had either just come in or was preparing to go out. She had a small face whose lineaments might have been admired when she was fourteen but had not bloomed as promised, leaving her with a pinched and impoverished face. She appeared to be compensating for its lack of physical character by keeping her chin higher than nature required and her sloe eyes dart sharp.

"That'll be all, Una," she said to the tall woman. "Though you might see if cook has any fresh tea and biscuits for our guest." She waved Una off and then turned the gesture into an invitation for Marc to sit opposite her on an embroidered Queen Anne chair.

After introducing himself, Marc spun his yarn just as he had done three times previously that afternoon. He was beginning to believe it himself. Matilda Hepburn showed no emotion or response of any kind at the mention of the fictitious imposter or his clandestine thievery.

Before Marc could ask the routine and obvious question about the ride home to the city, she interrupted him to say, "I do not see, young man, why the police would come bothering us about such a thing. Mr. Hepburn and I are not accustomed to giving rides to total strangers, and certainly not one cloaked and wrapped in secrecy as the man you have described. I am sorry for Lady Durham's loss, though I daresay neither she nor her affluent husband are pinched for pennies."

"You're telling me, then, that you and Mr. Hepburn rode home together, as you rode out to Spadina?"

The black eyes darted and pricked. "I hope you're being deliberately naive, Mr. Edwards. The point I made was quite clear and in need of no elaboration."

"You did not travel to the gala with friends or neighbours?"

"That should be of no concern to you, sir, but in order to show my respect for the law, I will tell you no: we travelled alone."

"Please forgive me, ma'am, but I have been asked by the highest authority to make these intrusive and less than tactful inquiries."

At that moment Una re-entered the room carrying a tea tray. She stumbled on the edge of the thick carpet and, in righting herself, let go of the tray. Teacups, teapot, biscuits, and steaming tea struck the arabesques on the rug.

"You *stupid* oaf!" Mrs. Hepburn cried, rising to her feet.

"I'm terribly sorry, ma'am, I—"

"Just get out! Fetch cook and get this mess cleaned up!"

Flushed and confused, Una staggered back and fled.

Her ruffled feathers quickly back in place, Mrs. Hepburn said to Marc, "She's been like that for two days. Family problems, I believe. Come, I'll show you the way out."

In the lane, Marc met up with Cobb and gave him the disappointing news. "Did you find the driver of the barouche?" he said hopefully.

"I did, Major. He says it was a quiet night. Just mister and missus—out and back."

"Did you believe him?"

"No reason not to, though I don't know him from Adam."

"Damn."

"I guess we wasted an afternoon and lost half an inch of shoe leather inta the bargain," Cobb said. "So what do we do now? You think we're likely to get anythin' more outta our four gentlemen if we was to ask them the same questions?"

"Not likely. I've been instructed to treat them with kid gloves. But there's still the McConkeys. I'm certain that when we know the whole story of Sarah's ten months in the city, we'll have more clues to work with than we need."

"You ain't thinkin' about ridin' all the way out to Streetsville now, are you?"

"It's only eighteen miles, and I have my choice of swift horses from Government House. I'll be back before dark."

"Well, then, I'll keep pokin' around town to see if I can help turn up Badger."

"Good. If anything develops, leave a message at Government House. I've got to have something positive to report to Lord Durham later tonight."

BETH HAD NO INTENTION OF DOING anything for Handford Ellice beyond bringing him back from his hallucinatory state to the real world. Whatever he had done, he would need to face it, the sooner the better, and perhaps begin to talk about it. But such decisions must be made by Ellice himself, not his doctors with their soporifics or the police with their interrogations.

Lady Durham, as discreet as she was intelligent, had a bowl of broth brought in but let Beth spoon it onto his lips. After a few mouthfuls and a smile at Beth that seemed more painful than purging, he sighed deeply and rolled back on his pillows. Beth was just about to get up and tiptoe away when he suddenly spoke again, keeping his eyes closed all the while and pausing frequently.

"I really thought I had killed you, Mrs. Edwards. You who befriended me and did not find my dancing laughable."

"You've been ill and had a bad dream, that's all."

"A horrible dream. It kept coming back, over and over." He opened his eyes briefly. They were full of tears. "But it's gone now. I can close my eyes—like this—and still see you sitting there. With no knife in your neck." He shuddered, then smiled wanly.

Beth leaned forward and took his hand. She used it to stroke her neck. "See, my neck is as good as it ever was."

"As pretty, you mean."

"What you need to do now, to keep the dream away, is take some soup, rest, and get yourself strong."

"You'll come again, though?"

"If you wish."

"Good. I think I might go mad if I had to endure that nightmare one more time. You are lying beside me in a strange bed, and I wake up and see a knife in your neck, and I think 'That's odd' and I reach over and gently pull it out. But no blood comes out with it. Isn't that strange?"

"Dreams are like that. But, see, you're starting to be able to talk about it."

"Yes, I am, aren't I? And I haven't st-stuttered once." He laughed, and Beth joined him.

She put the spoon in his right hand, dipped it into the soup, and guided it to his mouth. "You spoke yesterday with my husband."

"Mr. Edwards, yes." His face darkened and Beth was afraid she had gone too far. But he continued without further prompting. "After the dance I played cards with some kind gentlemen. I got very drunk. I don't re-remember anything else except c-coming to that place. This girl, I thought she was you. I felt sick and ashamed. D-d-don't remember . . ."

"Please don't think about it anymore, Mr. Ellice. It wasn't me and you're safe in the governor's bed."

"Very . . . tired." He closed his eyes and drifted towards sleep.

Beth waited. His breathing was regular. The dream had not returned. Yet.

Lady Durham left her post, came across the room, and whispered a thank-you to Beth. "I think he's on his way back," she said. "He did not stammer until he got to the part about what happened in the brothel. That's a positive sign."

"Please send for me, day or night, if you think I can be of help."

"Yes, I will."

Outside the room in the hallway, Lady Durham looked suddenly distracted, as if she were indecisive about her next step.

"Are you all right, Your Ladyship?"

"Yes, yes. It's my husband who suffers from migraine and neuralgia. He often has to disappear into a dark room for days on end. I'm terribly afraid the stress of Handford's situation will trigger another of those dreadful bouts."

"Mr. Edwards will find the killer."

"I'm sure he will," Lady Durham said vaguely. Then, unexpectedly, she gripped Beth's arm tightly. Her gaze held, for the merest fraction of a second, a glint of pure terror.

"Come into my sitting room, Mrs. Edwards. There is something I think you need to know about Handford."

ELEVEN

Marc rode through the mid-afternoon sunshine on the lieutenant-governor's second-best horse along the ill-named "trunk road" that would take him to Streetsville. Three years ago he had travelled this same route as part of a foraging expedition led by Major Owen Jenkin, who had since become his friend and avuncular adviser. Little had changed. The hardwoods flourished on either flank of the corduroy thoroughfare, still threatening to overwhelm the preternatural intrusion of road-making humans. Buttercups and violets foamed in rainbowed wavelets along the verges and native birds tumbled and sang in the liberating breeze. For a while Marc was able to forget the urgency of his journey and simply enjoy a landscape he was increasingly comfortable to call home.

But the brutal death of Sarah McConkey was never far from his thoughts. His hopes for the afternoon's inquiry had been dashed. Apparently none of the whist-playing enemies of responsible government had ferried Ellice to Madame Renée's, if the wives were to be believed. And, alas, he could see no reason why they should dissemble unless they, and the friends accompanying them, were part of a vast conspiracy. If so—and the likelihood was remote—then it would take more than a day to unravel, and a day was all the time he had left to save Handford Ellice. Moreover, the wives would certainly tell their husbands, and more than a few neighbours, about his afternoon visit and the so-called stolen jewels, thus alerting those gentlemen and half the Family Compact—putting them all on their guard. There would be little merit now in trying to interrogate anyone else using the same cover story (pilfered pearls *and* a missing snuffbox?) and a serious risk of having them circle the oligarchic wagons. Either the authorities had to capture Badger, or Marc himself must unearth something useful at the McConkey farm.

This deflating conclusion was mercifully interrupted by the thud of approaching horses' hooves a short distance ahead. Marc drew his mount to one side and waited to see who was pounding towards him around the next bend in the road. The flash of scarlet and green and the familiar rattle of swinging sabres told him it was a mounted troop. Half a dozen subalterns were soon bearing down on him at full gallop. When the leading officer saw Marc, he raised a hand and the squad pulled up around him. Marc recognized several of the men and smiled a greeting.

"You look smaller without your tunic, sir," Ensign Beddoes said with a grin, "if that's possible."

Marc exchanged pleasantries with the officers he knew, then asked Beddoes, "Are you fellows part of the search for Michael Badger?"

"We are," Beddoes confirmed. "We've been beating the bushes in three townships for most of the day and haven't seen hide nor hair of him."

"Folks out here, as far as I can determine, are suffering an outbreak of blindness," said the officer beside him. "They don't seem to know whether the sun's come up or not."

"A six-footer with an orange mane ought to be hard to miss," Marc said.

"There's another troop scouring the area north of the city and a third doing the same east of it," Beddoes said. "What's this fellow done anyway, buggered His Lordship?"

"You could say that," Marc replied.

AFTER BEING GIVEN FAULTY DIRECTIONS AND getting lost for half an hour, Marc finally entered a public house on the outskirts of the village of Streetsville and risked a game pie and a glass of wine. The tapster then directed him to the McConkey farm, about a quarter of a mile off the main road. He rode up to the half-log cabin, relieved to see smoke coming from the crude chimney and cows drifting barnward to be milked.

Mr. McConkey, who opened the door with undue caution, turned out to be no surprise. He was a lean-muscled, stern-faced farmer with intimidating black eyebrows. He glowered at the intruder, said nothing, and waited, the half-open door wedged against his sturdy left boot.

"Good evening. Am I addressing Mr. Orrin McConkey?"

"Who wants ta know?" The voice was gravel and spit.

"I'm Marc Edwards. I've just ridden out here from Government House in Toronto—"

"We don't have any truck with people from the city."

"I'm here representing Governor Durham, sir. I have been sent by His Lordship to bring you some very bad news. May I come in?"

"Is it about Sarah?" a shrivelled female voice came from somewhere in the room beyond.

"Go back to yer business, Hilda. This has nothin'—"

"Yes, it is about Sarah," Marc said loudly.

"I take it you're speakin' about the girl who used to be my

daughter?" McConkey's expression darkened, but whether with anger or some more vulnerable emotion was impossible to tell.

"What's happened to Sarah?" A wizened woman, aged beyond her years, poked her bonneted face around her husband's shoulder.

"Please, let me come in," Marc said.

"If you must," McConkey said, opening the door. "Hilda, you go and finish makin' my supper. Any news about Sarah oughta be given to me first."

Hilda McConkey looked stricken but turned dutifully and scuttled away to a curtained-off kitchen area. Marc noticed that no hair fluttered from under the bonnet.

"I won't ask ya to sit down, Mr. Edwards. I got a meal to eat and cows waitin' to be milked. Out here in the country we have real work to do."

"Very well," Marc said, taking in the neat, clean, well-tended sitting room. On a polished hardwood table, the Bible took pride of place, and embroidered religious homilies decorated all four walls. "I'm sorry to have to tell you that your daughter is dead."

This dreadful revelation had no effect on McConkey. He merely stared malevolently at Marc as if waiting for the next sentence.

"She was murdered early yesterday morning—"

The rattling of pans in the kitchen stopped abruptly.

"In a house of harlotry," McConkey snarled. "I already know that."

"How could you?"

"Our pastor was in the city this mornin'. That evil woman had the gall to approach him about takin' the funeral service."

Marc tried not to let his disappointment show. And he hoped "that evil woman" had not told the pastor any of the sordid, politically sensitive details. He nodded in the direction of the kitchen, where all was silent.

"I was gonna tell her," McConkey said with a guilty start. Then, with fierce accusation, "I guess I don't need ta, now."

"I am sorry," Marc said, "but I must ask you some questions about Sarah as part of my murder investigation, painful though they may be."

"Why're ya botherin' to look fer her killer: she was a whore."

"Now see here, McConkey——"

"'Wherefore if thy hand or foot offend thee, cut them off, and cast them from thee!'"

Marc held his temper with great difficulty: there were higher stakes at play. "You may have disowned your daughter, sir, but that is of no importance to me here and now. I'm going to ask you a series of questions about Sarah, and I want full and truthful answers from you. If not, then I shall return with the sheriff and a magistrate's warrant."

"All right, then," McConkey said with a show of petulance. He wasn't accustomed to being bullied in his own home, but he sat down. Marc pulled up a chair opposite. The kitchen curtain swayed and went still.

Slowly and systematically, Marc took McConkey through what he assumed to be the relevant details of Sarah McConkey's aborted life. Yes, there had been a suitor for her hand who had been willfully rejected. The ensuing confrontation had caused the "wayward witch" to pack a valise and strike out on her own for the city. Yes, the Reverend Finney was known in Streetsville, having been a circuit rider here in the past, and Sarah had headed straight there looking for work. Finney had immediately sent word to the McConkeys but was told to keep her if he so wished. He did, but three weeks later, in early October, a letter arrived from Finney informing them that Sarah had been found to have committed "abominations" and had been summarily dismissed with a stern warning to head straight home and beg her father's forgiveness. While certainly not inclined to forgive her, the McConkeys had nonetheless been willing to take back the prodigal. But she didn't come home. Worried now, they asked their own pastor, the Reverend Solomon Good, to try to locate her. He was able to learn only that she had vanished into Irishtown, whose iniquities dwarfed those of Sodom and Gomorrah. Then to their shock and consternation, Sarah arrived on their doorstep in mid-November, thin, pale, and pregnant. The malignant source of the pregnancy was not in doubt: Sarah had fallen as far as a Christian woman could. Despite her tearful pleading, McConkey had done his duty: he threw her out and publicly disowned her. Neither he nor his wife had seen or heard of her since.

Marc thanked McConkey and stood up. "The funeral is tomorrow morning at the old Mechanics' Institute building on John Street at—"

"We won't be there," McConkey said.

Marc glanced at the kitchen curtain.

"Mrs. McConkey feels exactly as I do," her husband said.

He followed Marc out as far as the gate, then turned without saying a word and trudged solemnly towards his bawling cows.

Just as Marc was untying his horse, Hilda McConkey emerged from the front door, peered anxiously about, then trotted out to Marc. The struggle to suppress her tears and the feelings they might assuage had made her small round face a constricted death mask.

"You goin' to the funeral?" she asked.

"Yes, ma'am."

"Say a prayer fer my Sarah, will ya?"

•   •   •

IT WAS A LONG RIDE HOME in the waning day. Marc wasn't sure what he had hoped to find in Streetsville. Perhaps a thwarted lover who had somehow contrived to take out his rage on the beloved? With a desperate Michael Badger happy to sell him a key to the hatch? Or perhaps some aspect of Sarah's tragic story not yet known and somehow relevant to her death? Instead, McConkey's account supported in every respect that of Mrs. Burgess and her girls, as well as that of Madame Charlotte. There were no missing weeks in the narrative, no further revelations to be made. He would have to work with what he now knew. Perhaps Finney or his young son was the father of Sarah's child. If so, then why would a Methodist minister arrange the demise of his mistress *after* the child was stillborn? Maybe the child had not died at birth! But where would Sarah hide it? Could she have been blackmailing Finney? Despite the risks, Marc knew he would have to interrogate Finney tomorrow, and interrogate him hard.

Still, in his heart of hearts, Marc clung to the notion that the primary target had been Handford Ellice. It was Sarah who was the random factor, not Ellice. The timing and circumstances were just too pat: Lord Durham and his mission had to be the efficient cause of the string of events culminating in that squalid death scene. But so far he had failed to find any real evidence implicating any of the whist players. And unless Badger were caught, such evidence was unlikely to turn up.

It was eight o'clock when he left Sir George Arthur's mount at the stables and plodded up to the verandah of Government House. An orderly led Marc not into the governor's office, nor the adjacent meeting room, but straight through to Sir George's living quarters and a comfortable drawing room. Lord Durham was seated in an armchair, smoking a pipe. One look at his face told Marc that Badger had not been found, and Marc himself was unable to disguise his own disappointment at the day's efforts on the earl's behalf.

"Sit down, Marc," Durham said wearily. His face was drawn.

"I've just spent three hours with the most tiresome, small-minded, and mean-spirited men imaginable." Then he smiled. "Reminded me of home."

"How is your nephew doing?" Marc asked, recalling that Beth was to visit him in the afternoon and wanting to delay his report as long as he could.

Durham brightened immediately. "Mrs. Edwards came to see Handford after luncheon, and according to Lady Durham's account of their meeting, she succeeded in bringing him out of the delirious reverie he's been in since they brought him here yesterday. Once he saw that she was alive, his nightmare of having stabbed her vanished. She stayed long enough to get him talking and feeling a bit more normal. Then Lady Durham spent the rest of the day convincing him that he did not murder anyone, that he was a victim of circumstance only. She has planted in his mind the notion that Sarah was murdered by someone else for reasons to do with the inmates of the brothel. Still, the horror of waking up covered in a girl's blood remains with him, and always will."

"I hope she emphasized that the knife was placed in his hand with malicious intent," Marc said.

"She did."

Though how anyone could have placed it there without himself wallowing in Sarah's blood was still a prickly question.

"I don't have to tell you that we have not found Badger," Durham said, "but I need to hear whatever you've discovered today, however dispiriting it may be."

Marc proceeded to describe the visits he and Cobb had made

to the homes of the four whist players, and the fruitless results. Alluding to Cobb's interrogation of Madame Charlotte and Mrs. Burgess and to his own trip to the McConkey farm, Marc sketched out Sarah's saga and the slim pickings to be inferred from it.

Durham sucked his pipe back into life. "Finney looks like our best bet, doesn't he? It's possible he may have had a double motive: to embarrass me and to get rid of a woman who might prove his ruin. Still, unless we can tie him to Badger, we don't stand much of a chance of proving anything."

Into the brief silence that followed this unsettling remark, Marc said, "When you mentioned the lost snuffbox to the whist players this afternoon, did you discover anything we didn't already know?"

"Alas, no. In fact, they were not only forthcoming about the two hours or so they spent with Handford, but positively voluble. They freely admitted escorting him to the bar—man to man, as it were—and were complimentary about his whist-playing skills. They said he simply excused himself shortly before midnight and headed, they assumed, to his private quarters. No monogrammed box was left anywhere within their sight. They all wished Handford a speedy recovery."

"Well, one of them is lying—Finney, by the looks of it. Do you want me to have a serious run at him?"

Durham thought about the suggestion. "No. You may interview him if you like on the pretext of getting background information on Sarah. But you must be tactful. I can't be seen bullying one of the province's significant churches, even indirectly."

"I'll be the soul of discretion, sir."

Durham smiled, then his expression darkened. "What if it turns out that none of the whist players is involved? What if it was someone else at Spadina who drove Handford into town?"

"But it had to be someone in that card room," Marc insisted. "That's where Mr. Ellice spent the last two hours before his disappearance."

"I thought so, too. So I sent word to Wakefield to get a list of all the guests seen by the staff in that room at any time after ten o'clock."

"How many are we looking at?"

"Well, excluding the women and several gents too arthritic to move without help, about eight."

"You have the names, sir?"

"Yes, but not one of them resides in the city. Three are from Brantford and west, two from Port Hope, and the other three from Niagara and beyond."

Marc did not reply. The futility of following up these possible leads needed no gloss put upon it.

Durham took a last puff on his pipe. "What will you do tomorrow besides interview Finney?"

"Cobb and I are going to Sarah's funeral at ten. I intend to keep a close eye on the women of the two brothels, who may be there. I want to study the dynamics of their relationship, if I can."

"Funerals and weddings often compel people to reveal their true selves, eh?"

"Exactly. Then I'll go to Finney's."

"I've been promised more troops to search for Badger. Sir George is more than eager to help. I have been impressed, I must say, with the absolute discretion of you and your policemen."

"Thank you. How much longer have we got before—"

Durham frowned. "Tomorrow night at eight o'clock, Magistrate Thorpe and Chief Constable Sturges are to appear in my office here, at which time, failing the discovery of the real killer, I shall turn Handford over to them."

"I'm sure that won't be necessary," Marc said, wishing it were so.

BETH WAS WAITING FOR MARC. CHARLENE, sensing excitement in the air, reluctantly went off to her room, where she contrived to sit reading very close to her door. Some cold roast, cheese, bread, and a flask of cider awaited Marc on the sideboard.

"No good news," Beth commented, watching him eat.

"I'm afraid not. Badger's still on the loose. I'm going to wait until morning to fill you in on all the details of the day. Right now I'm tired and discouraged. Perhaps in going over things with you tomorrow, I'll be better able to compose my notes, and one of us might even think of something that's been overlooked."

"All right, love, I understand." Beth poured herself a glass of cider. "But I have several things to tell you that can't wait."

"About Ellice? I know most of it already. His Lordship was very pleased with the miracle you worked on his nephew this afternoon. After you left, his aunt was able to engage him in conversation and at least begin to convince him that he too is a victim in this business."

"I'm glad, for Handford's sake. But there's more."

Marc was not sure whether he should be anxious or excited. "Did he tell you something important that happened at Madame Renée's?"

"He gave me a description of his nightmare."

"About stabbing you."

"About pulling the knife from my neck."

"I don't quite follow. Are you saying he has no memory—even in his fantastic nightmares—of pushing the knife in?"

"I am. His nightmare, which he's had over and over, was of pulling the knife *out*."

Marc reached across and clasped Beth's hand. "This could be critical to the case," he said with rising excitement.

"I thought it must be but didn't see how."

"Cobb and I have been mystified as to how the killer could have managed to plunge a dagger through Sarah's throat, pull it out, then reach over and place it in Ellice's hand without getting her blood on him or tracking through it as it spouted onto the bed and the floor. Now I think we know."

"Handford himself pulled the knife from Sarah's throat, then?"

"I'm sure he did, half-consciously, in a drunken doze, perhaps assisted by a little laudanum administered out at Spadina. We may never know for sure the exact sequence of events."

"So the killer could've just stabbed Sarah and run?"

"I'm certain of it now. It was enough that Lord Durham's nephew be discovered naked beside a murdered prostitute and covered with her blood. Ellice unwittingly capped the deception by pulling the knife out, as any human being would have done in those circumstances, drugged or not. Which means that one of the women could have committed the act without bloodying herself or even waking the others."

"Or anybody with a way to get in and out of that little door."

Marc sighed. "Yes. We have added another detail to the picture, but it doesn't point us in any one direction."

He swallowed the last of the roast. Beth hadn't stirred. "There's something else you need to tell me, isn't there?"

"Yes. It's not directly connected, like the nightmare business, but Lady Durham wanted you to know."

"Wanted me to know what?"

"When I left Handford's room, Lady Durham led me into her sitting room and told me something about her nephew, something not even her husband is aware of."

Marc felt the hair rising on his neck as Beth told the tale.

When Handford Ellice was fifteen, he was caught in the stable with a girl by his mother and a visiting prelate. The young couple were naked and basking in the afterglow of their sexual exertions. If the girl had been a servant or the daughter of a tenant, money would have exchanged hands and the matter been soon forgotten. However, the girl was the youngest daughter of the neighbouring squire, eighteen years of age, and a willing participant, it seemed. While this sort of indiscretion was bad in and of itself—considering the lustre of the Ellice name, the petty ambitions of the squire, and a priest's witnessing the transgression—the girl was found to be black and blue on every part of her body not normally camouflaged by clothing. Distraught at being discovered thus, the girl alleged that Handford and she had been often in that loft and that after sex, which she claimed he always initiated, he routinely beat her, being crafty enough to whack her with his riding crop only where the bruises wouldn't show.

Handford—stuttering, confused, ashamed—protested that this was only their second encounter and swore that he had never hurt the girl. When he had inquired after her bruises, she just laughed, he said. The upshot of all this was a stalemate in which the entire matter was hushed up and satisfactory accommodation reached. The squire received ten acres of prime hunting ground he had long coveted and the shocked prelate was given a living at the discretion of Bear Ellice, the lad's illustrious and absentee father. The Ellices of course got to retain their respectability.

Marc let the incriminating details accumulate before he said, softly, "Does Lady Durham believe her nephew was a sadist? And could be one still?"

"She doesn't want to believe it. You just said yourself she spent all day convincing him he couldn't have killed Sarah."

"Yet she wanted me to know, even though Lord Durham himself does not?"

"Yes. She thought you should. She wants to have the truth for herself, awful as it may be."

"Even if it means I have to go up there tomorrow evening and tell her that her nephew is not only a murderer but a species of madman?"

"I think you have to consider it a possibility."

Neither of them slept well that night.

TWELVE

Marc made his way along King Street to the police quarters at the rear of the Court House. There, referring to his notes and under the baleful watch of Gussie French—who resented any official document not transcribed by his own pen—he brought Chief Sturges up to date on the investigation. In turn, Sarge told him that the search for Badger would be intensified within the city. Ten supernumerary constables had been called in from the city and surrounding county, and a dozen snitches had been given cash advances to reinforce their loyalty to the Crown and its immediate objective. If Badger were still here, the chief vowed, he would be flushed from cover before sundown.

With this guarantee to buoy his spirits, Marc carried on to John Street and the Mechanics' Institute. He found a modest crowd of mourners gathered for Sarah McConkey's funeral and Cobb waiting for him in the stuffy vestibule.

"All the ladies are in there," he said with mild reproach. "They decided they might as well get on with it." It was clear that Cobb felt that his time and Marc's would be better spent in the hunt for Badger.

"This will likely be a waste of effort, Cobb," Marc said, "but I want to see who's here and how they react to one another. We may get a different perspective on Mrs. Burgess and the girls."

"Which ain't exactly evidence," Cobb muttered.

"I want you to stay near the back of the hall and scrutinize every face. You never know who might decide to show up."

They entered the hall. To Marc's surprise the main room of the former Mechanics' Institute, austere even in the days when it was a hub of self-improvement, had been transformed into something not unlike a simple house of worship on a back concession. Benches formed rows of pews and great sprays of freshly cut roses adorned tables along the windowless walls. Below the front wall, with the mid-morning sun pouring through its single, tall, plain window, a makeshift platform and lectern had been arranged to provide an altar. A casket of gleaming hardwood, the kind normally reserved for those rich enough to purchase ostentation, sat before it, bedecked with sprigs of wildflower. Behind the lectern, fussing with his Bible and notes, stood the minister, a youthful-looking chap, meagre of stature but fired with holy purpose and the zeal to propagate it. Where two or three are gathered in my name, there am I in the midst of them, Marc thought gratefully.

There were more than two dozen mourners. In the rear rows sat several families unmistakably of Irishtown: the women in touchingly inapt bonnets and drab hand-me-down dresses, the men in suit coats a size too large or small, the children scrubbed but otherwise unaltered. The second row from the front was occupied by women, housewives whose spouses couldn't or wouldn't come, tenants or neighbourhood acquaintances of Mrs. Burgess most likely. With a pang of guilt Marc realized that whatever its troubles and traumas, the ragtag and motley collective of Irishtown was still a community. Madame Renée's was not, as he had first thought, an isolated bastion in a random and hostile terrain.

The proof of such a conclusion lay before him as he observed the scene in the front row: Norah Burgess and Madame Charlotte stood embracing each other. Tears had excavated runnels in Charlotte's pancake makeup, but Norah Burgess, her face unsullied by cosmetics, looked utterly devastated. She trembled as she clung to her rival, and the latter eased her onto the bench and held her till she steadied. On either side of the older women and filling the front row, their employees sat with quiet dignity, despite the almost comic effect of their efforts to temper their flamboyant working attire with black bits of shawl, scarf, or cowl.

Marc took a seat in the back row. Cobb meanwhile perched on a dusty stove near the entrance and, satisfied that no grieving lover or drooling assassin had intruded upon the ceremony, proceeded to catnap. The Reverend Solomon Good, whose booming voice emerged almost miraculously from his narrow chest, began the service with a long and soulful prayer, of which Cobb caught only intermittent phrases concerning Mary Magdalene, casting the first stone, and the bounteous compassion of God's only begotten son.

Cobb was unaware how much of the service he had dozed through when an alien sound to his left brought him almost awake. It was the click of a door latch being opened and closed. It took him a half-minute to get his mind in gear and ten more seconds to come to the conclusion that someone had just joined the mourners.

Although in the shadow of the far rear corner opposite Cobb, the figure was obviously tall, well built, and intent on remaining unobserved and unidentified. Despite the warmth of the day, it wore a loose-fitting coat and had covered its head and hair with a flowered scarf. It was peering around the room, looking for someone or something. The congregation by then was standing, and the hall was swelling with their voices raised in song and the hope of heaven.

"Jesus!" Cobb hissed to himself, "it's Badger!" He sprang forward but managed only to stumble and alert the target. By the time Cobb regained his footing, Badger was out the door. Cobb did not think to call out to Marc; he simply gave chase as he had done a hundred times before in the execution of his duties. Blinking in the sudden sunlight of John Street, he looked quickly up and down the road and spotted the culprit running awkwardly into the service lane that backed onto the houses and shops along Wellington Street to the south. In seconds Cobb was up to full speed, a pace that never failed to be underestimated by fleeing felons. He wheeled into the alleyway. Badger was only thirty yards ahead, weaving and stumbling among the half-dozen carts, assorted donkeys and their masters, and the usual flotsam of these much-travelled lanes.

"Stop that thief!" he hollered, but the command produced only curious stares or irreverent rejoinders as he pushed aside man and beast blocking the way. The creature in flight was the key to the investigation! He had to be captured here and now. With excitement surging through him, Cobb quickly gained on his prey. Now only fifteen yards behind, Cobb spotted the narrow alley leading south to Wellington between two brick buildings. Every instinct told him that Badger would veer into it. That meant a straight, unimpeded dash to the main street. With his superior speed, Cobb would have the bastard well before he reached safety. Suddenly a dog ran in front of Badger, who tripped, righted himself, and headed for the alley. At that moment a gust of wind blew the scarf away, and Cobb got a split-second glimpse of thick, light-coloured hair. Got you now, you murdering bugger, Cobb said to himself as he nimbly sidestepped the mange-ridden mongrel and cantered towards the alley.

Which was precisely when his feet went out from under him

and, in trying to prevent himself from landing on his back, he overcorrected and went skidding on his considerable belly for several yards, coming to a stop with his nose an inch from a brick wall.

"Shit!" he cried aloud, just as he came to the conclusion that he was lying in the very stuff.

Those spectators who had interrupted their business to take in the chase burst into mocking applause. Fuming and scarlet-nosed, Cobb resisted the temptation to instruct these scoffers in the awful solemnity of the law, picked himself up, and ran into the alley. Too late. Badger had reached Wellington Street. Winded and huffing, Cobb made it onto the thoroughfare. It was crowded with traffic, human and animal. Cobb looked left and right.

Badger had disappeared.

WHILE THE ESCAPE OF MICHAEL BADGER was a blow to Marc and Cobb, at least it confirmed that he was still in the city. Constable Brown was dispatched to Government House with an official request from Chief Sturges that sufficient troops be deployed to surround the city limits. Constable Rossiter was put in charge of the deputized supernumeraries to scour the streets and alleys west of Yonge, and Constable Wilkie headed a similar squad to do the same east of Yonge. Cobb was ordered to go home and render himself less redolent.

Marc was left at the station to fret and ponder what might have been. But not for long. Just before noon he decided that, while Badger was being run to ground, he would start shaking the tree among the whist players to see what might fall out. He headed straight for the home of the Reverend Temperance Finney.

He got a cool reception. "My husband isn't in," Mrs. Finney told him at the door.

"Please tell me, then, where he has gone. I am on urgent government business, a matter of life and death. I must see him as soon as possible."

"He doesn't tell me where he goes," was the curt reply, and the door closed in his face.

It was while he stood on the road, angry and frustrated, that he recalled without conscious effort what it was he had overlooked even as he had made copious notes earlier in the day. The only uncorroborated account of the drive back to the city after the gala was that of the Hepburns. Apparently they had gone as a couple and returned as a couple, with only the dubious testimony of their stableman to back their story. What if, for reasons not yet clear, Mrs. Hepburn had lied and bribed her coachman to do the same? While the police, and perhaps even the Durhams, might be content to have the murder attributed solely to Michael Badger, Marc was determined to uncover any political conspiracy. If proven, its exposure would help Lord Durham's cause by undermining the extremist opposition to his proposals. Marc was not quite sure how he might go about the interrogation, but if he could just get the two Hepburns together in one room . . .

He was sweating and excited by the time he had marched to Hospital Street and entered the Hepburn property. Striding up to the door, he gave a peremptory rap with the brass knocker. The time had come to drop the polite niceties. He had less than eight hours to solve the case and liberate the Durhams.

It was Una who opened the door. She was dishevelled, hollow-eyed, and distracted, almost slatternly.

"I wish to speak with Mr. Hepburn, please. Tell him it's urgent."

Una nodded without speaking, turned and shuffled back towards a heavy interior door, leaving Marc a clear view of her movements. She eased it open and he heard her say something in a timid voice. A murmur of male commentary rose in the room behind Una's figure blocking the doorway. "He says it's urgent, sir."

"Damn it all, I told you *never* to interrupt me in here on Thursday afternoons!"

"I'll tell him you're busy, then."

"You do that."

Una stepped back to reveal her red-faced master.

"And keep this bloody door closed! How many times do I have to tell you, Miss Badger!"

Una pushed the door shut but not before Marc caught sight of three men seated around a baize-covered table, littered with upturned playing cards: Finney, O'Driscoll, and Harris.

Looking abashed and worried, Una hustled back to Marc. "He's with his whist club, sir. Come back at four."

For the moment, Marc was oddly uninterested in the whist-loving chums. "Is Michael Badger your brother?" he asked.

"He is," she said, and burst into tears.

Marc offered his arm and led Una outside. They found a stone bench in a shady part of the garden.

"Tell me about Michael," Marc said gently.

"I'd like to. I've been going crazy since I saw him on Tuesday, and nobody to talk to, nobody to help."

"You saw Michael on Tuesday?"

"He came here about ten in the morning. He looked terrible. I never seen him so bad."

"What did he want?"

"Usually he comes for money, but he knew I had no more to give him. He said he was in real trouble and had to get out of town before the day ended. He wouldn't tell me what it was about, but I guessed it had to do with his gambling."

"He was in debt?"

"He always was. But there was something about him this time that seemed different. Even when he was on the run, and that was more than once, he always kept a bit of a twinkle in his eye. He would be scared, of course, but I knew him well and I knew he thought it was all a game—a dangerous game he was willing to play."

"A born gambler."

"Yes. But there was another side to him."

"There usually is. But you say this time seemed different."

"That's right. He looked like he'd had the fright of his life. He told me he had to see Mr. Hepburn right away."

Marc leaned forward. This was what he needed to hear, the connection between the paid assassin and his sponsor. "Michael knew Alasdair Hepburn?"

Una seemed momentarily puzzled. "Of course. He worked here quite often."

"I see," Marc said, and he did, his mind racing ahead.

"Michael did odd jobs around the town; he's real handy with a hammer and saw. But lately he's worked only for Mr. Hepburn. He helped plant the vegetable garden over there in April and May. But . . ."

She looked down, and despite her mannish figure and plain face, she was suddenly fragile and abashed. "He kept going back to that wicked place and that wicked woman in Irishtown."

"So you knew about his being Madame Renée's bruiser?"

"He couldn't help himself. He had to go back there, whatever."

After a pause, Marc said, "Getting back to Tuesday, then, tell me: did Michael see Mr. Hepburn?"

"No. Mr. Hepburn was at the bank. I told Michael that, and he was terrified and trembling. Then he told me to fetch pen and paper, and he wrote out a note, which he said I had to give to Mr. Hepburn when he came home for his luncheon at half past one. He swore me to absolute secrecy, saying his life depended on it. Then he left without another word."

"Would he have left town, do you think?"

"Only if he had money. We got cousins in Port Sarnia. He's run off there before. But a steamer costs money." She brushed aside a tear and said, "I haven't heard a word from him since Tuesday morning and there's an awful rumour going 'round about him being wanted by the police."

Marc waited until Una Badger stopped running her fingers through her already thoroughly ruffled hair. "So you heard about the funeral of Sarah McConkey?" he prompted.

"That harlot from Madame Renée's? Yes. I heard that a girl from there had been killed. I thought that Michael . . ."

"Might still be in town and attend the funeral for one of the girls he must have known?"

She hung her head.

Marc noted the bright sun glancing through the leaves upon her thick auburn hair, and said, "And you went there in disguise this morning?"

"Yes. He wasn't there."

Marc resisted mentioning the chase and its misinterpreted results. The important point here and now was that Michael Badger might not be in the city after all. He was probably hundreds of miles away, heading for his cousins in Port Sarnia.

While Marc was contemplating the implications of this development, Una said, "He told me not to, but I peeked at the note."

"The note he wrote for Mr. Hepburn?"

"Yes. I gave it to him right at one-thirty on Tuesday, but I read it first. I was beside myself with worry."

"I'm glad you did. It may explain a lot of things and help me to find your brother."

"You think so?"

"I do. So please, if you can, tell me precisely what it said."

"Oh, that's easy, sir. It was very short and I have no trouble reading my brother's writing. It said, 'Send help now, as arranged.'"

In deference to this caring and distraught woman, Marc checked his elation. But here was proof of a direct link between Hepburn and Badger. The "help" was no doubt of the financial kind, for homicidal services rendered. Even if Badger was as far away as Port Sarnia—where it would take a day by steamer or express rider to order his capture and at least another day to have him brought back—he now had enough evidence to secure a warrant. He and Sturges would interrogate Hepburn until he confessed, search his house for further clues, and with luck implicate the other three. Whist club indeed!

"You'll let me know as soon as you find Michael, won't you?"

"Yes. I'll come and tell you myself."

"There's a good, sweet side to Michael, you know. We grew up in a decent family and went to a proper school."

But it hadn't kept him from becoming a gambler and a cold-blooded killer.

MARC'S INSTINCT WAS TO BARGE INTO the card game at Hepburn's and wreak havoc. But reason soon prevailed. His first duty was to inform Chief Sturges that Cobb's sighting and pursuit of their quarry had been misguided. Then he would ask Sarge to go up to Government House to convince Sir George to dispatch a party to Port Sarnia to check out the Badger cousins. At the same time, the hunt for the villain would have to be broadened again to include the surrounding townships. Marc was also concerned about the rumour mill, which Una Badger had alluded to. While those involved in the manhunt had been told that Badger was wanted for killing a woman and that Lord Durham himself had taken a special, but unspecified, interest in the matter, such a facile and patently incomplete explanation had fuelled local speculation. Even now such rumours could be doing Durham as much harm as the truth about Ellice's involvement might.

Chief Sturges took the news about Badger with stolid resignation, a legacy of his Cockney upbringing and long service in Wellington's army and Robert Peel's London constabulary. While not commenting one way or the other on Marc's claims regarding Hepburn, he readily agreed to send Gussie upstairs to fetch Magistrate Thorpe. Grumbling about having his mid-day meal disrupted and about a "lot of bloody fuss over a common hooer," Gussie trotted off to the adjoining chambers. The chief then left for Government House.

Marc sat down at Gussie French's table and, pulling rank, consumed the clerk's bread and cheese. Moments later, Magistrate Thorpe came in, shook hands with Marc, and sat down opposite him. Gussie was left cooling his heels in a hallway.

In as concise terms as he could manage, Marc outlined his theory of the murder. Michael Badger, in debt to the dicers up at the Tinker's Dam and fearing for his safety, arrived on Monday morning at Madame Renée's to tap his favourite source for cash in order to preserve his knees and perhaps his life. As it turned out, most of Irishtown, including Mrs. Burgess's girls, were at the Queen's Wharf welcoming His Lordship to the city. Luckily he found Madame at home, alone. When Mrs. Burgess refused to give him a farthing, the desperate Badger somehow got word to Alasdair Hepburn that a plot, which the latter had hatched in anticipation of the earl's arrival and to which Badger had been till now an unwilling party, was suddenly operative. Hepburn, in possible collusion with other Tory sympathizers—Marc did not yet name them—got young Handford Ellice drunk and possibly drugged, and drove him to Irishtown after the gala. From there he was dropped off at Madame Renée's. The plan was for Badger, who had stolen a key for the hatch, to slip into the brothel when the house was quiet and the couple were fast asleep, and cause some kind of mayhem in order to have Ellice found in a low-life stew—producing a sex scandal to discredit Lord Durham and his already morally tainted entourage. Initially in the plot purely for money, Badger agreed to carry out his part, but once inside that room, his rage against Mrs. Burgess and his abnormal fear overwhelmed him. He stabbed Sarah McConkey with the dagger he knew lay under her pillow. Perhaps horrified at his own actions, Badger went to Hepburn on Tuesday morning looking for his blood money and, finding him out, and afraid or forbidden to go to Hepburn's bank, he left a secret note, which Una Badger fortuitously read and whose incriminating contents she could attest to.

The magistrate, who had taken many a shocking deposition in his day, showed little emotion during Marc's ten-minute peroration. When Marc finished, Thorpe said matter-of-factly, "You're suggesting this affair started out as a Tory plot to embarrass Lord Durham and inadvertently ended up as a murder?"

"I am."

"But if Badger is guilty, why go to such lengths to demonstrate that he was, in effect, bribed to carry out what was intended to be no more than an elaborate and ill-advised prank?"

"A prank that could get Lord Durham recalled!" Marc was indignant.

"I'm speaking of the law here, Mr. Edwards. You yourself have just insisted that Mr. Hepburn's plot was to lure young Ellice into at worst a compromising situation. Handford Ellice is an adult. He has a free will. He can say no to a glass of whiskey. So, unless you can prove that the lad was drugged and his comatose body literally dragged to the door of this brothel, you have no case against Alasdair Hepburn—for conspiracy, public mischief, or anything else."

"I have testimony about the note."

"Ambiguous at best, sir. After all, Badger was a sometime employee of Hepburn, and his sister's been the household maid for several years. The mere fact that they communicated by letter is not an incriminating or even a suspicious activity."

Marc was flabbergasted. He felt like accusing this blue-blooded Tory of protecting his own but bit his tongue instead.

"Don't look so disconcerted, Edwards. If Lord Durham hired you to find the whore's killer and disentangle Ellice from the mess, then it is to his advantage if Badger turns out, as you imply, to have murdered for purely personal motives. In that way, we can charge and hang him without any reference to who was sleeping beside the victim, since it's irrelevant to the case. Nor has Badger any certain knowledge that it was Ellice. I take it that the madam is unaware of his identity?"

Marc nodded grimly.

"Well, then, Ellice is out of it, eh?" Thorpe gave Marc an avuncular and well-meant smile. "My advice to you is to leave the conspiracy stuff alone. It can only harm your effort to protect Lord Durham."

"You are refusing, then, to give me a warrant to search Hepburn's house and have him formally interrogated?"

"I am, but not for the reasons I just gave you as my personal advice. Until you produce Badger for me, you have not enough concrete evidence. No magistrate in the province would issue you a warrant on such flimsy grounds as you've provided."

Marc sat too stunned to even nod his thanks to Thorpe for hearing him out or to say a courteous good-bye as the justice left the room. Still dazed, he thought he heard Cobb clumping up the walk. Marc hauled himself out of Gussie's chair and went out to relay both the exciting and the galling news. As he closed the door behind him, he heard an exasperated squawk: "Where the hell's my cheese!"

Sure enough, a constable was puffing red-faced towards the station, but it wasn't Cobb. It was Ewan Wilkie.

"You've got news?" Marc asked, seeing Wilkie wide-eyed and abnormally awake.

"You gotta come, Mr. Edwards, sir," he huffed, clutching his side. "I run all the way."

"You've found Badger!" The world rolled upright again.

"Nestor Peck found him up on Jarvis Street. Cobb's there now."

"That's great news, Constable. But why didn't you and Cobb bring him down here? I need to question him."

"That'll be kinda hard, sir."

"Why?"

"He ain't breathin'."

THIRTEEN

Marc hurried to the corner of Lot and Jarvis, where the twisting lane to the Tinker's Dam and satellite shanties met civilization, and where Wilkie, now two blocks behind, had said the body of Michael Badger lay. Marc tried not to think about how hopeless their situation now was. Without Badger's testimony, no legally warrantable link could be made to the conniving whist players. And unless he could force a confession out of one of them or anyone else who might be involved, even Badger might posthumously be exonerated. It was after all only Marc's theory that connected Badger to the invasion of the brothel and the stabbing of Sarah McConkey. He realized, though, that the temptation for the police to pin the murder on a known scoundrel would be strong and, as Magistrate Thorpe had hinted, Ellice might be kept out of it entirely. But Lord Durham professed to be interested in the truth, and Lady Durham needed to have her own disturbing doubts about her nephew's sanity and sexual conduct unambiguously clarified. If only Beth had not relayed the tale of Ellice's sordid affair in his father's stable, then perhaps Marc too would be willing to go along with the events that seemed to be unfolding in their own way, despite his best efforts to deflect them closer to a true trajectory.

Cobb waved to him from a spot on the lane to the Tinker's Dam about twenty yards from the end of Jarvis Street. Marc slowed and walked disconsolately to his partner.

"Ya took yer time, Major." Cobb was sweating in a brown suit coat that had replaced his soiled constable's jacket, and his boots had been newly blacked and buffed. His hat had been tipped aside so that his spiked hair rose up like a terrified porcupine from its lair.

"Where is the body?"

"Good day to you, too." Cobb pointed down the slope of a dry stream bed that wandered parallel to the path. "He's been there a while. The stiffenin' ain't quite outta him yet."

"Yet no one found him till now?"

"You can't see him from the path unless you was lookin' fer him."

In fact Marc had to take two steps down the slope before he could clearly discern the corpse of the orange-maned giant they had been hunting since Tuesday. Badger lay on his back in the long grass where he had tumbled after someone had blown a hole in his chest where his heart had once been. The blow of the bullet must have knocked him straight backwards. He had likely been dead before he hit the ground. His arms were at his side, and although still stiff with rigor, they appeared to have been in a relaxed mode before death ended further gesturing. The eyes were open, gray and glassy, and the mouth as well, as if in surprise. The corona of golden-red hair sizzled with flies. Marc went down to the body, being careful not to disturb anything that might be evidence. Cobb was beside him. Wilkie clambered up to the path above but was content to look out for Dr. Withers, whom Nestor Peck had been sent to fetch.

"He could've stayed here till somebody smelt him," Cobb said.

"But I figure he was shot sometime in the night: rigid mortar and all that."

Marc was bent over the corpse. "I agree. But look at all that powder on his shirt. The shooter couldn't have been more than two or three feet away."

"I forgot you seen a few bodies with bullet holes down there in Quebec."

"And I'd guess that a pistol was used, but Angus Withers may be able to give us more to go on."

"You plannin' to solve this murder, too?" Cobb said with genuine surprise.

"It has to be connected with Sarah's death somehow."

"How do ya figure?"

"It's just too convenient that a few hours before I began closing in on that traitorous crew of whist-playing Tories, my star witness is himself murdered."

"But we ain't a stone's throw from the Tinker's Dam and half the villains in the entire county."

"You think one of those he owed money to did this?"

"That's the most likely prop-up-hillity, ain't it?"

Marc thought that over. "But if he was killed here in the dark, up on that path, and the killer was standing three feet from him, it doesn't make sense."

"Why not?"

"There's no sign of struggle. The arms were not even raised in self-defence. If one of the gambling thugs did this, would he take a chance on walking right up to Badger in the dark before shooting him? Would you come within a yard of those grappling arms? The fellow was a bruiser, remember. And he had been on the run for almost two days, wary and desperate. Would he let a stranger accost him in the middle of the night?"

"You're sayin' he was shot by somebody he knew and wasn't ascaired of?"

"I am. No other explanation fits the facts."

"Okay, I'll give ya that, Major. But let's say Burly Bettman or some other henchman decides to bribe one of Badger's cronies to do him in?"

"Now that's a real possibility, though it's hard to fathom how anyone would know where he could find Badger. However, if it comes down to that, I guess you and your fellow constables are the best people to handle the investigation."

"Well now, I ain't lookin' fer work," Cobb said with a grin. Then he pursed his lips. "What'd'ya think that bulge is in his shirt pocket?"

"Don't disturb anything until the doctor's had his turn," Marc said, as Cobb knelt down beside the body.

"I'll be real careful." Cobb slid two fingers into the vest pocket of Badger's shirt and drew out a familiar object.

Marc whistled. "A key."

"And I'll bet my wife's bloomers what lock it'll fit inta."

Marc tried to keep his hopes from rising inordinately. It had been a day of disappointment. "So Mrs. Burgess was right: Badger did steal the key to the hatch."

"Which don't mean he used it."

"I realize that. But this definitely makes Badger our prime suspect once again."

"Maybe somebody in Irishtown suspected the same thing and decided to save us the price of a rope."

Cobb stared at the fallen giant, awed by his vulnerability despite his size. "Looks like he's been sleepin' rough," he said. "Them burrs and bits of hay on his shirt front didn't get there from the tumble he took inta the ditch."

"And what's this?" Marc said, noticing for the first time something white and crisp sticking out of the side pocket of Badger's overalls.

"Better not touch the body, Major."

Marc ignored the dig and pulled out into the mid-afternoon light a single sheet of notepaper, its elaborate watermark clearly visible.

"What is it?" Cobb asked, coming around to Marc.

"What I've been looking for since Tuesday morning," he said. He passed the handwritten note to Cobb.

Tuesday, 2 p.m.

Badger:

Here is the 30 dollars you requested. My advice is to leave the city and all its temptations.

Sincerely,
Alasdair Hepburn

Cobb's eyes widened. "By golly, Major, I think you've got him."

Marc was patting the other pockets in the overalls, ignoring his own advice about contaminating the crime scene. There was too much at stake to fuss over protocol. "There's a wad of something in this rear pocket. I'll wager it's thirty dollars' worth of blood money."

"This sure wasn't no robbery, then," Cobb opined, "and I can't see any of the thugs up here shootin' him and not goin' through his pockets."

"This looks more and more like the work of a quick-strike,

paid assassin, somebody who knew exactly where to find his target. And I know who put him up to it."

"Where ya goin?" Cobb called, as Marc sprinted up to the path and startled Wilkie, who was dozing on his feet like a sun-drugged horse.

"To bring a blackguard to heel," Marc said, and disappeared down Jarvis.

WHEN UNA BADGER ANSWERED HIS KNOCK, Marc drew her quietly onto the stoop and, as he had promised, gave her the news that her brother had been found shot to death. Having braced herself for just such an eventuality, she accepted the news with stoic resignation. After a moment to collect herself, she thanked Marc, and then followed his advice that she go directly to the police station to wait for more details. She naturally assumed that one of Badger's cronies had done the deed, and Marc did not disabuse her, even though he now knew the matter to be less straightforward and more sinister. But the sight of that brave, grieving woman gave him added incentive to do what had to be done. He entered the home of Alasdair Hepburn with all the tact of an outraged bailiff, striding the short distance to the door of the "whist club's" lair and flinging it open.

Hepburn was sitting alone at the card-table. He looked startled for an instant, but as soon as he saw who it was, he gave Marc a grimacing little smile and rose halfway in his chair. "Miss Badger usually does that," he said with a glance at the open door.

"Miss Badger had to go to the Court House on an urgent family matter," Marc said, annoyed that he suddenly found himself short of breath. "I took the liberty of showing myself in."

Hepburn raised his brow slightly and said amiably enough, "So I see." Evidently he had no inkling of what was to come, which suited Marc just fine. "Well, now that you're fully in, please take a seat. Miss Badger said you had called earlier."

"I prefer to stand for what I have come to say."

"As you wish. As one of His Lordship's amanuenses, I presume you're here on some errand relating to the commissioner's agenda here in Toronto?"

Marc bristled at the barb but decided to maintain his post on the moral high ground. "I am here representing both His Lordship and the Toronto constabulary."

The banker's brow again lifted a single notch. "Indeed. Then you have my undivided attention, for I hold both offices in high regard."

"Do you?"

"Is that a question, sir, or an accusation?"

Marc ignored the riposte. "I have come here to ask you some questions in regard to the events of Monday evening and early Tuesday morning, and I demand—in the name of His Lordship, the governor of the Canadas—that you give me straightforward and truthful answers." With a sinking feeling, Marc realized that he should have brought Cobb with him, for even if he compelled incriminating testimony from Hepburn, he would have no witness to it, and it could all be retracted and contradicted after the fact.

"I have never been known to do otherwise, young man, though I would appreciate your putting your queries with a more courteous tongue."

"I'm not seeking a mortgage!" Marc snapped.

"You may thank your lucky stars for that." Hepburn calmly opened a humidor beside him. "Would you care for a cigar?"

"No, thank you." Marc began to feel a tad ridiculous standing in front of the card-strewn whist table while the accused sat peacefully in his favourite armchair. "Now, about the events of Monday evening."

"I assume you are referring to the unfortunate death of a whore somewhere in Irishtown."

"How do you know about that?"

"My wife told me. It's the talk of the town, apparently. You see, we don't often have murders of any kind here in Toronto— unlike London." He gave Marc the practised, pecuniary smile of a self-satisfied banker. "But I fail to see how I may have anything to contribute to your investigation, if that is what you are about."

"I intend, sir, to show you exactly how you did contribute to the death of Sarah McConkey."

"Then please, proceed. You have me intrigued." Hepburn reached for his tinderbox. "Do you mind if I smoke while you talk?"

"Let me start with the fact that, according to Mrs. Hepburn, you and she were driven, alone, out to Spadina."

"That is true and is our usual custom on such occasions."

"But I put it to you that her claim that you two rode home together in the same manner is not true!"

"Is that so? Are you now about to tell me that it was the anonymous 'jewel thief' you described to Mrs. Hepburn with such fanciful mendacity who joined us on the way back?"

Marc winced but was able to play his trump card: "Not at all. It was Handford Ellice you brought here to the city, Lady Durham's nephew."

The brow lifted again. "You are referring to the shy young man whom we invited to join us at whist in Baldwin's card room?"

"Don't play the naif with me, sir. You are perfectly aware

whose ego you flattered and whom you plied with drink for two hours before midnight."

"To be truthful, and I presume that's what you wish of me, the lad was too shy to introduce himself, but yes, one of the attendants indicated who he was sometime after he'd sat down at our table."

"Are you denying that you and your accomplices took young Ellice off to the drinks table at regular intervals, until he was thoroughly drunk?"

"This lad, though diffident, was old enough to insist on his right to drink whiskey. We accompanied him in order to limit his consumption, not increase it."

"The result was the same, either way. By midnight he was inebriated and ostensibly slipped away to his chamber to sleep it off."

"Ostensibly?" Hepburn lit a tinder stick and applied it to the end of his cigar.

"Someone in your group suggested to Ellice that a ride to town and its potential pleasures awaited him at the stables, should he so wish to take advantage of it."

"You know this for a fact?"

"We have testimony from several servants and grooms that place Ellice in a fancy barouche some minutes past midnight, when many of the older guests were departing."

"There were many such vehicles there when Mrs. Hepburn and I left about that time." The cigar end reddened and Hepburn took a soothing puff.

"But I am certain that it was your carriage that contained Ellice."

"Which implies that both my wife and I are lying."

"Yes."

Hepburn appeared not to take offence at this unseemly

imputation, but his eyes did narrow perceptibly. "And what are we supposed to have done with the lad? Dumped him onto Front Street in the middle of the night in a strange city?"

"Nothing of the kind. You dropped Mrs. Hepburn off here, then you and Ellice walked up to Lot Street, one block north, and entered Irishtown."

Hepburn guffawed, choking on his cigar. "You're jesting! Go into that den of thieves and cutthroats after midnight on my own?"

"You were well known in there, sir, and I have learned in the past two days that your status as one of Madame Renée's regulars would have given you immunity and right of passage. I suspect there may have been a system of passwords in addition to coded knocks on a scarlet door."

"You have a vivid imagination, I'll say that for you."

"You knocked on that door, pushed Ellice in, and left before you were recognized—knowing that the lad's ready money and harmless demeanour would get him serviced by one or another of the girls."

"I trust that you're not suggesting that the purchase of the favours of a female is a crime? If so, then few gentlemen in this town or any other would escape hanging."

Hepburn's feigned amusement was almost credible.

"The crime, if you like, was to have Lord Durham's nephew found in a sleazy brothel, in the certain knowledge that any sort of scandal among the earl's entourage would surely scupper his mission and lead to his immediate recall."

"But who would know of this indiscretion besides the man who directed him there?" Hepburn seemed to be toying with his accuser, as if Marc were an impecunious client begging for a loan he knew would be refused.

"What would Ellice do when he woke up in Irishtown?" Marc

replied. "He wouldn't even know what city he was in! By morning, Lady Durham would be in a panic and forced to raise the hue and cry for her missing nephew—who might have been kidnapped or murdered, for all she knew. In these times any such calamity is possible. The chances of keeping the sordid business quiet were slim indeed."

"So the perpetrator of this so-called crime must have had a political motive?"

"Exactly. For instance, a Tory banker and charter member of the Family Compact, whose fortunes are threatened by the continuing instability and the failure of the royal authority to calm the uppity natives."

"And if young Ellice had managed to crawl back to the city, hire himself a gig, and drive to Spadina undetected, then what?"

Was the man actually enjoying this game?

"That possibility was anticipated and forestalled."

"Indeed. Sure you won't have a cigar? Or a chair?"

"Because of that necessity the whole scheme went awry." Marc found himself pacing back and forth across the room like a Crown counsel, feeling just a bit foolish as he fired his barbs both obliquely and directly at the witness in his baize box.

"It did?"

"I suggest, sir, that you paid Michael Badger, a former employee who subsequently worked as a bruiser in Madame Renée's brothel, to sneak into the house in the middle of the night and create some kind of disturbance, something that would be certain to expose young Ellice publicly by involving the police."

"How very clever."

"Too clever by half, however. For what you didn't know was that Badger bore a grudge against the madam and her business, and in a sudden rage stabbed the prostitute to death and fled."

That remark got the banker's full attention. He removed the cigar from his lips and watched it slowly descend in his fingers to the table. "Ellice was found beside the murdered girl?"

"You know damn well he was!" Marc stopped and leaned on the baize cover with both hands. "You've already admitted knowing about the stabbing of Sarah McConkey, and since it was you who led Ellice to her, how could you *not* connect the two events?"

Hepburn looked genuinely shocked. Marc was pleased that he had finally pricked that maddening façade. "But Matilda only told me that some harlot had been stabbed in Irishtown. Even the rumour mill has been starved for details."

"Well, sir, now you know. Your conniving plot to embarrass Lord Durham resulted in the vicious murder of an innocent girl, however fallen we may think she was. You paid the assassin to enter the premises. You seduced the young man and led him to that door. In my book that makes you an accessory to murder. You are as guilty as Badger. What is more, I think you've known since Tuesday morning exactly what must have happened."

"You're certain it was Ellice there?"

Marc suddenly realized that Ellice's secret was now out. But then if the killers were not exposed by eight o'clock, all would be lost anyway. He plunged ahead. "There is more."

"How could there be?"

"We found Michael Badger's body an hour ago in a ditch at the end of Jarvis Street—where you left it after shooting him point-blank in the heart." While Marc didn't believe this, he felt justified in using it for its shock value.

Hepburn's jaw dropped. "Now, young man, this has gone far enough. I've humoured you because I've nothing better to do with the remainder of the afternoon. But Michael Badger was an employee of mine, and my housekeeper's only brother. In fact, he was

like a son to me—Matilda and I have no children of our own—
and I am shocked and grieved to hear of his death. I thought
he had got safely out of town and away from his creditors." He
started to get up. "I must tell Mrs. Hepburn immediately. Does
Una know?"

"Yes. She's at the Court House now. But I must, as a deputized
constable, ask you to sit down until my interrogation is completed."

"But your accusations are preposterous! You've spun a fantasti-
cal tale that would be more pertinent to *The Mysteries of Udolpho*
than to Toronto. You haven't offered a shred of proof—"

"Ah, but I have the proof, sir. Hard-and-fast evidence that you
did lead Ellice to the murder scene and did hire Badger to invade
the premises. That should be enough to get an indictment from
the magistrate."

"I don't believe you." Hepburn glared at his accuser but stayed
in his seat.

"First of all, we have testimony from your stable hand and barouche driver that you did have a third party in your carriage, one
fitting the description of Ellice."

"But I know for a fact that Willy Falmer did not give Constable Cobb that version of events."

"True, at least not yesterday. I'm sure that out of loyalty or
other more tangible considerations he backed up Mrs. Hepburn's
version, but he has since changed his mind."

Marc hoped this lie would be sufficient to unnerve the suspect.
Instead, Hepburn smiled tightly and stared hard at Marc. "That is
not possible, sir. Willy Falmer left town at dawn this morning. He
is on his way to join his brothers somewhere beyond the Missis-
sippi River."

Good God, the man was more cunning than Marc had

anticipated. It was time to play his second trump card. He drew out the note he had plucked from Badger's pocket. "I have here, sir, all the proof I shall need to link you to the paid assassin. This note, foolishly signed by you, was found on Badger's body, along with a stolen key to facilitate his entry into the brothel." Marc dropped the letter on the table and Hepburn glanced at it, looking puzzled.

"This is my letter to Michael," he said. "And?"

"And it accompanied thirty dollars, also found on Badger, the money he earned by entering the brothel and stabbing a girl to death. Mr. Hepburn, you have a clear motive for leading Ellice there, and here is incontrovertible proof that you hired a bruiser to cause some kind of mayhem that night."

Hepburn paused to gather his emotions and his thoughts. He stubbed out the cigar. He flushed and then paled. Beads of sweat popped out on his forehead. "This is all too much. I am over-whelmed."

"Do you wish to confess, then?"

Hepburn smiled wanly. "I'm afraid not."

"But you've just admitted that the incriminating letter is your own!"

"It is. But the money was Michael's, not mine."

"Surely you can come up with a more plausible explanation than that."

"It's true. You see, sir, Michael was in many ways a good man, a sort of gentle giant. He was not in the least violent, though he knew how to intimidate if he had to. He was more of a conniver and would-be confidence man, a charmer of gullible ladies. I don't believe for a second that he was capable of murdering anyone in cold blood. His principal weakness was gambling, and it looks as if it led to his death. He was a hard worker whenever he needed to earn money to feed his vice. I paid him well, and both his sister and I tried to get him to save money and straighten his ways. We were both upset when he went to work for Madame Renée."

"I am not a fool, sir. I suspect you were quite happy with that particular employment when you began hatching your little plot."

"Then in January he came to me and asked me to deposit his wages in my bank, wages from Madame Renée and from the odd jobs he was doing for me. The account was set up so that only I could withdraw the money or both of us in person. It was the only way he knew to stop himself from squandering his earnings in the dicing dens. If you wish proof of this arrangement, you'll find all the relevant and notarized documents at the Commercial Bank."

"But what else would he need savings for? He merely wrote worthless promissory notes and got himself into serious trouble at the Tinker's Dam."

"Incredible as it may seem, he was planning to go off to the Iowa Territory and try his luck at farming."

"So you're telling me that this note was in response to Badger's written request for his own money."

"I am. Una Badger brought me that request Tuesday at luncheon. I recognized Michael's handwriting, as I'm sure Una did when she surreptitiously read it."

The man was ingenious and abominable. His alternative explanation provided a foolproof cover story for the dastardly transaction that had resulted in Sarah's death. "But you did not go back to the bank to get his money, did you?" Marc said, trying to hide his desperation.

"No, I didn't. Una described how scared and distraught he had been that morning and begged me to help him immediately. According to our long-standing arrangement, I was to send him his money—in a dire emergency—by messenger to the post office on George Street, where he would pick it up. I assume he feared his pursuers would be watching this house. So I got the cash from my own safe here and had it delivered. I can give you the name of the lad who took it there."

Marc sat down at last. It was all coming unravelled. He could see no way to challenge Hepburn's devious account, especially if the notarized documents existed and Una Badger became his unwitting corroborator.

"I know you and your wife gave Mr. Ellice a ride to town, and I know you led him down to the brothel. And I'm equally certain that your whist-playing chums are co-conspirators. I am deeply grieved that, for the moment, I cannot prove these things. But I am warning you that I will not stop trying."

"You cannot prove what did not happen."

Marc sighed. "What still baffles me, though, is why your wife would lie for you. Perhaps when the grisly facts of what happened at Madame Renée's come out, as they must, she will change her mind."

Hepburn's withering look said, Don't count on it.

Suddenly Marc had another inspiration. "I think I can guess why she lied for you. I'll wager she knows all about your addiction to the girls at Madame Renée's, a squalid obsession that could potentially ruin your standing in the community. You're a banker and a pillar of your church and, alas, an habitué of Irishtown stews." For a split second Hepburn looked abashed. Marc pressed his advantage. "She is probably ashamed and afraid. I pity her," he said, without pity.

"Are you quite finished? If so, I have grieving of my own to do."

Marc showed himself out.

FOURTEEN

When Marc reached the station, he found only Gussie French scribbling frantically at his table, heedless of spattering ink and ravenous flies. "Has Cobb come back?"

"Gone off home," Gussie muttered without dropping a stitch. "Lucky bugger."

"And Sarge?"

Gussie appended an extra period for emphasis to the sentence he had just finished, and looked up. "Chief Sturges went off to find Sir George and tell him to call off the fox hunt." He nudged a sheet of paper with the feathered end of his quill. "Cobb left you that," he said, and resumed scribbling.

Gussie had taken down from Cobb a summary of Angus Withers's comments after he'd examined the body of Michael Badger in the ditch where it lay. The bullet appeared to have entered the chest in a slightly upward trajectory. The shooter must have been shorter than Badger. The lead ball had struck bone—a rib or vertebra—and thus had barely exited the body: Withers found its misshapen remnant in Badger's shirt. He concluded from its size and the probable force of the entry that it came from a small-bore pistol, the kind easily concealed and deadly only at close range. The debris found on the victim's shirt front included gunpowder, bits of grass, and wisps of dry straw. Thirty dollars had been wadded in one of his pockets. Estimated time of death: between one and four in the morning.

That was it. Not a lot, but Marc found himself unable to care very much. The interview with Alasdair Hepburn had left him angry, confused, and ultimately drained of emotion. He knew he ought to feel at least some sense of triumph in that Michael Badger—on the strength of the key he was carrying and the motive supplied by Mrs. Burgess (with intent to rob possibly thrown in)—would be fingered for the murder. There would be no trial, nor any need for anyone to know or care who the aristocratic stranger was. Handford Ellice could be released to accompany Lord and Lady Durham back to Quebec tomorrow. Sure, rumours would circulate and fester, though Marc doubted whether Hepburn himself would be the source: that spiteful sword could prove to be double-edged. But a public scandal would definitely be averted. Still, Marc did not feel in the least triumphant.

He decided to leave a note for Chief Sturges explaining why he had taken the letter from Badger's body and admitting reluctantly that it had turned out to be innocent and unrelated to either murder. He took a step towards the door of the chief's office.

"I wouldn't go in there if I was you," Gussie cautioned.

"I thought you said Sturges was out."

"He is. But there's a female in there, waitin'."

Marc had no choice but to conduct one more interview. He opened the door carefully and sat with Una for a moment before asking her to tell him about her brother.

"Michael was ten years younger than me," Una Badger explained. She dabbed at her eyes with Marc's handkerchief. "Our mother died when he was six, so it was me who raised him and looked out for him. I knew him, Mr. Edwards, as a mother knows her own child. I knew his good points and his bad ones—and he had plenty of both."

Una confirmed the essential details of Hepburn's story. Badger did have some sort of arrangement with his employer to help him hold on to his earnings. While she did not know for sure, she assumed the note she had taken from Michael and delivered to Hepburn on Tuesday was connected with that arrangement. And, yes, Mr. Hepburn had been very kind to Michael, despite his gruff manner and quick temper. He had tried to dissuade him from his gambling and binge drinking, but had always taken him back regardless and given him work. In fact, a makeshift bunkhouse had been set up in one of the unused barns at the back of the property so that he would always have a place to sleep, day or night. But he had not used it to hide out on Tuesday or yesterday. She had checked it many times.

"So your brother would have confided in you?" Marc said.

"About some things, yes."

"Mr. Hepburn told me that he noticed some change in Michael after the new year."

"That's so. Michael came and told me that he was twenty-five and it was time for him to do something decent with his life. He talked about going away to the States, far from his cronies and the habits he couldn't seem to break."

"For which he would need to earn money and not gamble it away."

"Yes. And he tried, Mr. Edwards. Only God and I know how hard he tried. And now he's dead, shot by those terrible men—"

She sobbed into Marc's hanky.

"I'm sorry, but it all seems so unfair. He stopped drinking, he really did. Mr. Hepburn gave him work making shelves and cupboards for his new library. I tried to talk him out of being a bruiser in Irishtown, but he said the money was too good and, besides, he liked being there. When he come here on Tuesday, I knew something horrible had happened to him, but I thought, He's going to get away now because he *has* to: not to our cousins in Port Sarnia but all the way across the border where he'll be safe from his demons and be happy."

Marc reached across the chief's desk and laid a hand gently on hers. "But we were told that Michael *had* run up more gambling debts in recent weeks. He may have been saving his money at home, but he was issuing paper promises up at the Tinker's Dam."

Una merely nodded. Then through a screen of tears, she said, "I knew he couldn't stay away from that place as long as he lived in the city and as long as he had ready cash from that madam woman. But I swear, Mr. Edwards, it was only two or three binges: most of the time since January he was sober and work-ing—for Mr. Hepburn or in Irishtown."

"Unfortunately, he had a serious falling out with Mrs. Burgess on Monday. He owed her a lot of money. We found on him a key to a secret door in the brothel, and you and Mr. Hepburn have confirmed that he came for money ostensibly to leave town. I'm sorry to have to tell you this, but the police are going to name him as the murderer of Sarah McConkey."

The shock of this revelation registered on Una Badger's face and was slowly absorbed. Then she straightened her back and stared directly into Marc's eyes.

"Mr. Edwards, Michael Badger was a gentle man. He never swatted a fly if he could avoid it. I know. I watched him grow up. As a boy, he was big and awkward with a stook of orange hair that stuck up every which way. He was teased something terrible. But he never struck back, even though he was twice as strong as his tormentors. Do you know what he did?"

"Please tell me."

"He would pick up the closest one, give him a bear hug until he said uncle, then tip him upside down and quietly shake him until the other boys laughed. Then he dropped him and laughed with them. They soon got to like Michael. He had his faults, but people liked him. And he was fun to be with. He could talk the ear off a donkey!" Her face lit up momentarily at the memory of what was past and would not return.

"Still," Marc said hesitantly, "he became a bruiser in a brothel."

"But don't you see, sir, if he couldn't sweet-talk a drunken sailor out of being belligerent, why, he'd just give him a bear hug and flip him topsy-turvy."

"And Madame Renée didn't entertain too many sailors?"

Una smiled. "Michael called her customers 'pillow-puffs.' His only worry was that he would meet one of them on the street and get in Dutch for recognizing him."

Had Badger possibly encountered Hepburn at Madame Renée's? Was that the reason for Hepburn's "friendliness" towards him? Or was it a simple and deadly case of blackmail? What did it matter now anyway? Badger was gone and Hepburn was too clever to be implicated in either crime.

Una Badger suddenly grasped both of Marc's hands. "Michael couldn't have hurt any of those girls, not a hair on their heads. He liked them. He treated them like younger sisters. He took them little presents. He wouldn't let any of the men be insulting to them. And he never touched them in that . . . that other way."

"But—"

"Mr. Edwards, you've got to tell the police and the magistrate that my brother couldn't kill anyone!"

• • •

UNA BADGER HAD LEFT TO GO up to Dr. Withers's surgery to claim her brother's body. Marc's head was spinning too much for him to be able to compose a note for Wilfrid Sturges, but he did not need to, for the chief himself soon arrived. Marc rattled off a highly edited and barely coherent explanation of why he had bearded Alasdair Hepburn in his home, but his embarrassment was scarcely noticed. The chief was a happy and relieved man and cared not that a prominent citizen may have been needlessly bullied.

"Stop worryin', Marc. We've all done our duty and then some. We'll have this whole business wrapped up by noon tomorrow. We'll make a sweep of the rot around the Tinker's Dam, but it's not likely we'll ever find out who done us a favour by poppin' off Mr. Badger. Still, we can safely go up and tell His Lordy-ship that his nephew's off the hook."

Marc nodded numbly.

"Do you want me to tell 'im?" Sturges offered affably.

"No. Thanks anyway. I'm to make a full report to him at eight o'clock. I'll just go on home to have some supper and compose my notes."

"Be sure and put in a good word fer us peelers."

"That will be a pleasure, Wilfrid."

Out on the stone walk, Marc found himself fighting for breath. Confused and frustrated he might be, but one thought rang in his mind clear and unequivocal: Michael Badger did not murder Sarah McConkey.

"MARC, STOP THIS PACING UP AND down," Beth said, "you're gonna wear a path in the new rug."

Marc halted, said nothing, then began to pace again.

"You're scaring Charlene."

"She's in the kitchen burning the dumplings."

Beth laughed, and Marc sat down, his head in his hands.

"I've never seen you like this before."

"I've never felt like this before. Don't you see how impossible the situation is? In two hours I've got to walk up to Government House and inform Lord and Lady Durham that the police have attributed the murder to Michael Badger for reasons that have nothing to do with Handford Ellice. And everybody is supposed to be happy about it."

"But you and Una Badger are the only ones who think he didn't do it."

"I'm certain of it. Just as I'm positive that Alasdair Hepburn lured Ellice to that scarlet door and bribed Badger to cause some sort of commotion in there—an elaborate prank perhaps, intended principally to embarrass Lord Durham and give him something besides Upper Canada to be concerned about."

"But you said Badger wasn't involved. You've lost me."

"He was supposed to sneak in there, but if he did—and we'll never know for certain—he must have got quite a grisly surprise."

"You figure he may've found Sarah dead?"

"It's possible. He arrived at Hepburn's later that morning in terrible shape, according to Una. But one way or another, he did not kill Sarah. Everything I've heard about him so far suggests that he would not have murdered in a sudden rage, and certainly not one of those girls."

"So an innocent man's reputation will be sacrificed to keep the bigwig safe?"

"I don't see how I can stop it."

"You're certain the key you found on Badger fits the little door?" Beth suddenly said.

Marc smiled. "Not yet. I suppose Cobb or Sarge will check that tomorrow. They're in no hurry now that they're sure they've got their man. Anyway, I wouldn't bet one of Charlene's dumplings on it."

Beth nodded, then said evenly, "And there's Lady Durham, too."

"What do you mean?"

"She has her own doubts about Handford. If you tell her husband what you've just told me about Badger, then she'll leave here never knowing for sure whether her sister's boy is truly blameless."

Marc groaned. It was getting worse. "But I can't lie to Lord Durham. He wants the truth."

"If he doesn't ask, you could just leave out some of the details."

"Don't tempt me."

There was a clatter of errant pots from the next room.

Beth said, "If Badger didn't do it, then who did?"

"One of the women of the house or someone from Madame Charlotte's, I suppose."

"You don't seem all that interested."

"I would be if I could find a motive. But I'll be damned if I can think of one. I've observed the women closely. While the two madams are rivals and routinely disparage each other, I saw them embrace at the funeral. Similarly, I could detect no serious tensions among the girls of either house. Sarah was stabbed to death with one brutal, savage blow. Petty jealousy and simple revenge do not seem appropriate to such a crime."

Beth looked thoughtful for a moment. "Have you considered betrayal?"

"Betrayal?"

"Sometimes love can turn to hate real quick."

Marc was about to question Beth further when the first whiff of burnt food struck his nostrils.

From the kitchen came a mortified cry: "Help!"

COBB SAT ON A STOOL IN the summer kitchen and watched Dora prepare supper. Beads of sweat dropped from her nose and chin onto the bevel of her half-exposed bosom. Normally he found this sight both appetizing and erotic. Today, though, had been a long way from normal. The shock of seeing, close up, his second bloodied corpse in three days had unnerved him. He thought he now knew why the Major had tossed his uniform aside. It was one thing to face the sanguinary results of fistfights in dives or alleys, but the stilted, blank gaze of dead eyes was something utterly different: it was like encountering the moment after your own death.

Dora was humming, a deep and satisfied sound from the vast drum of her diaphragm. He found this, too, irritating, for what he needed most was for her to give him leave to talk about the events of the week and lay some of the angst upon her unwarranted contentment. But the pact they had made was solemn and inviolable: no talk about the travails of one's profession without explicit, advance permission. Cobb realized, though never admitted it, that he was the principal beneficiary of this agreement, as it allowed him to escape yet another gory epic of childbirth and its messy aftermath. He shifted his bottom on the stool and coughed.

"Well, Mister Cobb, let's have it. I ain't gonna get a peaceful minute till you tell me what's eatin' ya." She continued stirring the stew.

Cobb proceeded immediately to pour out his complaint, providing Dora with enough detail to assuage his pent-up frustrations but not enough to give away any state secrets.

"But the worst of it was that bed with all the girl's blood

soaked into it and some so-called gentleman lyin' stark naked on them bloody sheets. I been havin' nightmares ever since."

"Don't I know it. You been pokin' yer elbows inta me and mutterin' more gibberish than you usually do."

Cobb shook his head. "I don't know how ya do it, luv—pullin' babies inta this world covered with slime and muck—"

"And you say this happened in one of them shady houses up in Irishtown?"

Cobb closed his eyes. "Christ, I can't get her outta my head! Poor Sarah."

Dora stopped her stirring. "A girl named Sarah, you say?"

"Sarah McConkey," Cobb said before he could catch himself. "Jesus! Nobody's supposed to—"

"I heard there was a funeral fer her up on John Street, but I didn't know how she died."

"You know her?"

"I oughta. I helped deliver her baby a couple of months ago."

Cobb listened with increasing interest as Dora narrated the story of her involvement with Sarah McConkey. One day in late March or early April, a message arrived around midnight that a young woman needed the midwife. Dora picked up her bag, which was always packed and ready for use, and headed out into the chilly dark as she had hundreds of times in her long career as a midwife. The anonymous lad led her up to some place around Hospital Street. She couldn't be certain of the exact location because it was an abandoned barn and they approached it through a field. To her surprise the barn was fitted out with a proper bed, two chairs, and a few domestic utensils. In the late stages of labour was a young, pretty, brown-haired girl who managed a gritty smile and said only that her name was Sarah. "McConkey," the boy had added before the woman's male companion shoved him away.

When Dora had requested hot water, the man, who was very nervous and obviously concerned, replied that he and his woman were impoverished squatters and had no access to hot water or anything else not already in the barn. Accustomed to such situations, Dora never pressed for more information than she needed to know. Her task was to deliver babies while doing her best to keep their mothers alive. While Dora tended to these duties, Sarah's man paced up and down near the door of the barn. About two hours later Dora pulled the infant into the dank air of that profane stable. It was dead. Sarah moaned and mercifully passed out. The delivery had seemed normal, but the child had choked on the cord and died moments before entering the world. Dora set its still body beside her and knelt down to look to the afterbirth. She heard the man come up behind her. In the lantern's light the dead gaze of the babe stared upward.

"He let out a cry of anguish the likes I've never heard before in all my years in this business."

Dora assured him that Sarah had come through the ordeal in good shape. She gave him a vial of laudanum and instructions how to administer it. She offered to take the corpse and see to its burial, but he said he would do so himself.

"It was such a beautiful child," Dora said, giving the stew a motherly stir. "A boy it was, with the brightest orange hair you ever did see."

It was Cobb's turn to go unnaturally still. "What did this so-called husband look like?"

"Big fella. With a bushel and a half of hair, just like the babe's."

COBB HAD NO NOTION WHAT DORA'S unexpected revelation might mean. But he knew the Major would want to hear it, and with less than two hours before he was scheduled to appear before His Lordship, Marc would want to know now. So it was that Cobb left one supper suspended without explanation and fatally disrupted another. He rushed into the Edwardses' cottage without knocking and burst straight into the dining room.

"I got somethin' to tell ya!" he cried, and his look alone prompted Marc to get up, push aside a charred dumpling, and lead Cobb onto the front porch.

"Let's have it, then, old friend," Marc said, alarmed at Cobb's beet-red face and anguished breathing. "Take your time. The world isn't about to end."

As coherently as he could under the circumstances, Cobb relayed to Marc the gist of Dora's tale.

Marc said nothing for half a minute, then, "Are you sure it was Sarah McConkey?"

"There ain't a doubt. And who else could the father be besides Badger?"

Marc nodded. "All right, then. Let's go."

"Where to?"

"To beard a lioness in her den!"

Trotting dutifully in his partner's wake, Cobb was heard to mutter, "Not again!"

FIFTEEN

Marc's mind churned all the way to Madame Renée's, but he was not yet ready to share his thoughts with Cobb. They arrived to find the place shuttered and still.

"They're gone off!" a voice called to them.

Cobb recognized the urchin loitering nearby: it was one of the lads who had tossed obloquy upon his nose the day before.

"All of 'em?"

"Yup. I seen 'em luggin' their things up the road."

Cobb threw him a penny. "I'm gonna ask fer a raise in pay," he said to Marc.

"I think Mrs. Burgess is still in there," Marc said.

"It sure looks deserted. They've scarpered, as Sarge likes to say. And why do ya figure the birds've flown the coop?"

Marc pounded on the door with his fist. "I know you're in there, Mrs. Burgess. Open up, please. I must talk with you."

Fearing his friend had slipped a gear, Cobb touched Marc on the shoulder. "I think ya oughta let it go, Major. We done our damnedest."

Marc wriggled the door handle. The scarlet door swung open.

Mrs. Burgess was sitting in the near-dark in her customary easy chair. The air in the parlour was heavy and stale, but she appeared to take no notice of it, nor of Marc when he sat down across from her.

"Mrs. Burgess?"

She did not look up or reply, but her slumping posture and gray pallor told Marc that here was a woman on the verge of collapse.

"Please leave me alone." The voice was hollow and without emotion despite the plea.

"I can't do that," Marc said. "There are important matters that you and I must discuss, however badly you feel."

No response.

"Where are your girls?"

"Sarah's dead."

"I mean Carrie and Molly and Frieda."

"I sent them away."

"For good?"

"They'll be fine."

"You're closing up shop?"

"Ruined," she mumbled. "All ruined."

"Cobb, would you bring Mrs. Burgess a glass of brandy from the sideboard?"

Cobb poured a generous glass from a decanter and brought it over. Marc put it into Mrs. Burgess's hands, noticing how icy cold they were, and helped raise the glass towards her lips. To his relief she drank a mouthful, coughed, then drank another.

Cobb and Marc sat waiting. After what seemed an eternity and with a clock ticking nearby as a reminder of the eight o'clock deadline, Mrs. Burgess looked up and let them feast upon the devastation of her face.

"You loved Sarah," Marc began. "So I need to know why you killed her."

"Why do we do anything?" she replied.

"I'm going to describe what I think happened on Monday last, then I want you to tell me where I'm wrong, if I am. Do you understand?"

"I'm not deaf and dumb," she said with an echo of her former aplomb.

"I'll begin with events you may not know about. Out at the governor's gala on Monday evening, one of your regular gentleman customers—"

"Callers."

"Callers—got a young man drunk."

"The pale gentleman."

"Yes, who happened to be Lord Durham's nephew."

"A toff's toff."

Cobb ahemed loudly but was ignored.

"This so-called gentleman got young Handford Ellice drunk and drove him from Spadina to Hospital Street, then guided him here. Using the coded knock, he got you to open the door even though you were shutting down for the night. He pushed the lad inside and ran off. However, I'm certain that you knew who it was."

Mrs. Burgess shook her head, discreet as ever.

"I accept your account of what happened next. As it was Sarah's turn, she led the pathetic and near-comatose fellow into her room, where, in all probability, he fell deeply asleep without doing a thing he had paid for."

"He paid for her time. The performance was up to him."

Marc was encouraged that his comments provoked some of Mrs. Burgess's familiar feistiness.

"Meanwhile, you and the girls went to your own bedrooms. When Molly fell asleep beside you, you got up—ostensibly to check on Sarah, if anybody asked—and padded into her chamber. As you expected, Sarah was slumbering and her gentleman caller snoring like an exhausted hog."

"And?"

"And you slipped to the bedside, slid a hand under Sarah's pillow, pulled out her dagger, and stabbed her once—viciously—in the throat." Marc delivered these words with an emphatic hiss.

Mrs. Burgess's response was almost plaintive: "Why would I want to kill dear, sweet Sarah?"

"That is a question I asked myself on Tuesday and in every hour since, but I found no answer convincing enough to accuse you or your girls of murder. But I'll come back to that in a moment."

Mrs. Burgess took another swallow of brandy. She was now watching Marc with a mixture of wariness and defiance.

"As Sarah's lifeblood spouted from her body, you scuttled back to bed and lay down beside Molly. A little while later, probably while your heart was still pounding with the enormity of what you had done, the wretched Ellice—awakened but groggy with drink or worse—discovered the horror beside him, cried out, instinctively pulled the knife from Sarah's throat, then fainted dead away. When you and Molly reached the room, you found Sarah dead and her caller unconscious with the knife in his hand.

"How convenient, eh? Here was a way out: fetch the police and put the blame on the pale gentleman with the murder weapon still in his grip. The lack of bloody footprints in the room was enough to give credence to your story. For the first time since your impulsive slaying of the girl, you began to hope there was a way to salvage the situation. By the time Cobb arrived, your natural intelligence had started functioning again. Your ruse worked and you were prepared to let the chips fall where they would."

"But my business was ruined. Why would I destroy what I'd taken years to create?"

Norah Burgess, it seemed, had decided to play out this game to the end, as if the sport of it was all that was left to her.

"That's what kept me from pursuing you or your girls. I observed you here and at the funeral service. The affection that obviously bound you all, extending even to your competitor in the profession, were not faked for public consumption. They were real and deep. I was sincerely touched by them, as I was by Sarah's undeserved death."

"You had no business coming to the service."

"What you didn't know until Monday morning, and what Cobb didn't learn until an hour ago, was that Sarah and Michael Badger were lovers. The child that you and your girls eagerly anticipated throughout Sarah's pregnancy was fathered not by some randy employer or anonymous sailor up at Madame Charlotte's, but by Badger himself."

Norah's gaze hardened.

"I've been reminded that betrayal can be the motive for murder among friends and lovers, or parents and children—turning love into searing hate in an instant. And here was a classic example. Sarah had become, by your own admission, a surrogate daughter. The girls pampered her like a younger and still innocent sister. As you intimated to Cobb, you harboured hopes that it was not too late to rehabilitate Sarah, to save her from the awful business that was your only choice after a failed marriage. I suspect you had too much schooling or were too independent a spirit to become a housekeeper or governess under the thumb of some doltish squire."

"I never found one who wasn't."

"But all the while, Sarah was leading a clandestine life of her own. I'm not sure how much of their relationship Badger revealed to you on Monday morning, to spite you after you refused to advance him any more money, but it was enough. In this house, they had given no sign of their liaison, and that must have taken much skill and subterfuge. They met when they could in a stable at the back of a property on Hospital Street. Badger may not have told you that they had met and become lovers just days after Sarah's arrival at the Reverend Finney's home last September. I imagine Badger was doing some work for Finney at the time. However, their shenanigans were seen or suspected by Mrs. Finney, who had Sarah abruptly dismissed. Days later, Sarah was found destitute on Lot Street and conscripted by the opportunistic Madame Charlotte."

"Some lover."

"Oh, I think Michael was hopelessly in love with the sweet and alluring Sarah. But according to his sister, he often had to leave town in a hurry when his gambling pals came looking for their money. Usually he fled to Port Sarnia, where he'd hole up until he'd scavenged sufficient funds to buy his way back to safety. That's undoubtedly where he was when Sarah got thrown out. She didn't know where he was and he had no inkling that she was pregnant—and alone."

"Like we all are, in the end."

"He must have been frantic when he got back. But she had disappeared off the face of the earth. Then, in the market for a bruiser, you somehow got a lead on this giant of a fellow and invited him to take the job. Imagine his surprise when he arrives for work and discovers Sarah, big with a child she assures him is his, and safe and sound in a gentlemen's brothel."

Cobb indicated the brandy bottle to Norah, but she shook her head.

"I can guess what a pleasant winter you all must have passed in this very parlour or in the cozy kitchen in your own quarters. Yours is a hard business, and though I suspect you are a kind person at heart, you had steeled yourself first to survive and ultimately to thrive. Suddenly you have in your midst a young woman who seems to have had little trouble attracting and holding the attention of all those around her: sweet yet earthy, compliant, genuinely affectionate, and yet coldly deceiving when necessary. Then arrives a gentle bear of a man, a bruiser who plays topsy-turvy with obstreperous clients, who makes everybody laugh, and who, incredibly, does not lust after your girls or rouse barbs of jealousy among them. The only blot on this happy landscape is Sarah's loss of the child in early April."

"We would've kept it."

"I don't doubt it. But at least the calamity happened away from here. You only learned of it a few days later when Sarah returned with her tale about the stillbirth."

Norah's eyes widened, bleary but suddenly alert.

"Yes, it was stillborn, whatever taunts Badger may have tossed at you Monday morning. After her return, I'll wager you tried to talk her out of joining the business. But little Sarah was very persuasive. What is more, you didn't know that she had a powerful incentive to earn money, which she soon did by becoming a favourite with your customers. She and Badger were planning to leave the country and start a new life in the United States. They were also likely scheming to leave behind her lover's gambling debts and the advanced wages he owed to you."

"It's only money."

"Maybe so, but the heat was being turned up on Badger. After a binge of gambling on the weekend, he and Sarah had to leave soon if they were ever going to leave at all. He came looking for her that morning, most likely to suggest that she secretly withdraw all her savings and meet him at some prearranged spot. Instead, he found the girls in the city at the ceremonies and you here alone. Ever the charming improviser, he decided to see if he could wheedle a final chunk of cash from his best and most gullible source."

Norah flinched.

"But you turned on him, fed up with his errant ways, his lies, and his truancy. You gave him his walking papers. Badger had been amusing, but he was expendable. However, the gentle giant surprised you and probably himself. Again, unbeknownst to you, I'm certain that he had been offered a bribe a day or two before Lord Durham's arrival to help with a prank some Tory gentlemen thought to play on His Lordship and Mr. Ellice. His role, I have reason to believe, was to steal a key to your hatch and slip in here at two or three in the morning and cause a disturbance—perhaps give whoever was sleeping beside Ellice a punch or two or else a nightmarish scare—enough to expose the earl's nephew as a found-in in a brothel."

"Michael wouldn't have touched any of the girls."

"You're right, but he was perfectly capable of tricking his sponsor out of the bribe money, or perhaps he planned to sneak Sarah out with him. Whatever his thinking, he did take the key. It was found when we discovered his body in a ditch this afternoon."

Marc watched her for a reaction but saw none.

"He had been lying there since the middle of the night when you shot him dead."

Cobb tipped sideways on his chair. Norah took a deep breath and let it out slowly. Her lower lip was trembling, and he realized that she was nearing exhaustion and a possible breakdown. He would have to hurry.

"But back to Sarah. When Michael turned on you Monday

morning, scared and excited and a bit desperate to carry out his bold plan to elope with Sarah and a suitable grubstake, he used the best weapon he had: the truth that Sarah and he were lovers, that they had been deceiving you for months and had made fools of you and your girls. Without giving away their exact plan, he told you—foolishly, imprudently—that Sarah was preparing to leave you for him. You were angry with him, of course, and hurt, and you justifiably gave him the boot and threatened him with bodily harm should he be caught again anywhere in Irishtown. That put Badger in a real bind. He could head up to Front Street to look for Sarah among the thousands of well-wishers, while avoiding Burly Bettman and his thugs, hoping she could get to the bank quickly and they could immediately flee. As it turned out, he also needed to see Mr. Hepburn to retrieve his own savings. Both moves were fraught with danger. What to do? I'm guessing but am pretty sure that he decided to risk everything on a last throw of the dice. I believe he decided to accept the bribe he had up to that point been resisting—he *did* like you and your girls—sneak in here early Tuesday morning, take Sarah out with him, get his earnings from Hepburn and Sarah's from the bank, and take off for the border. That meant lying low for the rest of the day, trusting that Sarah would be able to sweet-talk her way out of any jeopardy he might have placed her in by his unwise outburst. Who knows but it might have worked. Desperation will drive any man to recklessness and love will double the quotient."

"You know nothing about love."

"Imagine, though, his anguish when, lurking somewhere in the vicinity Tuesday morning, he learns Sarah has been murdered. All his hopes are crushed at once. Then he discovers he is a fugitive from the law as well as the dicers. Nowhere is he safe. Somehow he manages to find refuge for another day or two. He gets his

own savings from Hepburn on Tuesday afternoon, using a prearranged protocol. Then he heads for cover. Why doesn't he leave
town? Well, there are troops everywhere in the townships. Roads
are being watched. There is also Sarah's funeral on Thursday. And
perhaps he has his own suspicions of who killed his beloved."

Cobb glanced over at the clock. It was past seven. They had
less than an hour.

"While you were angry with Badger, you at least had the sat-
isfaction of dismissing him. Moreover, you knew men well, and
it must have occurred to you that Badger could easily have been
exaggerating in order to hurt you for spurning his facile charm.
Then Sarah comes home from the ceremonies on the wharf and,
when you finally get her alone, you confront her with Badger's
claims. Or perhaps you let them sit festering while you watch
Sarah for signs. You have made yourself the master of the poker
face and the ready-made smile. Sarah is worried, of course, because Badger was truant on the weekend and she knows his weak-
nesses. Whatever happened, by evening matters on the surface
appeared normal. A few regulars come and go. You close up. And
then Handford Ellice arrives."

Norah Burgess was beginning to flag. Only her dark, discern-
ing eyes seemed still to be alive and sentient.

"I cannot believe you intended to murder a young woman you
had grown to love and dream a future for. All day you brooded
silently about whether she had really betrayed your trust and, if
so, whether Badger was a passing fancy and whether, once he was
gone, things would be as they had been. I think you entered her
room intending to check on her well-being as you usually would.
But the sight of her there naked beside an inebriated scion of
someone rich and famous and lucky by birth—something caused
you to snap. Possibly you knew deep down that Sarah was already

lost to you. You grabbed the dagger and killed her before she could offer up another excuse for her betrayal. Love turned to loathing in a blink. And in a blink the deed was done."

"It's seven-thirty, Major."

"But I'm still not sure why you had to shoot Badger. Unless you concluded that he might finger you for the murder or, worse, take personal revenge on you or your girls. Perhaps you waited for two days, hoping to hear that one of his cronies had slit his throat. When that didn't happen, and the troops were called out to hunt him down, you decided to act. No doubt you keep a lady's pistol somewhere in here to protect yourself in extremis. You took it and somehow lured Badger to a rendezvous off Jarvis Street. You approached him as a friend and shot him through the heart."

"Please, no more."

"You're ready to confess your crimes?"

With great effort she raised her face high enough to look Marc directly in the eye. "You got most of it right." She sighed. "Michael never got in here Monday night. I was awake the whole time. There was only me." A fierce but momentary look of anger seized her. "But he did have that key. When you found it was missing on Tuesday morning, I knew for sure what it was those two had been up to."

"How did you get in touch with Badger when nobody else could—not the gamblers, the police, or his own sister?"

"He used to hide out in a duck blind along the marsh above the end of Jarvis. I sent Peter there with a note. The boy had no idea what he was delivering and, of course, Michael would spot him coming a mile off."

That would account for the straw and grass on Badger's clothing. "But he got the message?"

"Yes. I told him I had nothing to do with Sarah's death and

that I'd tell him exactly how she died. Then I offered him money. That he could never resist."

"So you killed the only person who might be able to implicate you while avenging yourself for his affair with Sarah."

"Something like that."

Norah Burgess moaned and tried to rise up in her chair, pushing with all her might on its arms but falling back with a resigned sigh. Still there was fire in her eyes and she emitted a dry, throaty, ragged laugh.

"But you got the only important point completely wrong," she cried, with a scathing contempt that was aimed at herself as much as her inquisitor. "Yes, I liked Sarah and I treated her like a daughter. But I didn't love her. I loved him!"

NORAH BURGESS FINALLY AGREED TO ACCOMPANY Cobb to the station and sign a deposition admitting that she had murdered Sarah McConkey and Michael Badger. When Marc had first proposed it, Norah had complained that she was too tired to move—or think or feel. In fact, during the course of their conversation, she had visibly shrunk into herself and was now as withered and bent as a crone.

"I just wanta curl up here and shrivel away," she said.

"But innocent lives and reputations are at stake," Marc said. "The police are declaring Michael Badger a murderer—a dead man who cannot confess or be tried, and who will appear to many to be an official scapegoat. Handford Ellice's reputation will be ruined by innuendo and gossip unless a public confession is forthcoming."

"Why should I care about Ellice?"

"The future of the province and the Canadas may depend on Mr. Ellice's being disentangled from this affair. You better than anyone know he was a blameless bystander."

"You mean that old Wakefield business?"

"Yes." Not much had escaped Madame Renée.

"I'm too weary to walk," she sighed, but her eyes indicated she would make the effort.

Cobb came back into the room from the other part of the house. He had a small pistol in his hand. "Ya got fifteen minutes to get to Government House."

"Mr. Cobb here is going on ahead and will bring a cab up Lot Street; I'll help you to the buggy."

"But you'll be late fer yer meetin'!" Cobb exclaimed.

"Send a message to Lord Durham that I'll be half an hour late. Let Sarge know that he should stay any declarations against Badger."

"Okay, Major." He grinned broadly. "You sure like to cut yer meat close to the bone." Then he was gone.

Marc helped Norah to her feet.

"I'm all right now," she said, pushing away his steadying arm. "I'll sign the necessary papers." Clearly she was drawing on the last reserves of her strength. She had lost everything that mattered: her business, her surrogate daughter, the man she had loved. Somehow, she maintained her dignity.

She headed not for the scarlet door but her own quarters.

"It's this way, ma'am."

"I'll need to get my bonnet," she said. "We're going to town, aren't we?"

SIXTEEN

Darkness was approaching when Marc arrived at Government House, almost an hour late for his appointment. He was shown immediately into the drawing room, where Lord and Lady Durham rose to greet him. If they were anxious, and surely they had reason to be, they were too well schooled in the social graces to let their manners slip. Lord Durham asked Marc if he would like a whiskey or a coffee, and Lady Durham inquired after the health of Mrs. Edwards. Durham then directed Marc to a chair, seated his wife nearby, and sat down himself. It was only then that Marc noticed, in a shadowy corner of the room, the presence of Handford Ellice. He was wrapped in a heavy robe even though the evening was warm.

"Mr. Ellice is feeling well enough to be party to our conversation, Marc, thanks to the ministrations of Mrs. Edwards and my lady." Durham nodded to his wife and she smiled faintly in acknowledgement. "He is still too weak to join us in discussion, but we felt that he had a right to be here."

"I agree," Marc said. With the necessary courtesies observed, he added, "And the news is good. Cobb and I have found the murderer and secured a full confession."

Ellice emitted a single, dry sob. Lady Durham's face remained as it had been, politely immobile; her gloved hands lay still and prim in her lap, but without fuss or fanfare, two tears of relief made their way down her cheeks. Durham gave Marc a satisfied smile, one that seemed to say, I knew you would not let us down. Then he rose to approach Marc, his hand outstretched. Marc stood to accept Durham's grasp, firmly held for three or four seconds. The look of gratitude on the great reformer's face was all the reward Marc would ever need.

Although the Earl of Durham was reckoned one of the finest orators in the House of Lords, he was that rare exception among gifted speakers: he knew when and how to listen. For the next half-hour Marc retold that version of events he now believed to be true and incontrovertible regarding the deaths of Sarah McConkey and Michael Badger. The identity of the gentleman who had initiated the tragedy remained unknown, but the order and import of each subsequent event was relayed with tactful brevity. Occasionally Durham interrupted with a probing question or a call for more explicit elaboration, which Marc willingly supplied. Durham had asked him to discover and disclose the truth, and it was clear that His Lordship had been serious in that request.

Marc assured his listeners that Norah Burgess's confession would make no mention of the particular gentleman caller unfortunate enough to have been present at the scene, as it was not germane to the indictment. That is, Norah would have stabbed Sarah to death regardless of who lay asleep beside her: a scapegoat was a scapegoat. Everyone in the room knew that rumours would spread like the infectious disease they were, but that would happen anyway and the effect would be limited to those already inclined to believe the worst. The important point, for the Durhams and for the earl's mission, was that it would be the madam's confession that would fill the front pages of both the Tory and Reform press in the week ahead. A lurid double murder would override political opportunism every time.

When Marc had finished, Lady Durham said, "That poor girl."

And her husband remarked, "That poor woman."

LORD DURHAM WALKED MARC TOWARDS THE foyer. He declined the earl's offer of a carriage ride home: a stroll in the tender air of a summer's night would be sustenance for the soul.

"I'm still certain that there was a conspiracy against you," Marc said, as they neared the front doors. "But I am unable to prove it."

"Don't worry, Marc. It won't be the last such plot, here or at home."

They stood together for a long moment on the verandah, as if neither wished to take their leave.

"Whether you had been successful or not," Durham said at last, "I'd decided that you deserved something valuable for your dedicated efforts."

"But I couldn't possibly—"

"It's not that kind of gift," Durham said with a twinkle. "Earlier today, one of the delegations I entertained included the Baldwins, father and son."

"Our hosts of Monday evening."

"And prominent citizens here in the city." Durham smiled enigmatically. "I've learned, from sources I won't reveal, that you spent two years in the Inns of Court before distinguishing yourself in the army, and that you have recently contemplated studying for the bar."

"Your sources are impeccable, sir."

"That being so, I have extracted a promise from Dr. Baldwin and his son that, should you require a firm in which to apprentice, theirs would welcome you unconditionally."

"Thank you, Your Lordship. I am honoured by your thought-fulness."

"The honour is all on your side and the thanks on mine."

They shook hands, and Lord Durham walked quietly back towards his quarters. Marc nodded to the sleepy corporal on duty and headed down the steps. On the pathway, in a pool of light from one of the bay windows, stood Horatio Cobb.

"Good Lord, Cobb, I thought you would be home and safe in Dora's arms by now."

"I figured you should hear what's happened down at the sta-tion," Cobb said with a sigh that was both frustrated and resigned.

Marc's blood went cold. "You did get the confession, didn't you?"

"Oh, yeah. That part went along fine. The magistrate was handy, which ain't always the case. He come right down with his own clerk and I helped the old girl give all the details pretty much like you did back in Irishtown. It took purty near an hour."

"And she signed it in the presence of Magistrate Thorpe?"

"He read it back to her and she signed it."

"Good. That's all that really matters, eh?"

"If you say so, Major."

Marc stared at his associate. "What else?"

"Well, the jailer comes in to take Mrs. Burgess to the cells through the tunnel, and there's been a whole lot of fussin' and fid-dlin' with the papers in that little room of ours—there's Sarge and me and Thorpe and the clerk—so we're not keepin' a close eye on the missus—"

"You didn't let her escape . . ."

Cobb was instantly offended and showed it. "'Course not," he growled. "But somehow when none of us was lookin', she man-aged to pull a little medicine bottle outta her floppy bonnet."

Marc immediately recalled that Norah had fidgeted with

something in her dress pocket throughout the interrogation in her parlour. Fearing she would be searched at the station, she must have concealed the vial in the hat he had foolishly allowed her to fetch from her private quarters.

"She starts to cough somethin' terrible," Cobb continued, having to relive yet another nightmarish image, "and then she turns blue."

"She poisoned herself? Right there in the station?"

"Whatever she done, she's now dead."

Marc didn't know whether to be angry at his own ineptitude or at the incompetence of the authorities at the station. Possibly he was more relieved. The thought of such a woman dangling from a gibbet in the Court House square was not one he wished to entertain. Then it occurred to him that she had probably been sitting in that bleak parlour for hours, fingering the deadly vial and trying to work up the courage to take her own life. She had deliberately sent the girls away with all their earnings and, no doubt, her own savings as well. She had killed the man she had secretly loved and who had, in her mind, callously betrayed her. She had seen to it that Sarah, whose unplanned death she must have bitterly regretted, was given a proper funeral and did not die unmourned. She had closed the shutters on her life's achievement. All that was needed was a final dose of courage to commit the ultimate act of a free will. Marc and Cobb had arrived not a moment too soon. Much later and they might have found her dead—and her crimes unprovable. Marc shuddered now, realizing what a close call it had been.

"I heard her last words," Cobb said solemnly.

"You did?"

"They was whispered, mind you, but I was leanin' over 'cause I could see she wanted to say somethin' to me."

Marc waited.

"She said, 'Tell Lord Durham I wish him well.'"

EPILOGUE

Fort St. Louis
Quebec City

September 3, 1838

Dear Marc:

As you have no doubt heard by now, I have decided to cut
short my mission here in British North America. The knives
have been out for me back home since the end of July. While
I expect the Tories to slip the blade in whenever they smell
an opportunity to do so, the failure of my own party to
support the decisions I have had to make given the gravity of
the circumstances has left me feeling abandoned by those I
counted as friends. My ordinance permitting the ringleaders
of the Quebec revolt to serve their sentences in Bermuda
was essential to my plan for a conciliated settlement to that
unhappy affair, but its being declared ultra vires by Lord
Melbourne—at the instigation of Lord Brougham—in a
pathetic and futile attempt to prop up his own government
has dashed all my hopes. Moreover, if I were to acquiesce
meekly to the prime minister's whim, I would lose any

*credibility I have managed to achieve in the four months since
my arrival. Hence, I shall wind up matters soon and depart
for England in late October or early November.*

*Nevertheless, I have already formulated a general plan
for the future governance of the Canadas. It remains only
for my associates—Wakefield, Turton, and Buller—to help
me flesh it out. There will be a united parliament with
equal representation from each province. The Baldwins may
prove me wrong about the French way of life fading away
or blending with the British to make something strange
and new, but for now a single assembly ought to compel
the leaders of the two races to say hello to each other across
a parliamentary aisle every day: who knows what may
happen then? My principal concern, as you know, has ever
been to create some kind of legislative forum in which the
people who live in the provinces and have a stake in its
future will be given the opportunity to work out their own
destiny.*

*Less optimistically, Wakefield assures me that the
atmosphere in the Whig cabinet is now so poisoned that we
shall be fortunate to get our report written and seriously
considered by an indifferent and self-absorbed Parliament.
Moreover, the chances of having responsible government—
the linchpin of any scheme I propose—accepted are doomed
from the outset. Of course this will not dissuade me from
promulgating it loudly from any pulpit provided me!*

*On a more personal note, Handford has begun to recover
from his ordeal. We offered to send him home to recuperate,
but when he realized that Lady Durham is essential to
me and my work and could not therefore accompany him,
he chose to remain here. All in all, I think it was a wise*

decision. Please write again and let me know how your law studies are progressing.

Yours sincerely,
John George Lambton
Earl of Durham

P.S. My congratulations to Mrs. Edwards on the blessed event you are anticipating next April. I hope your marriage turns out to be as fortunate as mine has been.

AUTHOR'S NOTE

While *Bloody Relations* is wholly a work of fiction, Lord Durham and his brief governorship of the Canadas in 1838 are as well known as they are controversial. The particular speeches, opinions, and actions of the earl and his wife, Lady Durham, depicted herein are fictitious, but I have attempted to make their behaviour and personalities consistent with the historical record. In doing so, I have relied upon books like Leonard Cooper's *Radical Jack* and Chester New's *Lord Durham's Mission to Canada*. The same is true for the brief appearances of the other historical personages: Edward Gibbon Wakefield, Charles Buller, Thomas Turton, Sir George Arthur, and Robert Baldwin. Handford Ellice is an invented character, and the murder plot involving him is imaginary. Any resemblance between other fictional characters and actual persons, living or dead, is coincidental.

For the record, Lord and Lady Durham did visit Toronto for a day and a half in July 1838, their stay cut short by the earl's suffering a recurrence of his migraine and neuralgia. I have extended the visit to four days and based his dealings with the local gentry and politicians on the pattern he established while in Quebec. I transposed the "royal arrival" in Upper Canada—with all its official pomp and fanfare—from Niagara (where it actually occurred and was lavishly recorded) to Toronto harbour (though upwards of three thousand Torontonians did turn out on Queen's Wharf to greet him). I have made Spadina House as described here an amalgam of several of the great houses of the period, including Davenport, Russell Abbey, and Moss Park. Areas like Irishtown did exist in early Toronto (the red-light district was north of Lombard Street in Devil's Elbow), but its depiction and location here are my own inventions.

Finally, lest the skeptical reader feel my portrayal of prostitution in 1830s Toronto to be an exaggeration, here is a contemporary view from the *Canadian Freeman*, May 26, 1831:

> Houses of infamy are scattered thro' every corner of the town, and one of them had the hardihood to commence operations next door to our office, last week, in a house under the control of a Police Magistrate! So besotted are some of our would-be gentlemen—so lost to shame and decency—and so dead to every feeling of Christianity—that they crowded in at noonday, and some of them that we know visited it in open day, last Sabbath!—Young lawyers, and others of respectable standing. We had no idea before that such wretched and shameless depravity existed in our infant community—in any other place that we have lived, such men would be viewed as a walking pestilence and scouted out of all decent society. It seems to us that some of our authorities, and heads of families too, connive at debauchery of this kind, which, if not checked, will be sufficient ere long to draw down the wrath of God upon the town, as in times of old upon Sodom and Gomorrah.

ACKNOWLEDGEMENTS

I would like to express my gratitude to Jan Walter, my editor, for her wise judgement and scrupulous attention to detail. Thanks also to my longtime, faithful agent, Beverley Slopen, and to Alison Clarke and Kevin Hanson for their robust support of the Marc Edwards series.